# MURDER AT A BOARDING SCHOOL

A 1920s Cozy Mystery

A Lady Felicity Quick Mystery
Book 6

ROSIE HUNT

ISBN: 978-90-834331-1-0

With thanks to early readers Peggy Craddock, Federica De Dominicis, Kelly Hodgkins, Nancy, and others

Editing by Effie Wilson

Cover art by DLR Cover Designs

*For my aunt, a beloved and stylish teacher*
*You are missed*

# A Note on Language

This book is written in British English. There are two reasons for this:

- the story is set in England, and
- I, the author, am British.

Part of my British writing style is the use of s where z is used in American English. For example: theorise instead of theorize, and vandalise instead of vandalize.

However, you may have noticed that in the blurbs and marketing for this book, it's called a cozy mystery and not a cosy mystery.

This is because the American spelling is standard for the genre. Spelling it this way helps people (and algorithms) recognise my book more easily.

But outside of book genres, it's cosy all the way.

# Cast of Characters

## Quick family

Lady Felicity Quick, journalist and occasional amateur detective

Pip, Felicity's Yorkshire Terrier

Lord Jasper Quick, Earl of Denbury, editor-in-chief of the Western Daily News and Felicity's brother

## Students at Liverton Ladies' Academy

Lady Cecily Summervale

Lady Jane Ingles

The Honourable Miss Dolores Gastrell

Miss Usha Ghatge

Miss Gwendoline Milligan

## Teachers at Liverton Ladies' Academy

The Honourable Miss Cora Armstrong, headmistress

The Honourable Miss Mathilda Driver, movement teacher

Miss Harriet Eversley, teacher of household management

Miss Ivy Petherick, music teacher

Miss Elise Vincent, French teacher

Mrs Johanna Ogden, needlework teacher

## Others

Mr Alexander Cooper, reporter for the Western Daily News and friend of Felicity

Chief Inspector Luscombe, police detective

Sergeant Wilcox, police officer

Mr Clark, butler

## Extract from the Western Daily News, 1922

**STOP PRESS: Incident At Girls' School**

WICKLEIGH, 28 May — An arrest has been made at a boarding school for girls in West Devon. Chaotic scenes at a private event prompted the police's involvement. Our reporters are at the location. More to follow in the next edition.

More than anything, I always wanted to be reunited with you. In your gentle way, you tried to tell me it would never happen.

Now I realise you were right.

I once imagined that I was somehow a victim, but I can no longer hide from what happened. From my role in it all. It consumes me, and I fear it might drive me to madness.

Sending you one last, long embrace. I shall miss you, my dearest.

*Extract from a letter intercepted by British intelligence services*
*May 1922*

## Chapter One

LIVERTON HOUSE, WEST DEVON, 22 MAY 1922

The door that flew open into the long, statue-lined corridor of Liverton Ladies Academy's southwest wing missed Lady Felicity Quick's nose by a hair's breadth.

Felicity had been hurrying, an exquisitely patterned Persian runner absorbing the fall of her modestly heeled dove-grey shoes. Her focus had been on disappearing outside into the sunshine and cool breeze while afternoon lessons were being held, with no one to see her trot across the gardens to the rendezvous point.

The door had, however, swung open without warning and came close to touching the brim of her grey felt cloche.

Felicity froze. It was the closest she'd come to physical danger since arriving at the school almost two months ago.

A pair of warm chestnut eyes blinked around the door, followed by a timid smile.

"Lady Felicity. What a wonderful coincidence."

Miss Elise Vincent, Liverton's French teacher, clutched the silver locket at the neck of her white cotton blouse, over which she wore a fuzzy lavender cardigan. Her native Belgian pronunciations gave her speech a rolling softness, yet there was a tautness to her tone.

"Perhaps you might assist us for a brief moment, your ladyship?"

In the classroom beyond, girls giggled nervously.

"I don't quite see what's funny."

The bark of the Honourable Miss Mathilda Driver, Liverton's movement teacher, quashed the laughter.

"Miss Petherick, from the beginning, if you please," instructed Miss Driver.

A piano struck up.

"Let's start again, shall we girls?" thundered the movement teacher above what sounded like a wedding march.

Glancing back into the classroom, Miss Vincent winced. "Please, your ladyship? While you are still with us."

Felicity had, over the past weeks, aided with demonstrations of table manners and even conversational French, but whatever was being taught in the room beyond fell far outside the scope of the writing advice Felicity had been hired to provide to the students.

Still, she had an urge to help.

Which she resisted.

"I'm terribly sorry, Miss Vincent." Disappointing the French teacher wasn't that difficult. Felicity's pedagogical duties were, after all, just a cover, and she had an appointment. "I'm afraid I can't spare the—"

Two more heads appeared around the door.

"The situation is almost too dire to describe." The Honourable Miss Dolores Gastrell's eyebrows were drawn low over ocean-blue eyes. One of the school's sharpest students, with her dry wit and wilful streak, Dolores could be rather a handful, yet Felicity was oddly fond of her.

"Miss Driver is attempting to teach us grace and poise," hissed Lady Cecily Summervale, her smooth, sun-kissed forehead gently creased with concern. She glanced back into the room. "I mean no offence, but—" She lowered her tone further. "Grace and poise from Miss Driver?"

It was unlike Cecily to speak ill of anyone. In the short time Felicity had known her, Cecily had proven herself to be a considerate and caring young woman, always aware of the needs of others.

Both girls were dressed in elegant white gowns, with cascading layers of tulle and taffeta that reached to their ankles. They were outfits reminiscent of those worn for a formal ball. For Queen Charlotte's Ball, in fact, which was the most thrilling and important moment in a debutante's career. Preparation for it was foundational to much of the studies at Liverton Ladies' Academy. Only the ostrich-feather headdresses were missing.

Miss Vincent raised her eyebrows but said nothing. It wasn't correct to speak ill of a fellow teacher, especially not in front of the girls, but the French teacher obviously agreed with the students' assessments.

Miss Driver was always well-intentioned and enthusiastic. But with her powerful thighs developed from years of competitive steeple-chasing, and her regimented approach to organisation, the movement teacher was perhaps not the ideal example of elegant form.

"Couldn't you show us, your ladyship?" suggested Dolores.

"Oh, would you?" Cecily's long eyelashes fluttered with excitement at the idea.

Miss Vincent's face lit up with hope. "You would be most welcome to join us, your ladyship." With dainty features and gentle movements, the French teacher was graceful in her own way, but she walked with a slight limp due to hardships suffered while trapped in occupied territories during the war.

Felicity smiled politely. How might she wriggle out of the situation without risking blowing her cover? The end of her mission — her real reason for being at the school — was almost in sight.

"I would love to," began Felicity, "but I've got an awful lot of letters to—"

"Splendid!" Dolores grabbed Felicity's wrist and whisked her into the classroom.

The music stopped. All eyes were on Felicity.

Wriggling away was no longer an option. She ought to have known better than to give Dolores even the slightest opening.

With luck, the ordeal would be quick, and with even more luck, Felicity's connection would wait for her.

Felicity hadn't seen most of Liverton House's countless rooms.

This one was set up as a rehearsal room, with a sprung wooden floor, mirrors lining one wall, and a shining black baby grand in the corner. Tall, thin-framed windows gave onto blue skies, white clouds, and the green rolling lawns and meadows of Liverton's vast estate. Vases atop tall lacquered wooden stands displayed the bounty of the house's well-tended gardens, the white and pink heads of peonies and sweet peas lolling in the sunlight. The sweet smell of wood polish and a heady floral perfume filled the air.

Seated at the piano, her hands in the lap of her long, dark grey wool dress, was the music teacher, Miss Ivy Petherick. The expression on her hollow features was even more dour than usual.

In the centre of the shining wooden floor, Miss Driver paced up and down, her chin held high. Her white cotton blouse had elbow-length sleeves for ease of movement, and a pleated, shin-length skirt in navy blue revealed powerful calf muscles. Simple thin-soled shoes in black leather and a headband that swept back her sun-highlighted brown hair completed the practical outfit.

"Like this, girls. Do you see?" Miss Driver had excellent posture, and her stride was smooth and feminine. However, her height — she was taller than most men — and her muscular frame seemed to confuse the girls.

They remained huddled in layers of white tulle at the edges of the room, for the most part watching the demonstration rather fearfully, wondering if they'd ever be ready for presentation to the Queen. Several girls from Felicity's letter-writing class were among them.

Miss Gwendoline Milligan, already wan with her white-blonde hair and barely visible eyebrows, appeared even paler than usual against the white of her dress as she nervously bit her lip, her ice-blue eyes flicking between Felicity and the movement teacher.

Lady Jane Ingles, her hair shining like sunlit caramel, nodded her head with each of Miss Driver's steps, moving her lips as though counting the paces and learning the rhythm, her frothy dress unfortunately a little on the short side for her willowy frame.

Dolores had crossed the floorboards to a window seat where she joined Miss Usha Ghatge. Usha looked splendid in creamy white silk, her dress emphasising the warm reddish tones of her brown skin, but she didn't appear interested in Felicity or Miss Driver. As the only student at Liverton already betrothed, Usha wasn't under the same pressure as the other girls. She was merely passing time while her husband-to-be prepared himself with studies at Oxford for his future ruling a princely Indian state.

Usha and Dolores giggled as they dug into a pouch that lay between them on the window seat. A harsh stare from Miss Petherick killed their frivolity. Dolores silently slipped the pouch onto the windowsill behind her.

"Imagine walking down the aisle on your wedding day," boomed Miss Driver as she continued her demonstration. "It's easy enough. What?"

"Miss Driver?" It was difficult for the petite and soft-spoken Miss Vincent to break Miss Driver's stride, but her persistence made the undertaking a success. "Lady Felicity is here to help us."

Miss Driver came at last to a standstill. "Lady Felicity?"

"Only briefly," added Felicity. "I don't wish to interrupt the flow of your lesson."

Miss Driver shook her head in a manner not unlike a horse. "Not at all. Not at all, your ladyship. You're just in time to aid us in the walk around. Miss Petherick?"

With an audible sigh, the music teacher put her fingers to the keys and once again struck up the march, its uplifting nature at odds with the pianist's sombre attitude.

"Come along, now, girls," commanded Miss Driver. "Follow myself and Lady Felicity."

Although not given instructions, Felicity quickly understood what was needed.

Miss Driver, head high, paced a circle around the room. With the rustle of skirts and the fall of hesitant footsteps on the wooden floor, the first girls fell into line behind her. Felicity joined the circle on the opposite side of the room to Miss Driver.

It wasn't that Felicity considered herself a shining example of elegance and poise. She had, however, been presented at court —

albeit at a time when there was hardly a suitor available — and she knew that practice and confidence counted more than anything else. Especially at the formative and vulnerable age of the girls.

Miss Vincent watched with her hands clasped and her eyes full of nervous hope as even the least self-assured girls edged away from the sides of the room and shuffled into the circle, their eyes flicking between Miss Driver and Felicity. Though bunched together and still uncertain, they were at least moving.

"Just a couple of rounds," Felicity announced. "Then I really must go."

"Did you hear that, girls?" called Miss Driver above the piano. "We ought to make the most of Lady Felicity while she's still with us. What?"

Miss Driver's comment had impact.

With their gazes switched firmly to Felicity, the girls spread into an even circle and swept along like swans on a moat, the embellishments on their white dresses shimmering in the afternoon sunlight.

"That's it, girls." Miss Driver stepped away from the circle, her voice booming through the rehearsal room. "You've got it. By Jove, you've got it!"

Felicity smiled. Teaching at Liverton had brought her an odd satisfaction. She was convincing in the role not only because of the writing techniques she shared with the girls, but because of her genuine delight at her students' progress.

"That's the ticket!" Miss Driver stood with her fists on her hips. "Summervale," she barked.

"Yes, Miss Driver?" Cecily seemed to enjoy gliding smoothly around the room.

"You've talent, my girl. You might have led this class yourself. You're almost as accomplished as Lady Felicity."

A light flush bloomed on Cecily's pretty cheeks.

Felicity suppressed an amused grin. 'Accomplished walker' would be a noteworthy addition to her list of achievements.

Dolores leaned forward to whisper to Usha, and both girls

giggled. Miss Petherick looked up from the piano with a scowl. Whether the music teacher's disapproval was for the giggling girls or for the accomplished Felicity, it didn't much matter. It was time to move on.

"You're all doing wonderfully well," said Felicity to the class as she eased away from the circle and headed towards the door. "Do keep it up."

"Thank you so much," whispered Miss Vincent as Felicity passed her. Tears of gratitude shone in the French teacher's eyes.

"Please, don't mention it." The whole endeavour had only cost Felicity couple of minutes. If she hurried, she might still be on time.

"I say, Ingles," barked Miss Driver.

Jane's already long neck extended further. "Y-yes?" she replied hopefully, the distraction upsetting her footing slightly.

"Skirt of yours is a bit on the short side, isn't it?" Miss Driver squinted at the offending hem. "Ask Mrs Ogden to sort it out, will you?"

The mention of the name sent a shiver down Felicity's spine as she put a hand on the door knob.

"Why, y-yes, Miss Driver. I shall—"

*CRASH!*

The piano stopped with a cacophony of discordant notes.

Jane had lost her footing completely and lay in a heap on the floor. Dolores, who had been behind her, had tripped over Jane. Both girls lay in a heap of tulle on the floor, as though trapped in a snowdrift.

Usha had been behind Dolores but had side-stepped the accident just in time. In doing so, she knocked into Gwendoline, who tripped and fell into a vase of flowers, which toppled against the baby grand. Water splashed into the piano's inner workings.

Gwendoline froze, her shoulders stiff. Her lower lip trembled.

"Oh, là, là!" Miss Vincent brought a hand to her mouth.

"Goodness!" Cecily rushed forwards.

Dolores' features glowed a livid red, her glossy brown hair escaping from a jewelled comb as Cecily struggled to help her up.

"If I find my dress has been torn..." Dolores spoke each word through gritted teeth, her anger focused on Jane.

Jane, however, was oblivious.

With her hair tumbled onto her shoulders, she sat on the floorboards with her stockinged legs exposed, frowning at her knee. A purple mark already showed through the powder-pale stocking.

"Mummy always said my feet were too big for dancing," she mumbled dejectedly.

"Oh, dear." Miss Driver had been on her way to help Jane but hesitated.

Miss Petherick was rising slowly and vengefully from her piano stool, her pale green eyes jumping between Gwendoline and Usha as water dripped from the baby grand.

Stepping in front of Gwendoline, Usha held up her palms. "I am so, so sorry, Miss Petherick. I can buy you a new piano. I mean, my father can buy you a new piano. Or my betrothed. In any case, I promise you'll have a new piano."

Something tugged within Felicity.

Moving gracefully. Arranging one's hair and make-up correctly. Using precisely the right form of address. It sounded frivolous, and on some level it was, but the pressure of a debut season could be immense. The girls' dreams and their families' ambitions were all at stake, and these were the daughters of the Empire's most powerful families.

But Felicity hadn't come to Liverton Ladies' Academy to soothe the nerves of debutantes.

Twisting the door knob, Felicity stepped into the corridor.

She had to make her rendezvous. She had news to share.

## Chapter Two

The sun warmed Felicity's back through her grey dropped-waist jacket as she hurried along a gravel path edged with a border full of scent, colour, and butterflies. In the distance, groundsmen carried spades and pushed wheelbarrows to and fro. There was always a project or two underway on an estate as large and decadent as Liverton's.

Felicity threw a glance back towards the house, its red-brick walls and white stone trims peeking over tall, dense rows of clipped yew hedging. Ducking under an arch dripping with fragrant purple wisteria, she headed towards a gate in the hedge bordering an access lane that crossed the property.

Despite the need to hurry, Felicity felt quite calm. She knew exactly what she would say to anyone enquiring where she was going. Not that such enquiries were likely. Liverton's grounds were vast and the corner of the estate designated for the rendezvous was remote.

But were she to be asked, she would say she was merely taking a breath of fresh air during a gap in her teaching schedule.

It came so easily to her now. Lying.

Not that long ago, telling an untruth would have caused Felicity to blush. She might even have stammered. She'd spent most of her life sheltered from the vagaries of the world, believing that lying was only ever wrong and telling the truth only ever correct.

How far she had come.

The latch on the gate was stiff. Bees buzzed around creamy elder umbels in the blossoming hedgerow as Felicity stepped out into the lane. Like many roads in Devon, where the straightest of Roman thoroughfares had barely reached, the lane twisted in a serpentine manner and offered no clear line of sight in either direction.

Which way to go?

The conundrum didn't last long.

The skitter-scatter of tiny paws across the road's stony surface heralded the appearance of a small Yorkshire Terrier. He came careering around the bend, his tresses pushed back by the speed of his running, his tongue lolling with a dizzy happiness.

"Pip!"

Surprised and delighted to see her faithful canine companion, Felicity bent and scooped him into her arms and received copious licks of her chin.

"Steady. Steady, old chap. I can't teach my next lesson looking like I've been for a bath."

"He's not the only one who misses you, you know."

The deep, familiar voice created a warm, blooming sensation in the pit of Felicity's stomach.

Mr Alexander Cooper, fellow journalist, former professional rival, and now steadfast friend, had rounded the bend in the lane and stood in his relaxed, effortlessly handsome way with his hands in the pockets of a navy three-piece suit paired with a crisp white shirt. His calm, blue gaze hinted at a smile as the breeze caught a lock of his dark blond hair and made it dance on his scarred forehead.

Since arriving at Liverton, she'd often thought about Alex and his scar.

Felicity opened her mouth to issue a response, but she was so overcome with Pip's enthusiastic licking she had to roll her head away.

Alex looked on, thoroughly amused. "Lady Henrietta insisted I bring him. Apparently, he's keeping everyone at Bradley Court extremely busy with his demands."

Felicity wrestled Pip to her side, tucking the little Yorkie firmly under her elbow and stroking his soft, warm head. A gift from her deceased father, Pip was usually always at Felicity's side, even on professional engagements. At Liverton House, however, the rules about animals were strict, with no exceptions. The girls would turn the school into a menagerie otherwise.

With the little Yorkie in his place, Felicity could finally speak. "Are you taking your orders from my grandmother these days?"

Alex looked down at his shining brown brogues. "I stopped to see Jasper on the way over here." He kicked a pebble. "Lady Henrietta cornered me." He met Felicity's gaze with a wry smile. "How could I, a lowly commoner, refuse the wishes of a dowager countess?"

Felicity sighed. "How could anyone?" Her grandmother didn't always meddle. When she did, there was no point in resisting.

Alex quirked an eyebrow. "Jasp says he's glad it's your last week here."

Lord Jasper Quick, Earl of Denbury, was Felicity's older brother. He was also editor-in-chief of the Western Daily News and Felicity's boss.

Female readership of the paper had grown significantly since Felicity joined the news desk the year before. It was understandable Jasper was keen she return to producing articles instead of teaching letter-writing etiquette.

"Is he, now?" Felicity's response was a little sharp. Her return to the newspaper was likely not her brother's only concern. Despite his role in getting her into the school, Jasper could be protective of his little sister.

But the pang of regret in Felicity's stomach was for something else.

It was indeed her final week at the school. The end of her mission was in sight, and what did she have to show for her efforts?

Alex looked down at his shoes. "I'm looking forward to you being back at the paper, too, you know."

The remark caused Felicity to blush slightly. It had been an absolute age since she and Alex had been to the tea house near the newspaper offices for a bun and a chit-chat. She missed it. Desperately so, at times. Their fleeting catch-ups on the edge of Liverton's grounds every couple of weeks weren't the same.

But newspaper business and tea house get-togethers weren't what they met to discuss. Felicity had collected information, and Alex was there to receive it. And not in his role as a journalist.

Tucking Pip more tightly under her arm, Felicity straightened. "I know who it is."

Alex blinked with surprise. "You do?" There was more than a hint of hope in his voice.

It had been Alex who'd first proposed the mission at Liverton to Felicity. He and Jasper had discussed and agreed upon it. The connection to British intelligence was Jasper's, a fellow he knew well from the war years, though it wasn't an official channel. It wasn't even an official request.

Felicity nodded. "I'm quite certain of it. I don't see who else it could be."

Alex pressed his hands further into his pockets. His expression became serious. "There's no need to deliver a culprit."

Alex had been the first to explain the mission to Felicity.

Despite the years that had passed since the end of the Great War, those who betrayed the Allies and helped the Germans were being brought to justice, even if the trials were no longer publicised like they had been in wartime.

British intelligence believed a former spy for the Germans to be hidden at Liverton Ladies' Academy. Jasper's connection wouldn't divulge how the authorities knew, but because of the exclusive nature of the school — the headmistress of which was extremely protective of her charges — their investigations had met a dead end.

Contacting the Quicks had been a last resort.

"Only one teacher has avoided speaking to me about her whereabouts during the war," added Felicity. "Or about anything, really."

The breeze picked up. Alex swept his hair back from his forehead. He'd been together with Jasper under bombardments caused by the likes of the spy suspected of being at the school.

He gave a frown. "That wasn't what was asked."

"I was asked to gather information," said Felicity, stroking Pip. "To listen and report back. And to stay undercover. That's exactly what I've been doing, isn't it?"

The headmistress of Liverton Ladies' Academy was an old acquaintance of the Quicks. Felicity and Jasper's father had made generous donations to the field hospital she'd set up from her own funds and ran near Amiens.

Keen to help the authorities if he could, Jasper had telephoned the headmistress to explore with subtlety the possibility of getting an agent into the very heart of the school without raising suspicion. Upon hearing about the headmistress' predicament — the need for a teacher with expertise in writing to attend to a group of struggling yet promising students — Jasper hadn't immediately made the connection with his sister.

Sending in Felicity had been Alex's idea.

Alex's thick, blond eyebrows drew lower still. "You're not to confront anyone."

Had he somehow come to regret his suggestion?

Jasper had only begrudgingly agreed Felicity was an excellent fit because the target was no longer considered dangerous.

Felicity frowned back at her friend as Pip wriggled under her arm. "Precisely how reckless do you imagine me to be?"

In the two months she'd spent at the school, Felicity had been exceedingly careful. While filling the temporary role of tutor in penmanship and letter writing, Felicity was under instructions to learn what she could about the inhabitants of Liverton House by listening and remembering. She wasn't to ask too many questions. She wasn't to write anything down. It was an initial reconnaissance mission that was to leave no trace, and upon which the intelligence services would build as they saw necessary.

Alex wiped a hand over his clean-shaven jaw. "Apologies. I know you're capable of doing things in the right way. More than capable. You have my trust. Absolutely."

Alex rarely doubted Felicity. The matter at hand was sensitive. It stirred all manner of emotions.

Felicity stepped closer to him. "I shan't be detected. I just want to do my bit."

During the war, Felicity's family home had welcomed wounded soldiers for convalescence, but she'd witnessed none of the conflict's horrors directly. Not like Alex and Jasper had. So when presented with the opportunity to help correct a wartime injustice, Felicity had jumped at the chance.

She'd reported what she'd learned to Alex every couple of weeks, face-to-face meetings being safer than the use of the school's telephones. He passed the information on to Jasper, who then shared it with his intelligence contact. The reporting line was protracted, but were she and Alex ever caught, a secret meeting with a man of similar age who wasn't a family member would be easier to explain away than clandestine meetings between brother and sister.

Felicity swallowed. "I've only got till the end of the week."

Alex smiled sadly. "You've done more than enough already."

Felicity felt otherwise.

"I have my suspicions about Mrs Ogden, the needlework teacher," she said.

A quarrel of sparrows flapped into the branches of a nearby dog rose and chattered urgently among the pale pink flowers.

The sudden activity startled Felicity. Pip's ears twitched in the birds' direction.

Alex folded his arms. "The needlework teacher," he repeated quietly.

Felicity tipped her head to the side. "Do you remember the handwriting sample?"

The three of them had been together in Jasper's office at Bradley Court when Felicity's brother had shared more detail about the informal yet highly secret mission. He pushed a sheet of paper with swirls on it across the desk for Alex and Felicity to peruse. The spy had been careful, but the swirls were from impressions pressed into type-written documents recovered by the intelligence service.

It was a ghostly trace of the spy's handwriting.

Although the swirls hadn't been complete words, the style was distinctive.

Felicity had reviewed and ruled out almost all the teachers' handwriting. All but one.

"Of course." A hint of hope had returned to Alex's voice. "What of it?"

A rustle in the hedgerow made Felicity turn, but it was just a blackbird. Being secretive could wear on one's nerves. Not even Liverton's headmistress knew Felicity's real reason for being at the school. The pressure would surely all be worth it.

"The handwriting will be the key," assured Felicity.

She would spare Alex the worry of the details, but Felicity had a plan.

## Chapter Three

The dining room at Liverton Ladies' Academy was as luxurious and well appointed as the finest restaurants in London.

Starched tablecloths shone pristine white. Rich velvet curtains were swagged at the windows. Candles flickered in silver candelabras. The delicate scent of tomato and herbs from the recently cleared soup course still hung in the air.

Serving staff bustled between the scattered round tables as the murmur of polite chatter rose towards crystal chandeliers. There were perhaps forty girls seated for dinner, their ages ranging from eighteen to twenty. All of them were fashionably attired in the latest colours and silhouettes, with many sporting silky bobs and long beaded necklaces.

Though there was no official rule, the school's teachers sat separately from its pupils.

On one hand, it indicated the teachers' authority over their students. On the other, it reflected the exclusive provenance of the girls compared to the teachers, who, except for the likes of Felicity, were mainly from lower rungs on the social ladder.

Felicity was seated in her usual spot at the teachers' table. Everyone had their own established place, which meant dinner offered limited opportunity for conversations with different people. There were also those, like Miss Petherick, the music teacher, who preferred to dine in their private quarters.

Felicity was, however, quite done with talking and listening. For her last week at the school, she had something else planned.

To one side of Felicity sat Miss Harriet Eversley, teacher of household management and the economics of philanthropy. She had a slight hunch, unruly curls captured in a bun, and a pair of round glasses that sat crookedly on the tip of her button nose. The sleeves of her brown tweed jacket climbed above her wrists.

She dabbed at the corners of her mouth with her napkin and sat back in her chair with a sigh. "That was most satisfactory."

"Indeed, indeed," boomed Miss Driver, who occupied the other seat next to Felicity. "Jolly good soup. What?" The movement teacher had changed out of the pleated skirt worn for the deportment lesson, although the loose-fitting red-cotton dress she'd chosen for dinner was perhaps more appropriate for the sidelines of a netball match.

"Quite delicious," responded Felicity to Miss Driver with a polite nod. But her attention was elsewhere.

Across the table, past the flickering flames of the candelabra, sat the needlework teacher.

Small, round, and with grey hair set in waves against her head, Mrs Johanna Ogden was unassuming. She had papery skin and wore old-fashioned dull-coloured outfits. Even the silk flowers on her hat, although delicate and excellently made, looked tired. She spoke very little, and when she did, she was always perfectly polite.

But her grey eyes flicked quickly and brightly, watching everything in the dining room, and her little mouth was quick to purse in a disapproving manner.

Over the past two months, she'd been successful in avoiding Felicity's every attempt at engaging her in close conversation. Suspiciously successful.

"I say," boomed Miss Driver, addressing the table. "Jolly good soup, wouldn't you say?" She was intent on a wider reaction. "Cook's outdone herself. What?"

Wrinkling her eyes, Mrs Ogden gave a curt nod.

"I can only agree," said Miss Vincent, who was seated next to Mrs Ogden. "We are quite spoiled. Really quite spoiled."

A shriek of laughter went up from one of the girls' tables.

Mrs Ogden fired a glare towards the merriment.

Unharmed from her fall during movement class, Dolores was the centre of attention, in a cigarette-straight burnt-orange dress with flutter sleeves. Her mischievous blue eyes glinted as she delivered another line — inaudible from the teachers' table — which created even more laughter.

Mrs Ogden's scowl deepened.

Miss Vincent smiled good-naturedly. "In my day, such bold character wasn't becoming for a lady," reflected the French teacher. "How times have changed. For the better, I mean."

Mrs Ogden turned her scowl upon Miss Vincent, but the needlework teacher's eyes lit up with the arrival of the next course.

"Tonight's fish is sole à la meunière," announced Liverton's grey-templed butler, Mr Clark, as the food was set before the teachers in a smooth, coordinated action.

"Delicious," murmured Mrs Ogden, her eyes fixed on her plate as the scent of the warm fish and parsley-and-lemon sauce filled the air.

One thing about the needlework teacher was clear: she enjoyed her food. She took generous portions at breakfast, lunch, and dinner, and always gave her meals her full attention.

It was this weakness that Felicity would exploit.

For despite the mouth-watering nature of Liverton's menu — the sole slid like silk off the bone and the sauce was buttery yet delicate — Felicity intended to miss a course or two that evening in order to execute her plan, which was as daring as it was simple.

Seeing a sample of Mrs Ogden's handwriting couldn't be achieved by picking up a student's work to read the comments written by their instructor. The other teachers' handwriting had been easy to check. Even Miss Driver created written reports for the pupils attending her movement classes, offering detailed instructions on how to improve their court curtseys.

Mrs Ogden's approach was different. She perused the yards of linen and Aida cloth that the girls toiled over with a pair of small silver scissors in her hand. When she saw a stitch she didn't like, she snipped it out.

If Felicity was to deliver results in her mission's final week, action was required. And it was action that had to be taken while Mrs Ogden — and preferably the rest of the school — was kept busy, because Felicity mustn't be caught sneaking into another teacher's room.

As the fish course was delivered to the students' tables, the dining room quietened to the gentle clatter of cutlery on plates and subdued conversation.

While everyone was still busy with dinner, Felicity would excuse herself, go up to the teachers' wing, and slip unnoticed into—

"Enjoyed your walk this afternoon, your ladyship?"

The reflection of the candelabra in Miss Eversley's glasses obscured her eyes, but the teacher of household management was turned towards Felicity. The question was clearly for her.

"My walk, Miss Eversley?" Felicity's stomach tightened, but she maintained a polite smile. Had her meeting with Alex been observed?

"You went on a walk today, Lady Felicity?" Miss Driver twisted in her seat, her tone disgruntled, perhaps upset someone had engaged in physical exercise without inviting her to join.

Miss Vincent blinked at Felicity with interest.

Mrs Ogden's focus was squarely on her sole.

"One must take fresh air daily," said Felicity. It was sometimes possible to wriggle out of a topic one didn't wish to discuss by being pleasant while also being terribly vague. "Don't you agree?"

"Quite agree, quite agree," thundered Miss Driver, tucking into her food.

"You went to meet someone, did you not?" Miss Eversley's eyes — and the emotion driving her enquiry — were still obscured by the reflection in her glasses.

Mrs Ogden's pale, judgmental stare flicked up from her fish plate and towards Felicity and Miss Eversley.

It was impolite to enquire into private affairs at a staff dinner table, but Felicity needed to remain calm. Had she been careless? With its high hedgerows, it wasn't possible to view the lane from the school building. Had Miss Eversley been close by, perhaps even listening in?

Felicity opened her mouth, ready to defend herself.

"Oh, come now, Miss Eversley." Miss Vincent spoke without raising her eyes from her fish. "You cannot probe people at the dinner table in this way. It isn't courteous."

Miss Eversley drew in her chin. As she turned her head towards the French teacher, the candles' reflection dropped from her glasses, revealing an expression of genuine confusion. "I meant no offence."

"A woman of such quality and beauty as our dear Lady Felicity no doubt has a string of suitors waiting for her answer to their breathless proposals." Miss Vincent gave Felicity a playful wink. "But this, of course, is none of our business."

Felicity smiled back at Miss Vincent. While the French teacher's interjection was appreciated, it wasn't entirely reassuring. Had Felicity been seen with Alex, and the assumption was he was her beau? The thought made her feel slightly giddy.

Mrs Ogden sent a disapproving look across the table in Miss Vincent's direction. The needlework teacher had finished her fish. The courses were counting down. Time was running out.

Felicity placed her knife and fork together next to her half-eaten sole, but before she could stand up, the doors to the dining room flew open.

# Chapter Four

With her sharp chin held high and her dark bob shining under the chandeliers, the Honourable Miss Cora Armstrong, the headmistress of Liverton Ladies' Academy, strode into the dining hall. She wore a short burgundy cape over a sharply cut charcoal jacket and skirt and had a stack of books gripped tightly under her arm.

All chatter ceased. The teachers and students stood up, and the servants retreated to the edges of the room.

*Dash it.*

Felicity's plan would have to wait.

Arriving at a lectern in the far corner, Miss Armstrong posited her books before her and surveyed the room. Her shrewd dark eyes gleamed as she made eye contact with practically everyone, looking at Mrs Ogden, Miss Vincent, Miss Driver, Miss Eversley, and, finally, Felicity, where her gaze seemed to linger.

Felicity swallowed.

Miss Armstrong gave a nod, and everyone sat down.

"Girls. Colleagues." The headmistress' voice rang through the room as clear as a church bell. "Please, continue your evening meal. We shouldn't allow our food to go cold."

The gentle clatter of cutlery resumed. Under encouragement

from the butler, the serving staff stepped gingerly away from the walls and continued their table service.

Mrs Ogden, who had already finished her sole, sat with her hands in her lap, her attention on the headmistress. Felicity sat likewise, her half-eaten fish still on her plate.

"I would like only to remind you," continued Miss Armstrong, "that our annual practice ball is merely days away."

A smattering of excited giggles and whispers rippled across the girls' tables.

Miss Driver lifted an eyebrow, and Miss Vincent smiled. Mrs Ogden and Miss Eversley seemed unmoved by the announcement.

The practice ball was the highlight of the school year. It was a dress rehearsal for Queen Charlotte's Ball, which had been held annually since the Eighteenth Century. The season's debutantes were presented to the reigning monarchs and — perhaps even more significantly — to the British Empire's most eligible bachelors.

"For the students in their final year here with us at Liverton—" Miss Armstrong looked at the table where the girls from the movement class were seated.

Jane straightened in her chair. The bruising from her fall was hidden under a teal dress with a loud yellow polka dot, but her green eyes were wide with nervousness. Usha wore a wry smile, her fingers worrying a long necklace decorated with gold filigree, which echoed the beading on her jade-green dress. Dolores sat stiffly, a mild scowl on her elegant features. Gwendoline, who was in a frock of layered peach voile, blinked hard and tucked her fluffy white-blonde hair behind her ears, as though concentrating carefully on the headmistress' instructions.

Miss Armstrong continued. "I would like to remind you in particular to make the most of this opportunity." She cast her stare at each of the final-year girls. "As your teachers and mentors, we can only bring you so far. You are the key to your own success."

While Liverton Ladies' Academy offered a well-rounded education, the institution's primary aim was no secret. It shaped its students to attract the best possible husband.

"Do your parents proud," concluded Miss Armstrong.

*SMASH!*

All eyes went to the side of the room.

A crystal decanter lay shattered and glittering on the floor. Nearby stood a young female servant, her hand clamped to her mouth, an empty tray at her side.

The headmistress sent a cold, hard stare in the butler's direction, but Mr Clark had already swung into action, ordering a footman to bring a dustpan and brush and ushering the stunned maid through the serving door.

"Oh, là, là," whispered Miss Vincent, a hand at her chest.

"Goodness." Miss Driver sounded shocked.

Mrs Ogden wrinkled her nose, as though offended by the interruption.

Giggles went up from the girls' tables. Felicity sincerely hoped they weren't laughing at the unfortunate servant.

Miss Eversley pushed her glasses up her nose. "It would cost a maid several years' wages to replace such an item."

Miss Driver frowned. "It was an accident, Eversley. The girl won't be charged."

Miss Eversley shook her head. "Oh. I know that."

The spell of her presence broken by the interruption, Miss Armstrong collected her books from the lectern and strode back across the dining hall. She gave an instruction to the butler — perhaps for food to be brought up to her private quarters — to which Mr Clark replied, "Of course, ma'am."

The headmistress' departure presented the perfect opportunity.

Felicity brushed down her grey linen skirt and pushed back from the table.

*CREAK!*

Mrs Ogden's chair scraped the floor. She rose from her seat. "Ladies, I bid you all goodnight," said the needlework teacher, stepping away from the table before Felicity had even stood up.

Felicity clenched her jaw to prevent the uttering of a mild oath.

Mrs Ogden always stayed in the dining room until the full service was over. Always. Had Felicity been rumbled? Surely, it wasn't possible. She hadn't even told Alex the full details of her plan.

As Mrs Ogden moved away from the table, she was approached by a flustered-looking young footman.

"Your books, ma'am."

"Thank you," said the needlework teacher as she received the tomes, which she must have given to the staff to look after while she was dining.

Felicity squinted. She couldn't exactly twist her head to read the spines, but what were the titles? There was a book on Chinese textiles, and was that a work by Dickens?

"The pork chops with apple, your ladyship." The butler had reappeared, offering to place a new plate of food in front of Felicity.

After a brief hesitation, she nodded and thanked Mr Clark as he set the plate down.

"Unlike Ogden to miss this," commented Miss Driver as she tucked into the chops.

"Oh, absolutely," agreed Miss Vincent. "Delicious."

"Quite," replied Felicity a little tightly as she set about finishing her dinner. Her plan for the evening had been scuppered, but her time at Liverton Ladies' Academy wasn't over yet, and giving up wasn't an option.

# Chapter Five

Low, grey clouds smothered the morning sky. Though there were patches of blue, there was no sunshine to give the conservatory a warm ambiance. Wind jostled the tall trees at the edges of the formal gardens as a charm of finches darted between the branches.

At a table positioned opposite the interior door, Felicity sat with the morning's Western Daily News spread on the table in front of her. She sipped tea, nibbled toast with apricot jam, and aside from Alex's latest piece about a robbery at a jeweller's in Torquay — which Felicity read thoroughly — she merely skimmed the articles.

After her plan for the evening had been quashed, Felicity stayed up late marking her students' attempts at letter-writing. She'd slept fitfully and awoke to the dawn chorus. Dressing in a long-sleeved frock of navy blue Georgette with a V-neckline and a simple string of pearls, Felicity was sure of being the first in the conservatory for breakfast.

Her plan to slip into Mrs Ogden's room for a look at her handwriting hadn't been cancelled. It had merely been postponed.

There was, of course, no firm evidence that Mrs Ogden was guilty. Being withdrawn and slightly superior didn't mean a person had done anything wrong. One couldn't convict a person on character alone.

However, the aloof Mrs Ogden seemed practically to make a sport of avoiding conversation and hiding her handwriting, and her strange behaviour at dinner had only heightened Felicity's suspicions.

Yet Felicity was perfectly willing to be wrong about the needlework teacher. Knowing the truth, regardless of the outcome, was what mattered. Just a glance at Mrs Ogden's handwriting would make all the difference. The sample Jasper had received from his intelligence contact had been so distinctive.

Felicity turned another page in the newspaper, her eyes roving distractedly over the columns of text in the pale grey light of the conservatory. She glanced up as students and teachers arrived for breakfast, their interactions subdued and mainly focused on steaming pots of tea and coffee and plates of eggs and bacon.

As soon as Mrs Ogden arrived for breakfast, Felicity would make her move. There would be no waiting around this time.

With her toast finished, Felicity poured herself another cup of tea, steam rising from the amber liquid. Her stomach fizzed with excitement as she stirred in the milk, keeping a subtle watch on the conservatory door.

The idea she might help catch a spy felt more important than almost anything she'd ever done. Yet even sipping it slowly, her tea was soon finished, and there was still no sign of the needlework teacher.

Felicity wasn't ready to give up, but with her impending departure from the school, her opportunities were dwindling.

Mr Clark approached. "Will there be anything else, your ladyship? Smoked kipper with poached eggs, perhaps?"

Felicity smiled at the butler. She'd placed such an order on previous occasions. "Thank you, Mr Clark, but my first lesson is starting soon."

"Very well, your ladyship." The butler withdrew.

With a little sigh, Felicity stood up from her table. She couldn't be late for her lesson.

Perhaps Mrs Ogden's had an enormous pile of embroidery hoops to review? Felicity now understood that most of a teacher's work took place outside the classroom, and she'd been wrong about people before. Perhaps the plan to sneak into a fellow teacher's room was completely over the top.

Felicity held on to that thought as a cold draught whipped at her ankles and the long corridor's Persian runner dulled her footsteps on the way to the day's first lesson.

Besides her commitment to help uncover the spy, Felicity had made a promise to the school. Crafting responses to social invitations felt frivolous in comparison to the stakes of her secret assignment, but Liverton's girls deserved Felicity's support.

Didn't they?

---

"May I go first?"

A ray of sunlight filtered through the clouds and lit up the small circle of students seated in the classroom.

Gwendoline looked like a French confection in a pale green chiffon day dress, her hair shining like finely spun silver. Usha's complexion glowed golden-brown against her olive-green tunic-style day dress. A smattering of freckles highlighted the bridge of Cecily's nose, although there was nothing outdoorsy about her silk crepe boat-necked dress in duck egg blue. Jane's deep green eyes sparkled handsomely, the dark shade of purple of her long-sleeved frock providing quite a contrast. Dolores' hair shimmered with flecks of reddish brown, which were perfectly complemented by the rust-coloured beading on the cream voile of her dress.

Each girl had a unique beauty. Each combined the verve of youth with the poise of a fully fledged woman. It was a potent mix.

"If none of your fellow students object, Miss Gastrell—" Eschewing the seat behind the teacher's desk at the front of the classroom, Felicity sat as part of the circle of students, which she surveyed for opposition to Dolores' request. "—then I don't see why not."

Dolores beamed, triumphant.

Felicity sought Dolores' paper among those on her lap. There was no need for the teacher to explain her method, as the girls were used to it by now. The drafts and feedback were shared aloud with the whole group, so that everyone might learn from the others, and so that the girls might encourage one another.

Felicity held Dolores' submission in front of her. "The task was a letter of general correspondence that would also function as a casual invitation to a friend for a summer get-together."

Dolores nodded confidently, although she pressed her knuckles to her lips as Felicity read her letter aloud. Jane and Gwendoline leaned forward, paying careful attention. Usha pushed back into her chair with her arms folded. Cecily's gaze drifted out of the window.

On the surface of things, this small gathering of students was Felicity's reason for being at the school.

They were all in their final year and all expecting to make their debuts that autumn. But the school's headmistress felt them to be lacking, particularly in paying attention during classes and applying themselves to their homework, and especially where writing was concerned.

Miss Armstrong refused to return any of her girls to their families without them being thoroughly improved. The headmistress had therefore been eager to welcome Felicity as a temporary addition to the staff at the school.

Felicity lowered Dolores' letter back onto the pile of papers in her lap. "On the whole, Miss Gastrell, this is excellently written."

Dolores' lips broke into a proud smile.

"You show marked improvement in your penmanship," continued Felicity, "and the flow from polite catch-up into the suggestion of a picnic was seamless."

Jane frowned. "Did it have to be a picnic? I didn't make it a picnic." She gazed fretfully at the other students in the circle. "Ought it have been a picnic?"

"No, Lady Jane." Felicity cut in, keen to nip any unnecessary worrying in the bud, particularly from Jane, who often doubted herself. "I didn't specify an activity for the get-together." She rifled through the papers till she found Jane's submission, which was easy to spot with its large, energetic handwriting. "'A hack over the meadows of Stapleford Manor.' That's what you proposed."

Jane lifted her eyebrows, still fretting. "That's wrong, though. Isn't it?"

Felicity shook her head. "Horse-riding is an appropriate activity for an informal get-together, if you know your invitee already has an interest in the pursuit."

Jane melted with relief, her long arms falling to her sides. The transition between girlhood and womanhood was a period in one's life when the smallest of things could take on enormous importance.

"Must you leave us at the end of the week?" implored Jane.

Gwendoline nodded eagerly. "Oh, please say you'll stay. There's not another teacher like you."

Warmth blossomed within Felicity. How much she enjoyed tutoring the girls continued to surprise her. "I'm afraid I must," said Felicity solemnly. Her engagement with the school was temporary, and she had her newspaper career to which to return.

Dolores cleared her throat. "Had you finished everything you wished to say about my letter, your ladyship?"

Felicity rifled back through the letters on her lap. A demanding attitude was perhaps a weakness of Dolores', but then Felicity hadn't always been as agreeable as she was now. Such developments came with age and, perhaps more importantly, experience.

Felicity cast her eyes over the comments she'd written in the margins of Dolores' work. "As we already covered, Miss Gastrell, you suggested a picnic to your correspondent. One point of attention I marked was what you suggested for afterwards."

Dolores gave a little shake of her head. "What did I say?"

Usha, who was seated beside Dolores, eyed her friend with amusement.

"You say, and I read this directly from your paper, Miss Gastrell, that 'after the picnic, we might sneak away into the woods'. Might you explain what you meant by that?"

Dolores blinked incredulously. "Exactly that. A walk in the woods. Without being overseen."

Felicity gave a gentle frown. "It's a rather unusual inclusion in a letter to a friend about a picnic. May I enquire what prompted you to include it?"

Dolores looked blank. "You didn't specify the type of friend we might address in our letter."

Felicity's frown deepened. She looked at the top of the letter. Where the name of the addressee ought to have been, Dolores had written 'X'.

"Dolly intended her letter for a male recipient, your ladyship," clarified Usha.

Jane gasped and clapped a hand over her mouth. Cecily brought her gaze back in from the window. Even Felicity was taken aback.

She did her best not to show it. "You're right, Miss Gastrell. I didn't specify the type of friend. I assumed we would all understand it to be a female acquaintance. That was my mistake."

Gwendoline straightened. She looked concerned. "Will we learn how to address men in our letters?"

Felicity hesitated.

The girls were at the school to prepare themselves to make unforgettable debuts and excellent matches. However, letters to and from 'beaux' — as the girls referred to young men in whom they had more than a passing interest — were not included in the list of exercises Miss Armstrong had given to Felicity to practise with the girls.

"Well," she began, but she was saved from answering by a knock on the classroom door.

A tall, red-headed girl entered with an apologetic expression. She was a pupil from the year below. "Awfully sorry to interrupt, your ladyship, but we're not quite sure what to do."

Felicity gave a shake of her head. "What to do about what?"

The girl looked uneasy. "We're in the classroom next door. We've been waiting for our teacher for rather a long while. Only... Well, she hasn't arrived."

"For which teacher are you waiting?" enquired Felicity steadily.

"For Mrs Ogden, your ladyship. We're her needlework class."

Felicity's stomach felt suddenly hollow.

She gave the red-headed girl a calm, reassuring smile. "Thank you for alerting me." She turned to her class, hoping no hint of the dread she felt was reflected in her countenance. "Class, please busy yourselves with the writing of a new text. You may draft a formal invitation to a dinner attended by foreign dignitaries. I shall return as soon as possible."

Assured by the tall, red-headed student that the needlework class had enough embroidery with which to keep themselves occupied, Felicity strode along the draughty, statue-lined corridor. Outwardly, she would remain serene and report the situation of the missing needlework teacher to Miss Armstrong, but her thoughts were flying ahead like a runaway train.

Was this a coincidence? Or, fearing discovery as a wartime traitor, had Mrs Ogden purposefully disappeared? Was it Felicity who had somehow rattled her?

It was a relief when Mr Clark appeared at the other end of the corridor. Drawing closer, however, there was nothing reassuring about the pallor in the butler's cheeks.

Felicity did her best to appear unmoved, but there was now a cold, hard rock of worry in her stomach.

"You've discovered Mrs Ogden to be missing, have you not, Mr Clark?"

There was a sheen of sweat on the butler's wrinkled forehead. "Missing, your ladyship?"

"Mrs Ogden's needlework class is currently without a teacher," clarified Felicity.

Mr Clark's head trembled as he nodded. "That's q-quite understandable, your ladyship. A maid went to bring Mrs Ogden her breakfast and found she couldn't be woken."

Felicity tipped her head to the side. “Because she wasn’t in her room?”

“No, your ladyship.” The butler swallowed. “Because Mrs Ogden is dead.”

# Chapter Six

News of Mrs Ogden's passing swept through Liverton Ladies' Academy like a Victorian miasma, casting a pall on everything it touched. Lead-grey clouds thickened in the sky, intensifying the gloom around the school.

Like everyone, Felicity was stunned by the news of Mrs Ogden's demise, but there was little time to reflect on its implications for her clandestine mission. Important teacherly duties required Felicity's attention.

She gathered together the girls from her letter-writing class and Mrs Ogden's needlework group and informed them of the bleak development.

A maid tending to the fireplaces had reported that the teacher was asleep and couldn't be woken. The butler discovered Mrs Ogden was no longer among the living when he touched the needlework teacher's wrist in a more forceful effort to wake her and found it to be cold.

A doctor was immediately called. Finding no obvious cause for Mrs Ogden's demise, he said it wasn't abnormal for her heart to have suddenly ceased its normal function, given her age.

Felicity left the most vivid details out of the report she delivered to the students gathered in her classroom, an electric light burning overhead as clouds continued to gather above the treetops outside.

The girls were deeply shocked. Jane sobbed quietly at the news. Gwendoline bit her lower lip and blinked back tears. Usha and Dolores exchanged solemn glances. Cecily rose from her seat to console a younger girl from the needlework class who was crying uncontrollably.

Felicity did her best to offer comfort to the girls, but when Miss Eversley appeared briefly in the doorway to say Miss Armstrong had decreed that classes for the day were cancelled, the students scattered to their respective apartments and common rooms, leaving Felicity alone in the classroom.

An unpleasant knot tugged in the pit of her stomach as she returned the disarray of the chairs to their normal positions. Was Mrs Ogden's death indeed natural, as the doctor had suggested? Had her early departure from the dining hall the night before been nothing more than a coincidence?

Or, knowing her dark secret was about to be uncovered, might Mrs Ogden have played a role in her own passing?

More disturbingly still, was there a chance a third party had a hand in Mrs Ogden's demise?

There was, of course, no confirmation that Mrs Ogden was the traitor the intelligence services were hunting. But wasn't that missing piece of information now more important than ever? If Mrs Ogden had met her end at someone else's hands, didn't that suggest Felicity wasn't the only spy hunter at the—

*Tap-tap-tap!*

The door to the classroom opened to reveal the sombre faces of Miss Driver, Miss Eversley, Miss Petherick, and Miss Vincent.

"Mind if we come in? Or would you prefer to be alone?" Miss Driver's questions were redundant as she was already striding into the room, the pleated skirt of her practical moss-green cotton dress fluttering in her wake. "Wanted to check up on you. What?"

Miss Eversley pushed her glasses up her nose and fiddled with the silver brooch at the throat of her high-necked ivory blouse. "We're all aghast."

Miss Vincent twisted her fingers together. She looked well put-together in a pink floral dress and knitted cream shawl, but her eyes were ringed red from crying. "What terrible news. What absolutely terrible news."

Hollow-cheeked Miss Petherick said nothing. She wore a black wool dress with a grey chiffon scarf. Her penetrating gaze had a sadness to it, but a state of mourning wasn't unusual for the music teacher.

"Yes. Absolutely awful." Felicity did her best to look shocked rather than worried, but a terrible possibility gnawed at her conscience. Had Felicity's presence at the school somehow triggered Mrs Ogden's demise?

Folding her arms over her navy blue dress, she swallowed. "I'm afraid didn't know Mrs Ogden at all well," continued Felicity.

"Oh, none of us did." Miss Driver flapped a dismissive hand as she settled herself into a chair.

Miss Eversley frowned. She remained standing. "Nothing wrong with keeping to one's self."

Miss Driver tutted. "Didn't say there was. Look—" She softened her tone. "Even if none of us knew the woman beyond pleasantries, and even if the old girl passed peacefully in her sleep, it's still rather a horrid shock. What?"

"Yes." Miss Vincent dabbed at her eyes with a frilly handkerchief. "Such a shock."

Miss Petherick, her arms folded, went to the window and gazed at the trees shuddering in the wind.

"And I'm saying that even after everything I saw in France and Belgium." Miss Driver was proud to have been among the voluntary aid detachments during the Great War. She'd driven teams of horses pulling ambulances that raced across terrain so pulped by artillery no motorised vehicle could handle it.

It was therefore Felicity's assessment that Miss Driver was unlikely to have betrayed the Allies. She'd put herself at risk to care for injured soldiers, going above and beyond what was expected of any woman during the conflict. It didn't fit with supplying information to the Germans.

"I quite agree." Miss Vincent continued to look sombre. Trapped in Belgium under the occupation, the French teacher had witnessed her share of horrors. She'd lost her parents and brother. Indeed, the conflict had wiped her village off the map.

At dinner, Miss Vincent had once joked that if it weren't for the war, she'd have married a wealthy farmer and not have worked a day in her life. Felicity smiled but couldn't laugh. It was impossible to imagine a woman who had lost so much spying to help the forces that had destroyed everything she held dear.

Miss Petherick remained with her back to the group. Felicity hadn't heard it from the music teacher herself, but Miss Petherick's severe countenance and preference for dark clothing stemmed from the loss of her betrothed on the battlefields of Flanders. Her love for the man had been unfathomably deep, and she'd yet to recover from the loss.

According to the other teachers, Miss Petherick had been a different person before the war, gay and blithe. Would a bereaved fiancée collaborate with the enemy to waste the lives of even more soldiers? It was hardly conceivable. There was also the fact Miss Petherick had served as a governess at a remote manor house in Scotland during the war.

"Mrs Ogden wasn't sick, though. Was she?" Miss Eversley's expression was glum, but the economics teacher didn't seem sad like the others.

Miss Eversley had worked as a surgical nurse in Miss Armstrong's wartime hospital, and her proximity to death had perhaps hardened her to it. It also made no sense for a nurse kept busy with the wounded to help the enemy to target its artillery strikes.

"I haven't the faintest idea." Felicity looked to the other teachers for a response to Miss Eversley's question. "Was she?"

Miss Driver sighed deeply. "Far as I know, Ogden was as healthy as a horse."

The affirmation did nothing to alleviate Felicity's unease, but she couldn't risk appearing overly preoccupied by the needlework teacher's passing.

She straightened. "I believe we can all agree that Mrs Ogden's passing is surprising and incredibly sad," she said. "And a loss to the school."

"Absolutely," agreed Miss Driver.

"Quite so," sniffed Miss Vincent.

*Tap-tap!* There was a knock at the classroom door.

"Come in," boomed Miss Driver.

The upright young footman who appeared in the doorway spoke with forced confidence. "A request from Miss Armstrong." He was not always on such duties. The disruption to normality caused by the discovery of Mrs Ogden's body had no doubt thrust him forward.

"What is it?" barked Miss Driver, unable to take a gentle approach in any matter, even in grief.

"A m-m-meeting," answered the footman, his nervousness now fully on display.

With a sigh, Miss Driver stood up and performed a couple of stretches, twisting her torso left and right. "Only natural to rally the troops."

Collecting the lesson's papers and hugging them to her chest, Felicity braced herself. As a teacher, she had a duty to be strong for the girls, even in the face of an uncertain outcome for her mission.

"W-with Lady Felicity," clarified the footman hastily. "Miss Armstrong has requested a meeting with L-Lady Felicity."

Felicity ceased collecting her papers. "With me?"

Miss Driver squinted at the footman. "Only Lady Felicity? Are you quite sure?"

Miss Petherick turned slightly away from the window and cast a look at the servant.

"Yes, are you sure?" echoed Felicity, hoping for a mistake. Being singled out wasn't a good sign.

The young footman cleared his throat and stood straighter. "Miss

Armstrong wishes to speak to Lady Felicity in her office. That is the message."

Miss Driver sent a look of disbelief in Felicity's direction. Miss Vincent wore a sympathetic expression. Miss Eversley blinked blankly.

The smile Felicity offered her fellow teachers was an uncontrollable mix of apology, embarrassment, and fear. Had her undercover mission been discovered? Why else would the headmistress single out Felicity so quickly after Mrs Ogden's passing?

*Remain calm*, she told herself. *Nothing is certain. Not yet. And whatever happens, you can handle it.*

"Thank you." Felicity addressed the footman without the remotest quiver in her voice. "I shall go to Miss Armstrong's office right away."

## Chapter Seven

The headmistress' office was at the heart of Liverton House, if a sprawling building that had grown organically over the centuries could be said to have a centre.

The office was a grand, symmetrical room. A pair of tall, sturdy filing cabinets flanked full-length windows in the middle of which was a set of French doors. Outside, neat rows of topiary pyramids decorated a paved terrace. In the distance, tall beech trees danced in the wind, grey clouds low overhead.

In front of the French doors was a wide oak desk with a red leather inlay. Atop it sat a pile of papers, perhaps applications from potential students, and a shining black candlestick telephone. The red leather chair behind the desk was empty.

Miss Armstrong was standing at the window, looking out at the windswept landscape. She wore a fine wool suit in muted red and smoked a cigarette in a short holder, which was the same ebony black as her severe bob.

"Lady Felicity, ma'am," announced the footman as Felicity advanced towards the desk, a plush blue-and-gold carpet absorbing the fall of her heels. With her back straight and chin high, she was determined to hide any sign of nervousness.

The headmistress didn't turn from the window. She held her

cigarette tightly, the smoke curling upwards, its bitter smell filling the room.

Felicity fought the urge to cough.

"Thank you, Mr Talbot," said the headmistress.

The footman bowed towards Miss Armstrong's back. As he withdrew, he closed the doors behind him.

Taking a last inhalation of smoke, Miss Armstrong turned, crushed the cigarette in a crystal ashtray on the corner of the desk, and settled into the red leather chair. She had sharp, prominent cheekbones and a dark, intense stare.

"Please." The headmistress gestured to a similar chair on the other side of the desk.

Felicity settled into her seat as Miss Armstrong picked up the stack of papers and tucked them noiselessly into a desk drawer. Then she leaned back in her chair, her elbows on the armrests, her fingertips tapping together.

While the cut of her jacket and skirt was as sleek and fashionable as her neatly trimmed hair, Liverton's headmistress had none of the fun, carefree attitude often exuded by fashionable women of the day. Yet there was no doubt she had a softer side.

During the war, she'd spent her entire inheritance on establishing and running a field hospital. When her personal funds ran out, she raised money from the likes of Felicity's father to keep the operation going.

After the war, she opened Liverton Ladies Academy, the house and grounds rented at a favourable price from a family whose son her hospital had saved, but the need to support herself through work wasn't Miss Armstrong's only motivation for starting a school.

She cared as fiercely as a lioness for the women and girls who depended on her for their livelihoods and education. And her dedication didn't go unappreciated. Every year, there was a long waiting list of girls whose families were desperate to boast that their daughter had been under the tutelage of Miss Armstrong.

All this amplified Felicity's discomfort at having been summoned to the headmistress' office alone. Disappointing someone as exceptional as Miss Armstrong would be truly devastating, even without the high stakes of Felicity's secret mission.

"You wished to see me, Miss Armstrong?" Seated on the edge of her chair with her hands folded in her lap, Felicity wished to appear concerned by whatever Miss Armstrong might have to say but not unduly worried.

Miss Armstrong continued to tap her fingertips together. The wind rattled the espagnolette of the French windows.

"I knew your mother, you know."

Felicity raised her brow. "You did?"

The game of cat and mouse had begun.

Miss Armstrong clutched the armrests of her chair. "Adelaide and I were at school in Switzerland together briefly. We were terribly young." Her thin lips tweaked upwards in a faint smile. "Your mother was a bright, intelligent woman."

Felicity felt warmth tinged with sadness at the thought of her mother.

Lady Adelaide Quick had passed when Felicity was still an infant. Despite having been extremely well cared for by her father, grandmother, older brother, and a retinue of staff, and with enough means for the best governesses and schooling, Felicity still wondered how her life might have been different had her mother lived longer.

"Adelaide would be awfully proud of you were she here today," added the headmistress.

Felicity smiled, but something snapped taut inside her.

Miss Armstrong's mention of her mother had caught Felicity off guard. Had that been the intention? Was the headmistress preparing to pounce?

"Thank you for saying so," said Felicity politely. "Although I must say I lacked nothing under my father's care."

Miss Armstrong sighed and lowered her gaze. "We lost a great man when we lost Lord Kingsley Quick."

Felicity's father had been taken by the influenza that swept through Europe in the Great War's wake. He'd not been young, but his death had been sudden and unexpected.

Though it saddened her further to consider the loss of her father, Felicity maintained an upright posture.

"Your words are appreciated," she said firmly. References to Felicity's parents or any other attempt to soften her guard wouldn't work. Alex and Jasper were the only ones who knew Felicity's true purpose for being at the school, and it had to stay that way.

Miss Armstrong met Felicity's gaze. "Are you enjoying your time at Liverton?"

Felicity gave a curt nod. She could answer this question honestly. "More than I expected."

"I'm pleased to hear it. It was rather fortuitous the day your brother telephoned. I'd been thinking of hiring in some extra manpower, so to speak, on the teaching side. When Jasper told me how you were finding it difficult to keep up with the demands of journalism but dreaded the idea of being bored—"

Felicity continued to appear calm as she dug her fingernails into her palms. Is that what her brother had told Miss Armstrong? That Felicity couldn't handle her work as a reporter?

Yes, the mission at Liverton was important, but that Jasper had sacrificed her reputation as a journalist without even consulting her... She would have words with her brother, that was for certain. But for now, Felicity had to maintain her composure.

"I do so like to keep busy," agreed Felicity pleasantly.

The headmistress tipped her head forward, her glossy bob shining in the grey light from the windows. "I'll admit I monitored the papers when you first arrived. Journalists have tried to sneak in before. I wondered if I'd let one in through the front door, so to speak."

"I quite understand."

Could Felicity relax a little? Miss Armstrong's honesty about suspecting Felicity of subterfuge related to her role as a journalist was reassuring, and Felicity knew for certain there'd been nothing in the Western Daily News about Liverton Ladies' Academy since she'd joined the school.

"I carry out the most rigorous of checks on all my staff," continued the headmistress. "In attending my school, the girls' reputations should be augmented, not depleted. But I know your family's newspaper doesn't thrive on scandal and that you didn't come here to report."

"That's quite correct." Felicity breathed a little easier.

Miss Armstrong brought her fingertips back to tapping. She narrowed her eyes. Her stare was intense. "Indeed, you came to my school to do something else, didn't you?"

Felicity's stomach dropped. Had the cat cornered her mouse?

*Tap-tap!*

The door to the office opened. It was the butler with a tea tray.

The tension was excruciating as Mr Clark poured tea for both Felicity and the headmistress. Miss Armstrong kept her eyes on Felicity practically the whole time.

When the tea service was finished, the butler withdrew.

Without even the slightest tremble, Felicity lifted her teacup, took a sip of the steaming, milky Assam, and returned it to its saucer while Miss Armstrong's words echoed around her mind.

*"You came here to do something else, didn't you?"*

The fight wasn't over yet. It had only just begun, and Felicity was ready for it. She was ready for anything.

Felicity smiled politely at the headmistress. "May I ask why you summoned me, Miss Armstrong?"

There was a pause as the headmistress sipped her tea and eyed Felicity. Carefully, Miss Armstrong returned the cup to its saucer and placed it on the desk in front of her. "I would like to offer you a permanent position here at the school."

Felicity's teacup rattled in the saucer on her lap. She'd imagined herself ready for anything, but she hadn't been ready for that.

"A permanent position?"

Miss Armstrong returned her grip to the armrests of her chair. Her expression was deadly serious. "Allow me to speak frankly. Your efforts as a teacher have not gone unnoticed. The girls like you. They like you an awful lot. In mere weeks, you've improved the writing skills of a group of girls I considered practically unreformable. You've guided them with such consistency and kindness, the change has been miraculous. Added to that, your mere presence is an inspiration. Not that my girls are necessarily as career-minded as you have been, but with your background at the newspaper, you illustrate the possibilities available in today's modern world. And you are, of course, the daughter of an earl. You carry yourself with such elegance and decorum. It's no wonder they all look up to you despite you being so relatively close in age."

Felicity's cheeks glowed a little with embarrassment at the praise. It was true her students had advanced, but was she really regarded as a role model?

"Well."

It was all Felicity could say. She'd steeled herself for a rather different encounter with the headmistress.

She took a fortifying sip from her teacup. "I'm delighted to have made an impact on the girls."

Miss Armstrong's gaze remained severe. "I don't expect an answer straight away. Take time to think about it. Should you wish to make the switch away from journalism, then a career in teaching is open to you. You clearly have a gift for it."

The blush on Felicity's cheeks persisted. She welcomed the praise, despite struggling to accept it. Giving up on her career as a journalist was out of the question, of course — it had been her dream since childhood — but looking past her glowing words, Miss Armstrong was clearly oblivious to Felicity's undercover mission at the school. For the headmistress, Felicity was wholly dedicated to her work as a teacher.

A defensive stance was no longer necessary. An opportunity had arisen.

Felicity sat up straighter. "Would the intention be for me to replace poor Mrs Ogden?"

The wind rattled the French doors.

Miss Armstrong lowered her elegant eyebrows. "Mrs Ogden's passing is incredibly unfortunate, but these things happen. While I'm certain my girls will miss her, the enrolment for her classes was dwindling. Needlework is simply no longer key among the skills eligible young men seek in a bride." The headmistress' brow furrowed. "Forgive me if I sound mercenary, but one must be pragmatic."

"Of course," agreed Felicity. A woman like Miss Armstrong had to separate practicality from emotion. How else would she have run a field hospital during the war?

"So, no," continued Miss Armstrong, "the intention would not be for you to replace Mrs Ogden as such. I shan't be looking for a new needlework teacher. But with a teacher down, there is room for a new member of staff, and based on your performance, I thought of you for the vacancy straight away. Please excuse my pouncing on the matter, but you're set to leave us at the end of the week. I didn't want to waste any time."

"Quite understandable," said Felicity. "And I shall certainly give the offer serious thought. Do we know anything about the manner in which poor Mrs Ogden met her end?" Felicity sipped from her tea to emphasise the casual nature of the enquiry while her mind raced with ideas.

"Doctor Underwood spoke only of natural causes." Miss Armstrong gave a little frown. "Had you heard something else?"

Felicity blinked rapidly. "Oh, no." There were multiple poisons that could create the impression of a natural passing, but it wasn't appropriate to steer the conversation in that direction. "I was simply wondering if we knew what sort of natural causes. Mrs Ogden was in good health, was she not?"

The headmistress' expression relaxed slightly. "Heart or some such, I expect. She certainly enjoyed her heavy puddings, although I heard she went up to bed early last night. Must not have been feeling too well."

"I see," said Felicity, though she remained unconvinced. The needlework teacher had seemed fine during dinner.

But what if Miss Armstrong herself had done away with Mrs Ogden?

Perhaps Felicity's discussion with Alex in the lane had been overheard and reported to the headmistress. Fearing scandal for the school, she'd taken matters into her own hands, and—

Felicity dismissed the idea.

If the reputation of her girls was chief among the headmistress' concerns, then she wouldn't jeopardise everything by murdering a member of her own staff. It also made little sense for Miss Armstrong to offer Felicity a permanent position if she knew her not to be a genuine teacher.

Felicity sipped from her tea as her mind continued to whir. She needed to think carefully. Very carefully.

Miss Armstrong brought her fingertips together. Her gaze was penetrating. "Please consider my offer. Should you require additional information, you know where to find me."

Felicity extended her thanks to the headmistress. "I will indeed give your offer thorough consideration." Although not the way Miss Armstrong intended.

# Chapter Eight

In a room off Liverton House's main entrance hall were three indoor telephone booths built from polished wood panels and gleaming glass. Considering the house's remote location and that public phone booths were only just reaching the villages nearby, it was quite a feat of modern technology.

Despite the booths being an oddity, they were often busy, with queues forming in the evenings and at weekends. With lessons cancelled for the day in the wake of Mrs Ogden's passing, the queue to use the telephone was rather long.

Felicity waited patiently, gripping the elbows of her navy-blue dress. There was no distinction between students and teachers. Everyone joined the same queue without preferential treatment. A meandering chat with a chum at a boarding school on the other side of the country wasn't regarded as any less important than a telephone call to one's family, which was what Felicity was waiting to make.

In addition to her meetings with Alex, Felicity telephoned home to Bradley Court on a weekly basis. The slot for her regular call was that afternoon, which was timely. The news of Mrs Ogden's demise needed to be shared with Jasper. Felicity's collection from the school at the end of the week also needed to be discussed, as did the meeting in Miss Armstrong's office.

*"Unable to handle her work as a reporter."* What a thing to have told Miss Armstrong! Jasper didn't actually consider his sister incapable. He looked forward to having Felicity back at the paper as soon as possible, but her brother's words echoed in her mind.

She would, however, save that conversation with Jasper until they were face-to-face. The booths were not entirely sound proof, which also prevented any direct discussion of her secret assignment over the telephone. Alex would already have reported the outcomes of his latest meeting with Felicity to Jasper. He should therefore understand the significance of the needlework teacher's passing.

Felicity had almost reached the head of the queue. Only Dolores was waiting in front of her.

Dolores sighed loudly, her arms folded across the beading of a chartreuse dropped-waist dress, which wouldn't have looked out of place at an exclusive soirée at Claridge's or The Savoy. Behind Felicity was Miss Eversley, her nose in a book, her bespectacled eyes scooting greedily across lines of statistics.

"No, Mother. I said dead. DEAD." Still in rugged tweeds from a solo and rather energetic hike, Miss Driver boomed into the mouthpiece in the booth at the far end. "Yes. Taught sewing. SEWING. Sad, yes. VERY SAD." Her mother being hard of hearing perhaps explained the movement teacher's habit of raising her voice even to those without hearing loss.

Next door to Miss Driver, Gwendoline sat on the little stool in the central booth, still wearing her delicate pale-green day dress from the morning's lesson. Her frizzy pale hair floated as she nodded, her ice-blue eyes wide and blinking, her fingers knitted in the wire attached to the earpiece.

Nothing of Gwendoline's conversation could be heard. Indeed, the stillness of her lips could be observed through the glass window in the booth's door. She was listening.

Cecily occupied the last of the three booths. She mumbled into the receiver, a sad pout on her lips followed by the hint of a smile. Tipping her chin upwards, she laughed, her sunshine-blonde hair sweeping the shoulders of a light grey dress with Peter Pan collar and cuffs.

Felicity was normally patient while waiting. It could even be interesting to observe the behaviour of the teachers and students in the booths.

Today, however, her palms itched to get hold of a telephone.

Miss Driver exited her booth, her shoulders slumped. She looked beaten down. "Gastrell," she barked in Dolores' direction, holding the booth's swing-door open.

Dolores stepped aside. "Lady Felicity, please. You may go ahead of me."

Felicity drew in her chin. Dolores had seemed so impatient. "Are you quite certain?"

Miss Eversley lifted her nose from her book.

Dolores fired a brief but intense glare at Cecily, who smiled dreamily, the earpiece cradled lovingly to her head.

"I don't mind waiting a little longer, your ladyship," said Dolores, although the tension in her jaw indicated otherwise.

Miss Driver lifted her eyebrows at Felicity. The movement teacher was keen to get away.

Thanking Dolores and Miss Driver, Felicity seated herself on the booth's cane-work stool. As she waited for the operator to connect her to Bradley Court, Felicity's stomach squeezed with an odd sort of nervousness. How should she break the news of her primary suspect's death to her brother?

"Awful business, that teacher passing away like that."

That was how Jasper greeted Felicity as he got on the line.

Felicity let out a sigh of mild disappointment. "Hullo, Jasp." As the editor-in-chief of the Westcountry's most popular newspaper, there wasn't much he didn't know about.

Felicity's grip on the earpiece was tight. "I believe Alex will have already told you about—"

Jasper cut her off. "Natural causes, as I understand it," he continued, "and I was jolly relieved to hear there's nothing more to it than that. Although I can't imagine the old girl Armstrong's too pleased." His tone was breezy and full of bluster, but there was so much Jasper and Felicity couldn't say to one another.

Jasper hadn't expressed it precisely — few returning soldiers wanted to discuss their experiences in the trenches — but the furrowing of his brow and the twitching of his moustache when talking about the mission had underlined Jasper's desire for the traitor hiding at the school to be held accountable. Alex wanted it, too. There wouldn't be a British serviceman who didn't.

This longing for justice compelled Felicity to accept the mission. It drove her onward.

Felicity sat up straight on the little stool. "Miss Armstrong has asked if I might consider staying on. She's offered me a permanent position."

There was a pause. The line crackled.

"And are you considering the offer?" There was tension in her brother's voice. "I've got Finnegan lined up to collect you on Friday evening. Got a story or two for you to dive straight into next week."

"I've already considered it." Felicity spoke forthrightly. She'd consulted no one but her own conscience, yet she was certain it was the right thing to do. "I've not yet informed Miss Armstrong, but I've made my decision. I'm staying on. Only till the end of term, which is just a few weeks away." A few weeks Felicity hoped would prove very valuable indeed.

"Cici. Upon my soul." There was another pause. Her brother was surprised. "Coop told me your thoughts on... He told me about the conclusions you'd drawn. And now this news of... Of..."

"I know, Jasp. I know." Felicity wanted to explain but couldn't. Her reasoning was, however, crystal clear. Her time at Liverton had to count for something, and there were still so many questions in need of answers.

Was Mrs Ogden really the spy? Did she die from natural causes? Had Felicity's presence at the school influenced the situation?

Felicity couldn't bring herself to leave the school without some amount of certainty.

The line crackled.

"Liverton House. Bradley Court." It was the curt, nasally tone of an operator. "Are you still there?"

"Still here," rushed Felicity before they got cut off. Whether or not one's booth had sound proofing, nothing said on the telephone was ever private.

"Well." Jasper cleared his throat. "We can cope without you at the paper for a little longer, I suppose. If you're certain about this decision? To stay on and help the girls you've been teaching, I mean?" he added, in case anyone was still listening.

"I am." confirmed Felicity. "I want to make a difference. To the girls." *And to bringing a spy to justice*, she vowed silently.

# Chapter Nine

The morning's weather was a complete turnaround from the day before. The wind was still. Birds twittered amidst the topiary.

It might have been the broad blue sky with barely a cloud in sight, or perhaps it was Miss Driver's constant urging that fresh air was the perfect antidote to grief. Whatever her reasons, Miss Armstrong had designated the entire day for outdoor activities in the sprawling grounds of Liverton House.

Tennis-inspired fashions were a popular choice among the girls. There were bandeaux to keep one's hair in place, pleated skirts allowing for full movement, and flat-soled shoes with laces.

Under the teachers' directions, the students dispersed across various lawns and courts, the whites and creams of their clothing brilliant against the many shades of green in Liverton's carefully manicured gardens.

Felicity's outfit wasn't enormously different from the students'. Though she was focused on obtaining answers about Mrs Ogden, Felicity had to continue to blend in. She wore an ivory cotton cardigan over a white dress with a pleated skirt and a broad brimmed straw hat to keep the sun out of her eyes.

The other teachers had chosen a variety of fashions.

Miss Driver had on a roomy white blouse paired with a sporty and quite daring pair of checked plus fours. With a set of clubs under her arm, she seemed intent on teaching the girls a thing or two about golf.

Miss Eversley had on her usual tweeds, although her choice of a heeled shoe implied she had no interest in physical pursuits any more serious than croquet.

Miss Vincent had on lace-up Oxfords in tan and white paired with a cream dress edged with frills. She looked ready for a stroll along a seaside promenade.

Aside from the servants, who wore their usual uniforms, Miss Petherick was the only person in the school to choose the darkest of shades for the day outdoors. Her stiff cotton dress was striped black and grey with long sleeves and tight cuffs. The addition of a veil to her outfit would not have looked out of place.

It was still early, and Miss Armstrong hadn't yet made an appearance outside, but her influence was felt, as the day's well-planned activities began in a timely and efficient manner.

Mr Clark oversaw the servants handing out lemonade and fresh strawberries from tables set up under the shade of canvas canopies. In the distance, the groundsmen continued their work, carrying wheelbarrows of rocks under the increasing warmth of the sun.

On a neatly mown lawn edged with borders frothing with white and purple blooms, Miss Petherick and Miss Vincent were erecting a ring of music stands and folding chairs for a string quintet made up of Miss Petherick's students.

"Lady Felicity, might you give us a hand?" enquired Miss Vincent as she struggled with a folding chair that was determined to remain folded.

Felicity agreed to help without hesitation. With no talent particularly suited to the outdoors, she hadn't any official role for the day. Her primary aim for the morning was to be seen outside. Once that task was complete, she would slip away from the activities. No one would miss her as she headed back to the house.

"I heard you are staying a little longer with us," said Miss Vincent as she continued wrestling with the folding chair.

Felicity had informed the headmistress the evening before of her decision to stay till the end of term. Miss Armstrong had given a small, knowing smile. "Very glad to hear it," was all she'd said.

Miss Petherick flashed a glance in Felicity's direction. She was busy erecting the music stands with which Cecily — one of the soon-to-play violinists — was helping.

"That's correct," smiled Felicity, hiding her disappointment as the chair she was attempting to set up collapsed yet again.

"It's quite wonderful news," said Miss Vincent, delight evident in her heavily accented speech. "Isn't it, Miss Petherick?"

Miss Petherick sighed with dismay. She'd turned her attention to setting up one of the folding chairs, and it had just collapsed.

Cecily stood up straight from successfully erecting the last of the music stands. The flutter sleeves of her pale yellow linen dress danced in the breeze as she gazed at Felicity from under her sun hat. "Are you staying on with us?"

Felicity nodded. "Just till the end of term."

Cecily's brow rose with joyful surprise. "Oh, what wonderful news. Just wait till I tell the others."

"I'm glad you think so." Felicity sounded relaxed and happy. She was, however, growing impatient. The chair she'd been trying to set up continued to resist her. Who would have imagined unfolding a handful of chairs to be so difficult?

Straightening, she stared out across the lawn. Might there be someone nearby who could help?

*Wham!*

"Oh, là, là!"

"I'm all right. I'm quite all right!"

In turning her attention towards Felicity, Miss Vincent had no longer been watching the chair she'd opened. While it looked as though it had been properly fixed in position, it hadn't been.

So when Jane — a cellist in Miss Petherick's ensemble — took a seat, the chair had collapsed, sending Jane to the ground, her garish pink crepe skirt entangled in the folding mechanism, her white leather Oxfords protruding from the heap.

"Really, I'm quite all right," protested Jane as Cecily dashed to help her.

The noise attracted the attention of the butler, who sped towards the scene. He apologised profusely for not having involved himself in the setting up of the chairs at an earlier stage and, with the help of a footman, had all the chairs sturdily assembled in no time.

Relieved to be freed from her battle with the musicians' seating, it was time for Felicity to put her new plan into action, although not everything about the plan was new.

With the quintet's rendition of Pachelbel's Canon rising behind her, Felicity began a slow stroll towards the big house.

Her goal hadn't changed. She still wanted to see Mrs Ogden's handwriting, and though it was awful to admit, it was potentially easier now that the needlework teacher was no longer among the living.

Felicity couldn't be seen to be hurrying along the garden's avenues and across the lawns, but she was soon out of sight of the students and teachers and their outdoor activities. There was no time to be wasted. Who knew how long it would be before Mrs Ogden's belongings were cleared out of her room?

"You're needed on the tennis court."

Felicity had reached the sweetly scented rose garden when Miss Eversley appeared from an opening in the dense yew hedging.

"They require an umpire," she added, pushing her glasses up her nose.

Miss Eversley could be rather blunt, often skipping please, thank you, and other standard indicators of politeness, but Felicity had grown used to it. It was simply Miss Eversley's way. She meant no harm.

Nevertheless, Felicity was mildly disturbed by the interruption.

"I'm ever so sorry, Miss Eversley, but I don't know the first thing about tennis." Felicity's answer was prompt and honest. After the debacle with the chairs, she wished to avoid any further delays.

Miss Eversley looked at Felicity's tennis-inspired outfit with a degree of confusion. "But the students..." She blinked behind her lenses. "They asked for you. They asked for Lady Felicity."

Felicity arched an eyebrow.

She couldn't protest too much and risk raising suspicions, and the fact the tennis-playing girls had specifically asked for Felicity made it even more challenging for her to neglect her duties as a teacher. Felicity was, after all, determined to leave Miss Armstrong satisfied with her performance.

Bidding farewell to Miss Eversley — who sank onto a bench under a rose arbour and pulled a book from her jacket pocket — Felicity hurried towards Liverton House's tennis court. The gentle breeze was welcome as the sun continued to warm the day. The scent of early summer blooms sweetened the breeze.

Felicity thought through what she would say to the tennis players. She couldn't assist with the match because of her lack of experience in tennis. However, she would offer to locate Miss Driver, who no doubt knew all the rules of every sport going.

But where she'd imagined she'd find the tennis court, Felicity instead found a tall, classical fountain, with water trickling from the mouths of ornate sea monsters and putti holding urns bursting with fruit.

In rushing to get the tennis umpire ordeal over as soon as possible, Felicity had got lost.

"Looking for something, miss?"

A groundsman holding a sturdy wooden wheelbarrow stacked high with roughly hewn rocks had arrived on the other side of the fountain. Grey-blond hair protruded from under his peaked cap.

"I was looking for the tennis court," said Felicity, unable to hide a quiver of desperation in her voice. What if the clearing out of Mrs Ogden's room had already begun?

The fellow nodded. "Something of a maze, these gardens, aren't they? It's that way, miss."

Felicity expressed her gratitude and headed in the direction indicated by the gardener. Thankfully, she hadn't got herself too lost, and the gentle and reassuring *pock-pock* of a tennis ball bouncing off tightly strung rackets soon drew her onwards.

But the voices of the students and what they were saying caused Felicity to pause.

## Chapter Ten

"You worry far too much."

Felicity had come to a stop behind a tall laurel hedge. She was hidden from view at the edge of the tennis court.

"You're worrying about something that hasn't even happened. And may never happen." Usha spoke with a perfect English accent. Only the rolling melody of her words carried a hint of the subcontinent.

*Pock!* The ball could be heard bouncing back and forth in a lazy volley.

"But look at Miss Petherick." Naturally, the response came in Dolores' voice. When were Usha and Dolores ever apart?

*Pock!*

"Her sweetheart never came back from the war," continued Dolores. "They weren't even married, and the poor woman's life is ruined."

"A sad waste of not one but two lives," concluded Usha.

*Pock!*

"It's different for you," protested Dolores. "You see marriage as nothing more than a hoop of tradition through which one must jump."

"Does it have to be anything more?"

*Pock!*

"It can be the merging of two souls," said Dolores surprisingly earnestly, "that were always destined to be together and forever will be so."

Usha laughed heartily.

Was it wrong to eavesdrop on the girls? Under different circumstances, perhaps it was, but the intelligence services were counting on Felicity to listen and learn.

"Consider Miss Vincent," offered Usha. "Her whole family is gone. Lost everything. Yet she's sweetness itself."

Dolores tutted. "If anything were to happen—"

*Pock!*

"—I would die. There'd simply be no point in continuing."

Usha laughed. "You underestimate your own resilience."

The rhythm of the ball hitting the rackets ceased.

"I promise you," insisted Dolores. "I would die."

Usha sighed loudly. "You are quite beyond help."

The moment seemed apt for Felicity to make an entrance. Lurking for too long carried risks, and she wanted to make it up to the house as soon as possible.

"Miss Ghatge, Miss Gastrell." Felicity greeted the girls as she rounded the hedge and appeared on the lawn tennis court, its painted white lines sparkling in the sun.

Usha and Dolores were alone on the court in their stylish tennis whites and bandeaux, with ties trailing across their shoulders. Their rackets were the latest models, the wood gleaming with varnish and the handles hardly blemished. Around them on the ground, scuffed white balls littered the court. The tins that had once held the balls lay haphazardly discarded.

For an adjudicator to be needed, Felicity had assumed a more serious game to be underway.

"I understand you're in need of an umpire." She kept her tone breezy.

Dolores scrunched her brow.

"An umpire, your ladyship?" echoed Usha as she approached the net.

"Miss Eversley informed me you requested my presence in particular," continued Felicity, her smile faltering a little. Something wasn't quite right.

Usha shook her head slowly, her glossy black bob shimmering in the sun, her racket held to her chest. "Miss Eversley was here, but I'll come clean to you, your ladyship. We practically sent her away. We told her we weren't in need of supervision. As you can see, it's just Dolly and myself, and we're not the most serious of players."

Dolores arched an eyebrow. "We did old Eversley a favour. She'd rather be off somewhere alone with her nose in a book." Dolores had that exactly right. She spun her racket in her hand. "But we didn't request an umpire."

"Indeed, we didn't, your ladyship," confirmed Usha. "Pleased to see you though we are, of course." Her smile was commiserating.

"I see." Felicity maintained her composure, but her skin prickled under her cotton cardigan.

If Mrs Ogden hadn't met a natural end, and someone else had been involved in her demise, it meant there was a killer at the school, hiding in the shadows. Miss Eversley had lied to Felicity, but was it the behaviour of a murderer? The lie had been easily found out. Why tell it, then?

Felicity straightened. "Very well. If you've no need of me... I mean, neither of you are particularly upset, in light of..."

Usha blinked her big dark eyes somewhat blankly.

Dolores squinted. "Oh. Mrs Ogden, you mean?" Her tone denoted surprise but also disdain. Catching herself, and with a glance at her friend, Dolores adopted a rather more sombre expression, her racket no longer spinning at her side. "It's tragic, of course. A terrible thing to happen, but we weren't close to the woman. Hardly knew her."

"We never took a needlework class," confirmed Usha.

Felicity nodded. It wasn't just Dolores and Usha. There was no grand outpouring of sadness around the teacher's passing. A day of outdoor activities, while beneficial for the girls in taking their minds off the matter, could even be considered disrespectful towards the deceased woman's memory.

"Forgive my bluntness," began Felicity, "but was Mrs Ogden not well-liked?"

Usha bit her lip and threw a glance at her friend.

Dolores spun her racket. "As I said, your ladyship, we didn't know her. I dare say few did. She wasn't exactly the outgoing, friendly type. Not like yourself, your ladyship." Dolores smiled.

Felicity smiled back. It was sometimes difficult to tell when Dolores was being sincere. "Thank you for your honesty, Miss Gastrell. I shan't interfere with your game any longer."

"Thank you, your ladyship," said Usha, backing away from the net. She sounded relieved.

"Sorry that you came over here for nothing." Dolores swung her racket as she returned to her position on the court.

*I've dealt with worse*, thought Felicity as she made a beeline for the red-brick manor house, which was now visible above the high hedges.

The girls hadn't shared their full opinion on Mrs Ogden, had they? Students weren't always inclined to be honest with their teachers, but Dolores' and Usha's answers would have to suffice for now.

Weaving quickly through the sundial garden, past neat rows of scented silver-leaved lavender, it wasn't Mrs Ogden's lack of popularity but Miss Eversley's lie that stuck like a bone in Felicity's throat.

Was it an ungainly attempt to stall or even stop Felicity from gathering evidence from the house? No one but Felicity knew the details of her plan to find a handwriting sample. So why tell such an easily discoverable untruth? What was Miss Eversley trying to achieve? Might she have had a hand in Mrs Ogden's demise?

Felicity was getting ahead of herself.

Before diving into all the potential scenarios, Felicity had to be certain about one thing.

Was Mrs Ogden the spy?

Felicity entered the cool darkness of the house through a side door left open for ventilation. As her footsteps echoed along the narrow, tiled corridor, Felicity steadied her thoughts and refocused on the task at hand.

The teachers' quarters were in a wing quite separate from the students' apartments. The plushly carpeted stairs and long corridors decorated with paintings, busts on pedestals, and the occasional piece of antique furniture were deadly quiet. Practically everyone was outdoors in the sunshine.

Felicity pushed through the double doors that separated the teachers' wing from the rest of the house. What she was about to do was beyond what had been requested as part of her mission. However, it wasn't her first time sneaking somewhere she ought not be, and she'd already considered how she might explain herself were she found rifling through the dead woman's belongings.

Hopefully, it wouldn't come to that.

Built from dark stained oak and with a brightly polished brass knob, the door to Mrs Ogden's room was just as unremarkable as any of the others along the corridor.

*Tick-tock. Tick-tock.*

A grandfather clock stood at the head of the corridor counting the seconds. A faint cheer went up outside. Perhaps a victory on the croquet lawn or the conclusion of a crowd favourite played by the string quintet.

Felicity put her hand on the cool metal of the door handle.

Her stomach tightened a little as she twisted the knob.

## Chapter Eleven

With a gentle creak, the door to Mrs Ogden's room swung slowly open to reveal a surprising amount of disarray.

The bed had been stripped and the curtains taken down. The scent of wood polish mingled with traces of violet perfume. Several trunks were scattered across a thinning rug with a busy pattern that took up most of the floor. Some trunks were already closed. The rest lay open, half-filled with books, picture frames, and clothing draped over the sides.

Positioned by the window, which provided abundant light without direct sunshine, a tall stand held a sizeable wooden hoop. On a nearby stool, a basket contained a lustrous rainbow of threads.

In the hoop, a work of embroidery was stretched taught. Half-finished, the work depicted a large bouquet in an exquisite vase. The colours of the flowers were so expertly blended and the stitches so fine the work looked like a watercolour.

Felicity hesitated in the doorway. When a life ended, the items connected to the person remained as a trace of their presence, like a deep footprint in sand. As time passed and the items scattered, the footprint was washed away.

Mrs Ogden's presence was still very much in the room. It was, however, already disappearing.

"Can I help you, your ladyship?"

A small maid with a slight build and mousy brown hair had approached noiselessly along the corridor.

*Dash it!*

Still standing in Mrs Ogden's doorway, Felicity had been caught in the act.

"There's someone coming to pick up the trunks before lunch." The little maid kept her gaze meekly averted as she stood before Felicity, but her tone was businesslike. She had work to do and a deadline.

"Actually, yes," said Felicity, recovering quickly from the maid's interruption. She'd already considered a ruse for such a scenario. "You can indeed help me. I lent a book to poor Mrs Ogden. *Dombey and Son*. I do hope it's not too selfish of me to think of it under the circumstances, but the edition has sentimental value. I was hoping I might retrieve it."

Felicity had lent no such tome to the needlework teacher, of course.

Based on information gathered at dinner the night before, Mrs Ogden was a reader of Charles Dickens. *Dombey and Son* was a fitting novel to loan, but it was one of Dickens' more obscure works. When, after a search, no such book was found among Mrs Ogden's belongings, Felicity would apologise and say she'd found the book in her room. Mrs Ogden's returning of it must have slipped her mind.

"*Dombey and Son*, your ladyship?" echoed the maid, her forehead creasing slightly under her starched white cap.

"That's correct." Lying about the loan of a book was surprisingly easy. Hiding her disappointment was more difficult.

Short of breaking into Miss Armstrong's office and rifling through the headmistress' files — a risk even Felicity wasn't willing to take — how might Mrs Ogden's handwriting be checked now?

The maid nodded and gave a little curtsey. "I shall do my best to find it."

"Thank you, Miss..."

"Brown, your ladyship." The maid's tone was flat and rather curt.

"Thank you, Miss Brown."

Felicity cast a solemn gaze over the room with its half-filled trunks as the grandfather clock continued its *tick-tock* in the corridor. Where would the trunks be going? A local women's charity, perhaps. Miss Armstrong said the needlework teacher had no family of which to speak, at least no one with whom she was in any discernible contact.

"Will that be all, your ladyship?" The maid was eager to return to her work.

It wasn't correct to obstruct servants in their duties, but the opportunity couldn't be overlooked.

"Quite terrible, isn't it? How Mrs Ogden was here one day and gone the next." Felicity's statement was honest, and she paired it with a sad, anxious expression. "Might you have any knowledge of how the poor woman spent her last hours?"

The maid blinked impassively. If her impatience with Felicity was growing, she hid it well, just as she hid any emotion at the loss of the needlework teacher. "Mrs Ogden left the dinner hall earlier than usual, but she had her evening drink delivered at the normal time. Well, nearly the normal time."

The maid's correction caught Felicity's interest. "Her evening drink?"

The maid shifted a little, her hands clasped before her white apron. "Mrs Ogden always took a mug of cocoa before bed, your ladyship."

*Poison. Poison in the cocoa.*

The thought caught Felicity off guard. Yet was it so farfetched? Cyanide, digitalis, and a host of other substances could mimic the symptoms of a sudden, natural death. If no one suspected foul play and tests weren't done in time, a poisoning might go undetected.

Under normal circumstances, the chances of Mrs Ogden being poisoned were extremely low. But what if Felicity hadn't been the only person at Liverton Ladies' Academy looking for justice?

"Were you the one to bring the drink up to her room, Miss Brown?"

The maid's eyes flicked away. She nodded.

"And did everything seem well with Mrs Ogden to you?"

"Yes, your ladyship." Miss Brown fixed her gaze on the floor. "Only she wasn't too pleased with me," she mumbled.

"Oh?" Felicity raised her brow. "May I ask why?"

Another gentle cheer and a smattering of applause rose from the gardens.

The maid fidgeted with her apron. "I let the drink get cold, your ladyship."

Felicity felt sorry for the maid. Cold cocoa was unpalatable, and Mrs Ogden was rather intolerant of mistakes. It was easy to imagine the needlework teacher expressing her displeasure forthrightly.

"I don't suppose you were in the habit of delivering Mrs Ogden's evening cocoa at the incorrect temperature."

The maid looked up at Felicity with relief. "Oh, no, your ladyship. I'd never done it before."

"What distracted you from your work?"

"I got called away, your ladyship. To help with the preparations for the practice ball. I said I was busy with the evening drinks, but she wouldn't take no for an answer. She said it'd only take a moment, but it took much longer than that." Miss Brown's lower lip trembled. "So by the time I delivered Mrs Ogden's cocoa to her, it was cold. Her last cocoa was cold."

So the little maid was moved by what had happened to Mrs Ogden. She was just very good at hiding it.

"Who called you away?" pressed Felicity gently.

"It's my fault, your ladyship." The maid was adamant. "I'm the one who has to take responsibility for my duties."

"It's quite all right. No one's in trouble." Felicity had to proceed carefully. "It's my role to instruct the girls. They have to learn how to operate in harmony with servants such as yourself. They'll be running their own households in the future. If you tell me who it was, I'll give her gentle instruction on the topic without bringing your name into it. Ultimately, it will be of benefit to the student in question."

The maid paused. She swallowed. "It was Miss Gwendoline Milligan, your ladyship. The very pale girl. She's the one that distracted me from my duties."

## Chapter Twelve

The sun warmed Felicity's shoulders and bees buzzed above drifts of nodding flowers in wide borders as she ducked under archways covered with rambling pink and white roses, the strains of Debussy's Clair de Lune drawing her onwards. The weather was perfect, the gardens immaculate, yet there was a knot in Felicity's stomach.

*Clack!*

A game of croquet was underway on a pristine, bright green lawn. One of the younger girls had just made a roquet with her stroke. Smiles were on the lips of students and teachers alike.

Miss Armstrong was now present, in a dark green pleated skirt, cream long-sleeved blouse, and a sleeveless knitted vest in dark red. She stood at the side of the lawn, watching with satisfaction as the girls engaged in polite rivalry among the hoops. Even Dolores and Usha had abandoned the tennis court for the croquet lawn.

Deck chairs were available under parasols for those not participating, where tea and cake were being served by the butler and footmen.

It looked idyllic. But Felicity sensed a dark undercurrent swirling beneath it all.

"Joining us, are you, your ladyship?" boomed Miss Driver as Felicity made her way around the edge of the lawn. The movement teacher was refereeing the croquet. Her clubs lay abandoned under a bench, the girls having not been as enthusiastic about golf as she'd hoped.

Felicity shook her head politely in Miss Driver's direction. "I'm afraid not." Before descending from the teachers' quarters, Felicity had collected a book from her room — *The King's English* by the Fowler brothers — and tucked it under her arm. Though she had no intention of perusing it, she now gestured towards it.

*Crack!*

The young student who'd made the roquet took her croquet shot. The two balls went barrelling over the neatly trimmed grass, which the groundsmen must have attended to daily.

"Bravo!" Miss Driver applauded. "I say, what a shot!"

Miss Armstrong's eyes flicked away from the croquet to watch Felicity. Miss Petherick, who was still conducting the string quintet, also glanced at Felicity as she chose a deck chair seemingly at random.

Felicity had been exceptionally watchful since arriving at the school. Now she was more vigilant than ever.

"May I?" Felicity enquired with a casual nod towards an empty deckchair in the shade of a broad parasol.

From the adjacent seat, Gwendoline looked up at Felicity, her ice-blue eyes thoughtful. She had on a wide-brimmed straw hat and an airy lavender linen dress, her pale skin protected from the summer sunshine by a gauzy white cardigan.

"Of course." Gwendoline sounded mildly surprised.

Was there any chance she was aware that Felicity's choice to sit next to her was no coincidence? Might calling the maid away from Mrs Ogden's final cocoa have been a calculated act?

Felicity had to find out.

Gentle applause went up around the croquet lawn as the string quintet stopped for a break. Miss Petherick, Cecily, Jane, and the other players set about putting their instruments to rest in their cases.

Gwendoline had put down her book — a cloth-bound edition of *The Letters of John Keats* — to applaud the musicians. Felicity also gently clapped.

"Will you be joining in the game at some point, Miss Milligan?" enquired Felicity as play resumed on the croquet green.

Gwendoline smiled shyly, as though flattered. "I much prefer to read."

"As do I," said Felicity, propping open the pages of *The King's English* at her bookmark, which she'd thrown into the book quite haphazardly before heading outside. "One learns so much," continued Felicity. "However, one has to at least occasionally join the action going on around us. We're also characters in our own stories."

Felicity hadn't lied to Miss Armstrong when she'd said she enjoyed teaching more than expected. Through gentle coaxing, Felicity had done her best to aid the girls in overcoming their own obstacles.

With Gwendoline, the improvements didn't come as easily as with the others, yet Felicity persisted. There was something of herself that she recognised in the girl. Gwendoline, like Felicity, was a keen observer.

Closing her book, Gwendoline looked up at the croquet players. "Oh, I know, your ladyship." There was a hint of regret in her voice.

Felicity sensed it wouldn't help to push the matter.

Gwendoline's family was exceedingly well-to-do, but their wealth had been acquired relatively recently. Her pale skin and hair also made her stand out. While Felicity had never witnessed meanness from the other girls, Gwendoline was self-conscious and lacked confidence.

Yet to deceive successfully, boldness was required.

When Gwendoline called the maid away from Mrs Ogden's cocoa, was it part of a wider plot?

*Clack!*

Cecily had taken up a croquet mallet and sent a ball spinning across the lawn. It went straight through a hoop.

"Excellent shot, Lady Cecily," bellowed Miss Driver.

Cecily smiled and shrugged as though it were nothing but a fluke, the short sleeves of her pale yellow dress fluttering in the breeze.

Dolores looked distinctly displeased, her narrowed eyes darting towards Cecily as she tossed the tie from her bandeau over her shoulder and lined up her mallet to take a shot.

"Father says I ought to put myself out there more." Gwendoline smiled sadly at Felicity. She was as pretty as any of the other Liverton girls, but her fingernails were bitten down, and there were worry lines on her young forehead. "I suppose that's why he sent me here."

The students at Liverton could expect lives full of comfort and wealth, but they still faced challenges. Familial expectations could be an extraordinary weight to bear.

"Do you feel well-prepared for the practice ball?" asked Felicity.

Gwendoline frowned a little. She watched Dolores finesse the alignment of her shot. "Not particularly. But that's the whole point of a rehearsal, isn't it? To test ourselves before the real thing."

*Thwack!*

Dolores swung her mallet.

"Have you been using your evenings for extra practice?" enquired Felicity.

Dolores' ball missed the hoop by quite some distance. She fumed, her jaw tight.

Gwendoline's lips turned downwards. "Miss Petherick has been helping me with my rhythm. I'm awful at keeping time. I know all the steps by heart. I just can't get them on the beat."

The music teacher stood on the other side of the croquet lawn, her arms folded tightly over her black and grey dress. She always looked unhappy, which made her difficult to read.

Felicity leaned forward in her deckchair. "I say, Miss Milligan. Might you know anything about a servant being distracted from her duties the other evening?"

Gwendoline turned towards Felicity, her pale eyebrows drawn tightly together. "Have I done something wrong?"

Felicity gave a little frown. She never enjoyed chastising others, and Gwendoline's confidence was already lacking. Yet she had to push forward.

"Not wrong, as such. Might you know about the incident to which I'm referring? The maid was already busy with a task. She had hot cocoa to deliver."

Gwendoline blinked rapidly. "I asked Miss Brown to assist in closing the window in the rehearsal room. The evening air was rather cool, and the window was very stiff. Miss Petherick sent me to fetch help while she went to inform the butler of the issue, so that it might be dealt with properly the next day."

A chill ran through Felicity.

The music teacher was responsible for the maid's distraction.

Might Miss Petherick have found out Mrs Ogden was a spy for the Germans during the war? Did she blame the woman for the death of her sweetheart and sought revenge?

As her thoughts swirled, Felicity did her best to remain calm. "So Miss Petherick left you alone with the maid in the rehearsal room while she went to inform the butler about the window?" The question wasn't entirely subtle.

Gwendoline looked pained. "Have I done something wrong?"

Felicity hesitated. Her question hadn't been answered, but she couldn't openly interrogate the girl. Tact and camouflage were essential.

"You should understand, Miss Milligan, that when a servant is involved in a task above stairs, it's important not to distract her." It felt rotten to berate Gwendoline, but Felicity couldn't allow anyone to imagine she was at the school to do anything other than teach. "If you're not the overseer of the household, you don't have the full picture. There could be unintended consequences."

"But I—" Gwendoline stopped mid-sentence, her forehead pinched. Her gaze dropped to her lap. "I quite understand, your ladyship. It was wrong of me. I ought to have fetched a footman. Thank you for making me aware of my mistake."

Felicity smiled sadly. "I've made similar mistakes in the past, myself," she offered.

The girl didn't look up. The damage had been done.

But a new suspect had emerged.

Had the music teacher engineered Mrs Ogden's cocoa to be left unattended so that she might administer poison? There were many missing pieces to this hypothesis, yet people had been murdered over less, and the unattended cocoa was suspiciously coincidental.

On the other side of the croquet lawn, Miss Petherick drank lemonade served by the butler. She gulped it down, taking no pleasure in the taste.

If she had taken revenge on Mrs Ogden, the music teacher didn't seem at all satisfied. The only thing that would perhaps ever make Miss Petherick pleased was the return of her sweetheart. Which, tragically, would never happen.

Even with the chance to assess Mrs Ogden's handwriting now gone, Felicity had learned useful information from the maid and from Gwendoline. She couldn't inform Jasper over the telephone, but Alex would hopefully visit the following week, and she could—

"Lady Felicity, might you have a moment for me?"

Jane had approached the deckchairs, her pleated pink skirt catching around her knees as she walked.

Gwendoline sniffed and reopened her book.

To fortify herself, Felicity remembered the scar on Alex's forehead. It could so easily have been more than just an injury.

With a glance at the music teacher, Felicity stood up. "What is it, Lady Jane?"

Jane came to a sudden stop, stunned to have so easily captured Felicity's attention. "Oh." She plunged a hand into a skirt pocket and, after a small amount of rummaging, produced a folded sheet of paper, which she held out towards Felicity. "I re-drafted it. In accordance with your feedback. Do you think you might take a look?"

Stepping away from where Gwendoline was seated, for the least she could do was leave the girl in peace with her book, Felicity took Jane's paper and slowly unfolded it. The handwriting was a hurried scrawl.

"You wish me to look at it now?"

Jane glanced around her. "I was rather hoping to put it in the post today. It's to a friend all the way up in Scotland. Mavis does so love to hear my news, and after what happened to that poor embroidery teacher, I simply have to share the details with Mavis. It'll give her something to tell her school chums about, and they are rather starved of goings-on up there. It's awfully quiet for miles around."

Felicity winced a little. A teacher's death shouldn't be treated as school-girl gossip, but that's why Jane was at the academy. To develop appropriate social behaviour.

"Seeing as you're in a hurry, I shall take a look now, Lady Jane," began Felicity. "But before I've even read your letter, I can tell you that Mrs Ogden's passing, or the passing of anyone, is a delicate matter. The act of racing to share the news with someone without a direct connection to the deceased is, on the whole, indelicate."

"Oh." Jane's shoulders sagged. "I see. Botched it again, have I?"

"Let's not jump to conclusions," continued Felicity. "Shall we move into the sunlight so I can read it better? You wrote this in a rush, if I'm not mistaken?"

Jane nodded as she accompanied Felicity in stepping away from the parasol's shade.

As they moved into the sunshine, Felicity did her best to keep her focus on Jane and her letter, but she couldn't help glancing at where Mrs Petherick had been enjoying a glass of lemonade.

The music teacher had gone. In her place, the groundsmen had been invited to the lemonade stand.

Dressed in linen shirts and flat caps, the workers set their shovels and wheelbarrows carefully down on the sidelines of the croquet match, which was still ongoing. Among them was the man with greying hair who'd helped Felicity find the tennis court.

Miss Armstrong oversaw the filling of their glasses and encouraged the men to help themselves to biscuits offered on a large platter held by a young footman.

The groundsmen looked awkward and out of place, their shirts damp from the effort of their toiling, their caps tucked under their arms. Only one man among them looked relaxed enough to enjoy his lemonade

He raised his glass at Felicity as she stared at him across the croquet lawn, Jane's letter having fallen to her side.

"Is it really that bad, your ladyship?" enquired Jane anxiously.

"It's not your... It's just..." Were Felicity's eyes playing tricks on her?

## Chapter Thirteen

It was only after the groundsmen had finished their lemonade and returned to work that Felicity could engineer the opportunity to investigate what had surprised her at the refreshments stand.

She speedily concluded her review of Jane's letter, which wasn't as insensitive on the topic of Mrs Ogden's passing as first feared. There was also a brief exchange with Miss Vincent, who enquired whether Felicity could oversee a game of quoits, which was thankfully scheduled for later in the day, after the picnic lunch.

Having agreed to the commitment, Felicity declared the need to stretch her legs and announced that she was going for a stroll. Once out of sight, the stroll became a brisk march in the direction in which the groundsmen had disappeared with their wheelbarrows.

Passing the trickling classical fountain, Felicity found herself in a shady avenue lined with horse chestnuts. It appeared to be an impasse, ending at a curved wooden bench situated before a wall of ivy.

A trail of small pieces of broken rock and the sound of tools on stone drew Felicity onwards. At the end of the avenue, beside the bench, an arched gate stood open. Beyond was something like a rockery. However, due to its scale, it was unlike any rockery Felicity had seen before.

Dinosaur-sized ferns sprouted from jagged cliffs. Boulders topped with bright green moss lay in imposing clusters, as though from an ancient landslide. A waterfall splashed into a stream that trickled beside a meandering stone path. The air felt cool and damp.

One of the 'cliffs' was undergoing major work, the bank of red earth behind it on display. The groundsman who'd given Felicity directions to the tennis court seemed to be in charge, directing the exact placement of each rock. A train of workmen with wooden wheelbarrows carried ragged chunks of grey limestone to the cliff face, each toiling with great effort, the iron-rimmed wheels of their barrows creaking under the weight.

A broad-shouldered fellow with dark blond hair and powerful forearms captured Felicity's attention. She couldn't take her eyes off him as he tilted the barrow, his muscles flexing impressively as the stones clattered onto the growing pile.

Just what the blazes was Alex doing working on the rockery?

His face glowing slightly from the effort as he steadied the empty barrow, Alex spotted Felicity and gave a slow smile. *I wondered how long it'd take you.* Setting down his wheelbarrow, he tipped his head towards the waterfall. *Follow me.*

Felicity couldn't smile back. The glare she gave Alex was narrow-eyed, but she had to follow him. They had to talk. My goodness, did they have to talk.

The waterfall's roar filled the air as Alex led the way through a rough stone gateway adjacent to the water feature, with Felicity following at a careful distance.

She glanced over her shoulder. Were any of the groundsmen watching them? None of them were, but that didn't mean they hadn't been seen.

Beyond the rockery was a covered seating area tucked behind an orderly colonnade of smooth, honey-yellow pillars. Benches in the same yellow stone stretched along the back wall. At the seating's centre was a small door painted to mimic the sandstone of the columns and benches. Dark leaved jasmine curled around the columns and dripped swathes of white star-like flowers. The sounds of the waterfall and the wheelbarrows were completely gone. The noises from the croquet lawn could also not be heard.

"You found me, then." Alex removed his cap. His hair was unruly, his scarred forehead glistening. He wore a white linen shirt rolled up to his elbows, burgundy braces, and sturdy grey trousers. He was dusty and glowing from physical effort. It was an appearance utterly unlike his usual smartly cut suits and slicked-back hair.

A blush threatened to invade Felicity's cheeks. She fought it. "Don't make me say it."

Alex sank down onto the stone bench, his cap in his hands. "The usual Lady Felicity greeting, you mean?" He leaned back wearily against the stone wall. "'What are you doing here?'"

Felicity put her fists on her hips. "Have I not a right to know?"

Alex shrugged. "Extra hands were needed. I'm an unskilled labourer." He looked at his palms, which were rather red. "Very unskilled."

Felicity tutted. "I know for certain you've still got your job on the paper. Jasper would never let you go."

Alex rested his head against the wall. "Your brother didn't send me, if that's what you were wondering."

Felicity folded her arms. "The thought didn't enter my mind."

She'd accused Alex of being her brother's spy in the past, but she knew better now. In less than a year, she and Alex had gone from being professional rivals to firm friends. But that didn't mean everything he did filled Felicity with delight.

"I'm not silly." Her tone was abrupt. "I'm aware you wouldn't be here if it weren't for me."

Alex lifted his head away from the wall. "When did I ever say you were silly?"

Felicity approached the pillars. The view beyond was of gently rolling parkland leading down to a shadowy stand of trees.

Thankfully, no one else was about. In the heat of her vexation, she'd perhaps been a little careless.

Felicity returned her attention to Alex. "I'm doing my best to stay undercover—" she kept her voice low "—and you appear from nowhere, without warning or explanation. And now we're having a meeting within the grounds in broad daylight."

Alex stood up. "Easy, now. The head gardener won't rat us out."

Felicity's stomach dropped. "You told him you're here to see me?" Her voice came out shriller than expected.

Alex half winced and half smiled. "It's understood there's an, umm... How should I say? That we have a..."

Felicity shook her head a little. She didn't understand.

Then the penny dropped.

"He thinks you're my beau?" she gasped.

Alex looked down at his rugged hands and squeezed the cloth of his cap. "You know why I'm really here, though." He brought his dark blue gaze to meet hers. "Don't you?"

Despite feeling suddenly rather flustered, Felicity folded her arms. "Enlighten me," she commanded, genuinely puzzled at how having Alex onsite was supposed to help.

"Jasp told me you were staying on. He told me about the needlework teacher. She was your suspect, wasn't she?"

"And you wanted to be first on the scene for the scoop?" It was all making sense now. "You know we can't report from the school."

"If there's ever a story, I want it first." Alex was always more dogged about getting the truth in print than Felicity. "But I know the school is out of bounds. And your mission — our mission," corrected Alex. "It'll probably never see the light of day in the papers. It's all closed-door military courts these days."

Felicity quirked an eyebrow. "It's *our* mission, now?"

Alex shrugged. "We're a team, aren't we?"

Felicity eyed her friend carefully.

She didn't exactly object to the implication she had romantic interests in an unskilled labourer, but she would have preferred to have been consulted on the ruse. And while it wasn't clear how they would work together on 'their' mission, Felicity and Alex had indeed collaborated to excellent effect in the past.

Considering the headmistress' concerns about the press sneaking into Liverton, there'd been a large degree of talent involved in Alex charming his way into employment as a groundsman. It would be a shame to waste his skills.

Felicity's mission had, after all, become even more delicate and complex.

Alex cocked an eyebrow. "Will you fill me in? Or shall I go back to shifting rocks?"

Felicity glanced beyond the colonnade. Aside from a covey of pheasants, with bright red cheeks and long speckled tails, the parkland remained empty.

Keeping her voice low, she explained to Alex how she'd intended to sneak into the needlework teacher's room to see her handwriting and how Mrs Ogden's unusual behaviour had scuppered Felicity's plan, only for the woman's lifeless body to be discovered the next morning.

After smiling and shaking his head at Felicity's willingness to resort to burglar-like behaviour — which Felicity countered with, "I was only going to look, not steal" — Alex went quiet for a moment.

He looked thoughtful. "Could all be a coincidence." Alex was never afraid to challenge Felicity's or anyone's thinking. "There's no suspicion of foul play, is there?"

Felicity shrugged. "There's no proof of anything. Not of a spy, a murder, or a killer."

"Except... You have an inkling. Am I right?"

He was.

Felicity began pacing. "There are countless ways to do away with someone and for it to be mistaken for natural causes. Poison, for example. Poison administered to a mug of nightly cocoa that the maid told me herself she left unattended. Left unattended because she was called away..."

"By someone who knew exactly what they were doing and who had plans for murder?"

"Well. Almost. Called away by a student at the request of a teacher."

Alex dipped his chin. "Your suspicions are still firmly on the teaching staff?"

"And if it is murder," continued Felicity, her heels tapping on the sandstone paving as she continued to pace, "doesn't that make it more likely the needlework teacher was our spy?"

She stopped and stared at her friend.

Alex held Felicity's gaze. "It would also mean there's a murderer at the school." His tone was solemn.

Was this his motive for becoming a groundsman? Did he imagine Felicity to be in danger?

Was she in danger?

Murder as revenge was a precise and calculated act. With the war traitor now punished, what would be the point of further crimes?

Alex folded his arms. "A murderer who might not appreciate your efforts to uncover his or her ruse."

Felicity frowned. Alex had a horrible habit of making good points. "I have a suspect in mind, but I shan't do anything silly."

Alex continued to sound rather serious. "You might have been caught in your now-dead colleague's room."

It wasn't the moment to mention Felicity had been caught that very morning.

"To listen and to learn," she said. "That was my task, wasn't it? I've extended the period, that's all. You want answers. That's why you put me forward for the mission, wasn't it?"

Alex tightened the fold of his arms, his cap still clutched in his hand. He looked conflicted. "I've a contact I can call for clarity on the official status of the teacher's death. Perhaps even some background on your murder suspect, if you give me her name. Another of the teachers, is it?"

"Miss Ivy Petherick. She had a sweetheart who never came back from the war. I'm not sure of the details, but that's my idea for her motive."

Alex nodded. "I'll make some calls when I get back to Exeter tonight."

Felicity smiled at her friend. "Thank you."

Alex mussed the hair at the back of his head. "Look. You know I'd never stand in the way of you doing whatever you felt was right."

"I know." It was one of Felicity's favourite things about Alex.

"But it's my fault you're here," he continued. "I brought you into this situation."

"Alex." Felicity sensed where he was going.

"If you feel I'm exposing you, I can leave. I'll say the rocks are too heavy. I don't mind losing face."

Felicity took a step towards him. "There's no need for that. We're a team, aren't w—"

"Oh, dear. Am I interrupting?"

Her pale hair shining like a halo in the sunshine, Gwendoline had appeared at the edge of the colonnade. She had a book under her arm and a little wooden box with a silver handle clasped at her side.

Alex straightened and pulled on his cap. He gave Gwendoline a brief, polite nod. "Miss."

"You're... You're not interrupting anything, Miss Milligan." Felicity smiled faintly, but her stomach was a knot. How much had Gwendoline heard? "I was simply informing the groundsman, Mr Cooper here, of damage I noticed to a... To a pathway near the fountain."

It was nonsense, of course, but what else was she supposed to say?

"I'll inform the head gardener right away, your ladyship." With a tug on his cap, Alex left the seating area, striding purposefully towards the rockery.

"I can leave, if you like, your ladyship." Gwendoline looked surprised and uncomfortable, which hopefully meant she hadn't been listening before her arrival on the scene.

"No, Miss Milligan, it is I who shall leave you in peace. It's the perfect spot to spend time with a book. I wish you pleasant reading."

Felicity stepped out into the parkland, sending the pheasants clucking across the grass. Avoiding the rockery, she took a hedge-lined gravel path she hoped would lead her back to the croquet lawn. There was the game of quoits she'd promised to oversee, and there was Miss Petherick to watch and learn more about.

Though the sun was still warm, Felicity shivered.

The stakes had been raised.

# Chapter Fourteen

A fire crackled in the great hearth of Liverton House's library, its light dancing on the gold lettering on the spines of the leather-bound books that filled the towering bookcases. While the sunshine had warmed the day's croquet, picnic, and quoits, it was still too early in the year to count on warm nights.

Felicity was seated at a large oval table, making her way through a stack of letters written by her students. Using a fountain pen loaded with burgundy ink, she added notes of encouragement and corrections, but progress was terribly slow. Felicity's attention was elsewhere.

After Gwendoline interrupted her meeting with Alex, Felicity had returned to the croquet lawn in time for a picnic lunch of sausage rolls, egg sandwiches, and slices of madeira cake. The afternoon passed peacefully, with Felicity mainly engaged in overseeing multiple rounds of quoits, all while keeping a clandestine eye on the music teacher.

Miss Petherick spent the afternoon conducting the string quintet, whose seats and music stands were in full view of the quoits pitch. There had been nothing odd about the music teacher's behaviour, neither during the afternoon nor during dinner, which was served in the dining hall. Discussion at the teacher's table was muted, most of everyone's energy having been spent on the outdoor games.

Felicity had looked up from her entrée when Gwendoline arrived for dinner. Felicity smiled at Gwendoline, but the girl looked away promptly. Was her unease from Felicity's chastisement about the maid? Or from her disbelief of Felicity's story about reporting damaged paving to Alex?

Neither option was desirable, but what could Felicity do to mend things without drawing further attention to her own odd behaviour?

Miss Eversley had also been at dinner and was now in the library, poring over books filled with columns of statistics at a walnut desk in the room's corner. In normal circumstances, Felicity would already have confronted the teacher of household budgeting about her mendacious behaviour concerning the need for a tennis umpire.

The circumstances at Liverton were anything but normal, however.

If Felicity was to bring her mission to a successful close — including making good use of her extra weeks at the school and of Alex's support — investigation of the hypothesis of Miss Petherick having poisoned Mrs Ogden was the next logical step. Reverting to her original mission brief but with an updated aim in mind, Felicity would return to watching and listening while remaining undercover.

It was with this *modus operandi* that, after dinner, Felicity had stood under the portico of Liverton House's front entrance, pulling her cardigan tighter against the night air, which was scented with freshly trampled grass. From this vantage point, it was possible to watch the after-dinner comings and goings through the house's lit windows.

Upon seeing Miss Petherick moving with purpose along the east corridor towards the library, Felicity had gone up to her room, collected a stack of letters, and went to sit among the students and teachers engaged in quiet study among the bookshelves.

Her back to the snapping fire, Miss Petherick was seated almost opposite Felicity at the large oval table. She was perusing a large pile of sheet music, her fingers lightly tapping the mahogany table top as her eyes skimmed the notes.

Was this Miss Petherick in a good mood because her sweetheart had been avenged? Or was this behaviour quite normal? Before Gwendoline's testimony about being sent by the music teacher to distract the maid, Felicity had been looking for a wartime spy, not a murderer. Miss Petherick hadn't been a person of interest. Felicity hadn't studied her behaviour in detail.

Only a smattering of students were present in the library, far fewer than usual. The merriment and fresh air of the day outside had perhaps tired them.

Dolores and Usha were seated in a corner in a pair of plush leather armchairs. They had jotters open on their laps, but they were mostly whispering and giggling together.

Jane was also present. She was restless, flitting between her desk and the bookshelves that lined the walls. She selected a book, brought it to her table, then after reading only a page or two, returned the tome and selected another one.

"Your ladyship?"

The voice startled Felicity.

Mr Clark's silent approach was, however, appropriate for the library, and his tone was gentle.

Felicity hoped her skittishness wasn't noticeable. "Mr Clark?"

"Your book, your ladyship."

The butler held out a silver salver. Atop it was a thick tome with fabric binding and tatty corners.

Felicity blinked down at it, confused. When had she requested Mr Clark fetch her a book from the shelves? It didn't look like any of the library's leather-bound editions.

"I understand you loaned this book and wished it returned." The butler spoke with as much discretion as possible.

Felicity glanced at the spine.

*Dombey and Son*.

The ruse had only been intended to explain away Felicity's

presence in Mrs Ogden's room. She never expected a book out of it. The needlework teacher had clearly been more of a fan of Dickens than first thought.

"Of course. Thank you, Mr Clark."

As Felicity lifted the book from the tray, its pages fell open. Papers and a bookmark fluttered to the library carpet.

"My apologies, your ladyship," said the butler as he stooped to retrieve the fallen items.

The scene attracted attention. Eyes Felicity didn't want upon her flicked in her direction, including those of Miss Petherick.

The items Mr Clark collected from the floor included a bookmark, a train ticket, and a clipping from a newspaper.

There was also a small, hand-written note.

"Do you wish me to dispose of these articles, your ladyship?" enquired the butler. Besides the bookmark, which was intricately embroidered, the papers that had fluttered to the floor had the appearance of worthless clutter.

But to Felicity, they were extraordinarily valuable.

"No," she said, perhaps a little too sharply. "Thank you, Mr Clark. I shall sort through them myself."

As the butler withdrew, Felicity maintained her composure as her insides fizzed with excitement. The book in her hands contained samples of Mrs Ogden's handwriting. Felicity had practically dismissed the idea of seeing anything written by the needlework teacher, yet here it was, delivered to her.

Conscious of maintaining her cover, Felicity remained in the library and continued to review her students' letters. Miss Petherick's attention continued to be fixed squarely on her sheet music, her fingers occasionally working imaginary keys.

As Felicity tried to maintain focus on the letters, the tattered copy of *Dombey and Son* on the table beside her was an enormous distraction.

Surely a review of Mrs Ogden's handwriting was more important than maintaining a watch over Miss Petherick? If the needlework teacher wasn't the spy, it undermined the music teacher's motive for wanting her punished.

Felicity stood up from her seat, with her students' letters and Mrs Ogden's copy of *Dombey and Son* clutched to her chest.

This was surely the breakthrough she needed.

# Chapter Fifteen

Servants had already visited Felicity's room to close the heavy blue velvet curtains and light a fire in the small hearth. The room was much smaller than her own bedroom at Bradley Court, and there was no Yorkshire Terrier to sleep atop the counterpane. But the single bed was comfortable, the furniture, fixtures were sturdy and of high quality, and Felicity had slept in much less luxurious conditions before.

With the door to her room closed behind her, she went to the modestly sized desk opposite her bed and switched on the small green lamp. Putting the letters she'd been marking to one side, she cleared away that morning's edition of the Western Daily News and placed the copy of *Dombey and Son* squarely atop the desk's dark blue leather inlay.

The fire snapped in the grate as Felicity lowered herself onto the hard wooden chair in front of the desk.

There was something rum about acquiring a deceased person's intimate property through deceitful means, yet now was not the moment to become overly concerned with the moral mechanics of how Mrs Ogden's book had been acquired. Suspecting someone of being a wartime traitor was extremely serious indeed.

Granted, the only two people aware of Felicity's suspicions —

Alex and her brother — were two of the most trustworthy and honourable men in the world. But it was just as important to clear Mrs Ogden's name as to condemn it, and it was no longer only the needlework teacher that Felicity suspected.

What if both Mrs Ogden and Miss Petherick were entirely innocent?

Felicity opened the book's front cover, resting it on a domed glass paperweight to be gentle with the spine of the well-loved tome. A hint of violet perfume clung to its pages. The butler had neatly reinserted the papers and bookmark that had fluttered onto the library floor. They lay in a small heap between the flyleaf and frontispiece.

Felicity gingerly lifted the first paper from the little pile. It was a neat newspaper clipping of a recipe. The recipe was for a drink intended to aid with sore throats, containing sage and honey and apparently inspired by a traditional medieval remedy.

Felicity put the cutting to one side.

Next, there was a train ticket. Wickleigh to Exeter. A journey made in June 1921, precisely a year ago. What was the reason for keeping the ticket? Mrs Ogden had seemed such a purposeful, neat creature. The collection of little items stuffed in a tattered book appeared so out of character.

But then had Felicity — or anyone else — really known Mrs Ogden?

She put the ticket to one side.

Underneath it was the handwritten note.

In dark blue ink on a scrap of thick cream paper was written:

*2 sk. Curacao Blue*
*1 sk. Deep Ochre*
*3 sk. Shady Green*
*Milliners*
*Tapestry*

*Milliners* and *tapestry* were types of needles. *Sk.* likely stood for *skein*, but what was written didn't matter. It was how.

Felicity had been sitting next to Alex in Jasper's office when she'd seen the impressions collected from the spy's envelope. The sample of the handwriting wasn't complete, and she hadn't a copy with her for direct comparison. Any physical evidence of her mission was forbidden.

The handwriting's loops, however, had been large and distinctive. Felicity had imagined a match would be easy to spot. Indeed, through the absence of distinctive flourishes, she'd been able to rule out the handwriting of all the other teachers.

Looking at Mrs Ogden's handwriting now, however, Felicity's excitement dwindled.

She shifted the paper back and forth under the bright light from the desk lamp. There were large loops in the tail of a small Y and grand flourishes in the generous bulk of the capital letters.

Was it a match?

Felicity squinted. It was possible, but she couldn't be sure. Without the original sample of the loops for a direct comparison, there could be no definitive answer. The expertise of a handwriting specialist might even be required.

Disappointed, Felicity sank back in her chair. It felt like a blow. But it wasn't, really, was it? She could pass the sample onto Alex. He could get it to Jasper, and the intelligence services could test it.

The discovery of Mrs Ogden's handwriting was still an important breakthrough.

So then why did Felicity suddenly feel so glum?

The introductory pages of *Dombey and Son* still lay open. Across the page lay a piece of greyish linen that had been neatly pressed and shaped into a bookmark. The fabric was decorated with the most elaborate and delicate needlework. Tiny stitches depicted a small bundle of meadow flowers, as one might collect on a summer's day. Yellow buttercups, blue cornflowers, and red poppies, all tied with a white ribbon. At a glance the flowers looked real.

Mrs Ogden had possessed considerable talent. She had an eye for nature. She cared for and loved things, just as every person did.

Even if she were a criminal, did she deserve to be murdered in her bed? And what if she wasn't guilty at all?

*Tap-tap-tap!*

There was a knock at the door.

Quickly, Felicity returned the items to the book and placed the tome under the newspaper on her desk. Smoothing her skirt, she went to the door and opened it.

Miss Petherick stood as straight as a guardsman in the hallway's gloom, the collar of her long dark dress tight at her throat, her cheeks wan and hollow.

A chill ran down Felicity's spine. The grandfather clock at the end of the corridor ticked steadily.

"Miss Petherick," said Felicity after too much of a pause. "How may I help you?"

The teacher's mouth was down turned. "You're to accompany me," she said. "Right away."

# Chapter Sixteen

What could Felicity do?

Say to Miss Petherick, *I shan't go with you because I suspect you of murder, and I fear I may be next?*

Nothing had yet been proved. And even if Felicity's suspicions were right, there was no advantage in signalling to Miss Petherick that she was being investigated.

"Might I ask where you intend to take me?" was Felicity's only form of protest.

"You shall see," said Miss Petherick, who then turned and began along the corridor.

Despite a feeling of deep unease, Felicity followed.

As they climbed the central stairs, Miss Petherick's movements were no more tense than usual. If the music teacher had done away with Mrs Ogden, she was playing it extremely coolly.

Felicity's pulse rose steadily, nevertheless.

Following Miss Petherick along a thinly carpeted landing on one of the mansion's top floors, Felicity recalled confidently telling Alex she wouldn't do anything silly. Wasn't following a suspected murderer to a remote corner of the house a tad ill-advised?

They reached the foot of a steep, narrow staircase. A chilly draught swept down from above. Miss Petherick began the climb. Felicity put her hand on the banister and hesitated.

Voices.

They were muffled, but the voices carried down the stairs.

Wherever Miss Petherick was taking Felicity, she wouldn't be alone.

She started up the stairs behind the music teacher.

---

Miss Petherick opened a door at the top of the steps and stood aside. Solid heavy beams in bare oak criss-crossed the attic, which was lit by candles flickering in the draught. Wooden trunks and chests were stacked against the walls, and there was a hint of mustiness to the cool air.

At the centre of the space was a small ring of chests serving as seats. In the middle was a steamer trunk being used as a table. Atop was a pot of tea with a knitted cosy, a milk jug, several cups and saucers, and a large plate of biscuits.

Their voices rang out clearly now. Huddled around the tea and biscuits were Miss Vincent, Miss Eversley, and Miss Driver.

"Her heart gave out, as I understand it." Miss Vincent wore a fluffy pebble-grey cardigan, a powder-pink scarf wrapped twice around her neck, and slate-grey knitted fingerless gloves. She dropped the H from 'her' and 'heart', but she was, as always, fully understandable.

Miss Eversley nodded eagerly, the candlelight glinting in her glasses. "That's what Miss Armstrong told me." She had on her usual tweed jacket and skirt but had added a thick hound's tooth scarf to the ensemble.

This was perhaps not the teachers' first gathering in the coolness of the attic. But it was the first such meeting Felicity had been invited to attend, and the needlework teacher's passing was on the agenda.

There were two wooden chests with square pillows atop but no sitters. As Miss Petherick took one of the vacant seats, Felicity took the other, shivering a little as she did so.

Miss Petherick appeared unmoved by the talk of Mrs Ogden's death. Having recovered a jet black lace-trimmed shawl from beside her seat, she busied herself draping it around her shoulders.

"Lady Felicity," said Miss Driver by way of welcome. She had on a long-sleeved navy blue tunic with black knee-high riding boots. A grey fur stole was pulled tight at her neck. "Glad you could join us."

"Yes." Miss Vincent smiled as Felicity sat down. "Very glad."

Felicity nodded in appreciation. "Thank you for inviting me."

Miss Eversley took a loud bite from a ginger biscuit. The lie the bespectacled teacher had told Felicity about the girls' request for an umpire remained baffling. It wasn't the time to confront anyone, however. It was time to listen.

The movement teacher frowned at Felicity. "Did Petherick not advise you to bring something warm?"

"My apologies," mumbled the music teacher as she poured herself a cup of tea. Thankfully, the tea pot seemed to be a self-service affair. It was one thing to have followed Miss Petherick up to the attic. It would have been something else to accept a drink from her.

"It's quite all right," said Felicity, doing her best not to allow her teeth to chatter. The moss-green woollen skirt she'd changed into for dinner was warm enough, but she'd left the jacket in her room. At least her cream silk blouse had a buttoned collar and long sleeves.

"Good, oh." Miss Driver was leaning forward with her elbows on her knees. Her blue-green eyes sparkled in the candlelight. "Realise it's a bit queer, what? Dragging you all the way up here."

"Miss Armstrong wouldn't like it if she knew we were discussing matters without her." Miss Eversley sounded oddly thrilled about meeting without the headmistress' knowledge.

"And seeing as you're staying with us, at least till the end of term," added Miss Vincent, blinking long eyelashes, "we thought it best to involve you in our discussions."

Felicity nodded. On the topic of Mrs Ogden's demise, she could answer honestly. "It does rather need to be spoken about, does it not?"

Miss Vincent paused. Frowning a little, she looked at the movement teacher.

"Petherick already told you, did she?" Miss Driver's gaze went from Felicity to the sombre-looking music teacher.

Miss Petherick shook her head firmly. "I did not."

"Oh." Felicity's stomach clenched. She'd made a misstep. "I appear to have misunderstood."

"What did you think we were here to discuss?" Miss Eversley spoke flatly. "What needs to be spoken about?"

"Well." Felicity hesitated. All eyes were on her. Was there any harm in forging ahead? "Poor Mrs Ogden. We all put on a brave face for the girls today, but it's all rather upsetting, isn't it?"

Miss Petherick's eyes fell to her lap. Miss Vincent blinked, as though still confused. Miss Eversley continued to crunch on her biscuit, her mouth working like a rabbit's.

"Yes, yes. Rather." Miss Driver allowed the volume of her voice to dip slightly in acknowledgement of the difficult topic.

Felicity nodded solemnly. At such close quarters, she couldn't risk watching Miss Petherick too closely. The meeting in the attic provided opportunities, but it also carried risks.

"Problem is—" Miss Driver sighed "—it leaves us a man down."

"But Lady Felicity is staying with us, remember?" Miss Vincent smiled encouragingly at Felicity.

"At the end of term, they'll both be gone," said Miss Eversley, brushing biscuit crumbs from her lap.

Miss Driver let out a sad sigh. Miss Vincent pressed her lips together and looked anxious.

"'Both'?" enquired Felicity.

Miss Driver looked at the music teacher. "Petherick is also leaving us at the end of term."

Miss Petherick sat as straight as a poker, her eyes on her hands in her lap. She looked distinctly uncomfortable.

"I see." Felicity hoped her reaction sounded entirely neutral, but the timing of Miss Petherick's departure was uncanny, and the decision must have been recent. Why else hadn't Felicity heard about it till now?

"It is a chance not to be missed," said Miss Vincent, smiling sympathetically at the music teacher. "Miss Petherick will become a private tutor in a delightful house somewhere near London."

"How lovely," agreed Felicity, but the music teacher didn't look up from her lap.

Having wrought her revenge on the spy who'd caused her sweetheart's demise, was this Miss Petherick's escape?

Miss Driver cleared her throat. "That's why we need to make the most of our resources in the time we have. Only a few weeks till the end of term. What?"

Miss Eversley nodded with urgency. "Exactly. Exactly."

Miss Petherick glanced up from her lap and at the movement teacher.

"I'll talk bluntly," said Miss Driver, as though she ever did anything else. "There's a bunch of final year girls not doing too well. Miss Armstrong knows it. Their parents know it. It's why you're here, Lady Felicity."

"Of course." Felicity knew exactly to whom Miss Driver was referring.

Dolores was often defiant, sometimes even rebellious. When not distracted by Dolores, Usha spent good chunks of time daydreaming. Cecily practised such concern and kindness towards others, it was often to her detriment. Jane needed to develop more control over the impression she created on others. And Gwendoline's confidence, while growing, was still far behind that of her peers.

Despite their faults — or perhaps because of them — these girls had become Felicity's favourites among the students, although her relationship with Gwendoline had been regrettably rather damaged earlier that day.

Miss Vincent clasped her hands together. "You have done wonders with them, your ladyship."

"But it's not enough," added Miss Eversley.

Miss Driver frowned. “Now hang on just a moment, Eversley, old girl. Lady Felicity has done more than was expected of her.”

Felicity didn’t react, even though the comment was mildly — and hopefully unintentionally — offensive.

“But the girls aren’t as fully formed as they should be.” Miss Eversley was defiant in her plain, serious way. “Otherwise we wouldn’t be here discussing them.”

“It’s Miss Armstrong who needs our help.” Miss Petherick spoke, lifting her gaze only briefly from her lap.

Miss Vincent nodded with enthusiasm. “You are quite right, Miss Petherick. Quite right. Every Liverton girl at Queen Charlotte’s Ball is a reflection of Miss Armstrong’s standards. She has helped each of us. We should help her. There is no question of it.”

“Absolutely,” agreed Miss Driver. “It takes years to build up a school’s reputation, and only one disaster of a season to decimate it. Believe me. I’ve seen it happen.”

Miss Eversley’s lenses flashed in the candlelight. “We can’t let it happen to Miss Armstrong.”

The teachers’ loyalty to the headmistress was understandably fierce. Miss Driver and Miss Eversley had remained dedicated to Miss Armstrong since working with her at her field hospital. Miss Vincent appreciated the professional opportunity provided to her as a refugee.

Miss Petherick’s concern for the headmistress was less easily explained. To Felicity’s knowledge, she hadn’t a special connection with Miss Armstrong. Did she feel guilty for committing a crime at a school overseen by a woman of such excellent character?

“Miss Armstrong is an admirable woman,” agreed Felicity.

There was a pause. A sharp draught nearly blew out the candles.

“Miss Armstrong cared for my Jonathan.” Miss Petherick spoke without lifting her gaze.

Felicity straightened. This was a story she hadn’t heard before.

“She did so personally,” continued the music teacher. “She reduced his suffering immensely. I should like to help her however I can.”

Miss Driver and Miss Vincent nodded sadly. Even Miss Eversley looked moved, blinking behind her lenses.

The headmistress having cared for Miss Petherick's sweetheart in his last hours was a powerful motivation for loyalty. Could the music teacher's need for justice have outweighed the risk of damaging Miss Armstrong's reputation by committing murder at the school?

The picture was becoming less clear.

At least there was the handwriting sample. Felicity had to get it to Alex. The next day's weather would hopefully be clement enough for an early stroll in the gardens.

Miss Driver sighed brusquely. "We must do our best for the girls. Their parents are powerful, well-placed people. They want a return on their investment when they send their daughters to our school. They want the best possible marriages for their girls."

Miss Vincent gave a sad shrug. "No match. No future."

Felicity nodded. In some ways, society had progressed immensely in recent years. In others, it hadn't.

"No future for the girls or for the school," added Miss Eversley. "Their parents could close this place down in a heartbeat."

Miss Driver frowned. "It won't come to that. We won't let it."

Miss Vincent turned pleading eyes on Felicity. "You'll help us, won't you?"

Miss Petherick lifted her gaze in Felicity's direction. Was there a hint of shame in her eyes?

Felicity straightened on her makeshift seat. "Of course. I shall continue to help the girls improve their writing skills."

"And improve them you have," concurred Miss Driver. "But I'm afraid it's going to take more than that to carry it off."

Felicity swallowed. "It is?"

"It will work like this—" began Miss Eversley.

Miss Driver cut her off. "Here's the plan. Each of us will align closely with one of the struggling girls. Take her under our wing, so to speak. We shan't tell them about the project, of course. That might offend."

Felicity blinked. As a new teacher, she was already exerting herself in preparing lessons and marking assignments. The rest of her attention was taken up by her secret mission. What capacity was there for a new project?

Miss Vincent wrung her hands. "Please, your ladyship. The girls need our support."

Had the French teacher noticed Felicity's reticence?

She adjusted her expression to appear less unwilling. "I quite understand. It's why I'm staying on till the end of term. It's just that—"

Miss Driver cut Felicity off. "Petherick will keep an eye on Lady Cecily Summervale, because of the musical connection."

Felicity glanced up at the music teacher. Miss Petherick's sombreness had lightened slightly.

"I'm taking Lady Jane Ingles," said Miss Driver. "She's rather weak in callisthenics."

"Miss Dolores Gastrell needs my attention," chipped in Miss Eversley. "Her grasp of basic mathematics is extremely weak."

"I'm already giving Miss Usha Ghatge extra tuition," said Miss Vincent with a satisfied smile. "Her betrothed wishes to tour France once they are married. She needs to impress with her French."

"May I ask—" Felicity's second attempt to object was interrupted.

"You've got Miss Gwendoline Milligan, your ladyship." Miss Eversley spoke with commiseration, as though Felicity had drawn the short straw.

*Gwendoline?*

It was too much.

Felicity smiled politely at her fellow teachers. "I think it's a wonderful idea to support Miss Armstrong, and I'm certain the girls will appreciate and benefit from the extra attention. Miss Milligan is, however, already quite the bookworm and has made incredible progress in her writing. I'm not sure what I could help her with beyond the lessons of mine she already attends."

Miss Driver tipped her head to one side and frowned. "You don't wish to help us?"

Felicity's smile faltered slightly. "It's not that, it's—"

"Do you dislike Miss Milligan?" suggested Miss Eversley.

"Goodness." Felicity was getting flustered. She hadn't prepared herself for this. "It's not that at all. Miss Milligan is a very likeable character."

"Then you'll help us?" urged Miss Vincent gently.

All eyes were on Felicity, even Miss Petherick's. A glint of hope shone in the music teacher's gaze.

Felicity was cornered. Where could she turn?

## Chapter Seventeen

The morning sunshine was warm, but the breeze was stiff. It shook the tall pink spikes of foxgloves and brought the heady scent of phlox through the open French doors of the classroom where Felicity sat before the small circle of girls.

"*It's going to be a truly fabulous event.*" Felicity was reading aloud from a letter written by Jane. "*I should so like it if you could come.*"

Jane sat on the edge of her seat, her elbows on the desk in front of her, a finger twirling a lock of caramel hair.

"*Do let me have your answer by Friday.*"

Jane's lips moved as Felicity read aloud. She'd worked so hard on the letter she knew the words by heart.

"*I shall send a motor to collect you on the afternoon in question.*"

Although Felicity was reading the letter aloud, she was doing so automatically, her mind not fully engaged with the text. She had other matters to think about.

"*Your dearest friend, Jane.*"

Felicity lowered the letter.

Jane continued to lean forward in her chair, the elbows of her loud green-and-yellow tartan blazer on the desk in front of her. Cecily was also still paying attention, her sage-green pinafore dress and white long-sleeved blouse much easier on the eye than Jane's ensemble.

But not everyone's attention was rapt.

With the loose, draping sleeves of her cream knit dress pulled back, Usha was sketching flowers onto the inside cover of her jotter. Dolores stifled a yawn with the back of her hand and folded her arms over the front of her white cotton jumper with a navy stripe. Gwendoline's gaze had drifted outside, her fingers worrying the cuff of her soft pink cardigan.

Felicity was usually more skilled at holding her students' attention. It was, however, hard to keep her mind away from the handwriting sample sitting in the pocket of her blue-and-green floral day dress.

Felicity smiled brightly. "Thank you, Lady Jane, for allowing me to read your letter aloud to the class."

Jane nodded bashfully, as though receiving a compliment.

Felicity hadn't been paying enough attention to what she was reading to draw any helpful conclusions about the text. "Who among you has comments for Lady Jane?"

The question was met with silence. The small battery-operated clock on the teacher's desk ticked quietly. It wasn't long till the morning's first break.

"I believe it to be a very good letter." Cecily cast her calm, amber-brown gaze on Jane. "I should be quite honoured to receive such a message from a friend."

Jane thanked Cecily with a nervous giggle.

Felicity quickly scanned the letter again. Cecily had a tendency to be generous, but Jane indeed seemed to be improving.

"Are there any further remarks for Lady Jane?"

Her arms still folded, Dolores shook her head slowly. Usha glanced up from her drawing and offered a dreamy smile, making no effort to hide her lack of attention.

Gwendoline brought her gaze in from the window but wouldn't meet Felicity's eye.

The little desktop clock continued its gentle tick.

Felicity had chosen her words carefully at the attic meeting the night before. She'd said she wanted to help and would do what she could but couldn't commit to a specific student. The excuse she gave to her fellow teachers was that, as a newcomer to the profession, she struggled to keep up with the workload.

In reality, as much as Felicity had become quite smitten by the girls and loved seeing them flourish, her priority had to be her mission.

Which was why Felicity struggled to take her mind off the handwritten note in her pocket. It felt as if it might burn a hole through the cotton of her dress at any moment.

Usha leaned back in her chair, tapping the end of her pencil on her desk. "Writing to a friend is one thing. But what about writing to one's beau?"

Dolores straightened in her chair, suddenly attentive.

Felicity was jolted away from considering the paper in her pocket. "What do you mean by 'one's beau', Miss Ghatge?"

Dolores spoke up. "I mean, that's why we're here, isn't it? To prepare ourselves to nab the right fellow and live happily ever after. We've only been writing letters about events and engagements as married women. What about before that, when we're trying to seal the deal, so to speak?"

Gwendoline looked with interest at Dolores. Cecily's cheeks took on a little flush of pink.

Jane frowned. "But the Honourable Miss Mavis Cavendish is a very important friend of mine. I should like her to receive only the very best letters."

"Yes, Janey, dear. Of course." Dolores sounded both concerned and dismissive. "But let's say you have a gentleman friend who's interested in you. Seriously interested. And let's say you wish to invite him somewhere. All above board, of course."

"Wouldn't you like to know how to address him in the correct way?" enquired Usha of Jane.

Jane thought for a moment, her forehead puckering.

Felicity ought perhaps to have taken back control, but her distractedness had loosened her authority over the class. She was also curious to see where the discussion might end.

"Yes, a very correct letter to a gentleman friend that also leaves some room for a different level of understanding," concluded Dolores. "That is what we ought to be learning, wouldn't you say?"

Jane squinted. "Is it?"

"Our fearless writing tutor will be able to help us." Dolores swivelled in her seat, her wavy chocolate bob swinging at her cheeks. "Won't you, Lady Felicity?"

Felicity smiled serenely. "I'm afraid there was nothing about letters to gentlemen in the instructions I received from Miss Armstrong." Felicity had been asked to ensure the girls were proficient in the composition of event invitations, cancellations, acceptances, and apologies, as well as the offering of appropriate wishes around events such as births and illnesses. "Only correspondence in the feminine domain."

Recovering from her confusion at Dolores' proposal, Jane looked intrigued. Gwendoline also followed the conversation closely.

"We ought not distract Lady Felicity from what she's been asked to teach us," offered Cecily gently, her cheeks still glowing.

Usha raised an elegant eyebrow. "But how many times have we written invitations for picnics, teas, and luncheons? Surely, we're proficient by now."

Usha had a point. Each girl had practised every exercise on Miss Armstrong's list multiple times and made significant improvements. And since the school's goal was to prepare the girls for their futures as wives, teaching communication with men seemed logical.

"Please, your ladyship," begged Dolores.

Gwendoline met Felicity's eye with an imploring look.

Felicity held Gwendoline's gaze for a moment.

"Very well," she said.

"Hurrah!" said Dolores, triumphant.

Usha smiled broadly. Jane looked excited but nervous. Cecily shrank a little into her seat.

Gwendoline smiled gratefully at Felicity, and Felicity smiled back. She couldn't take Gwendoline under her wing, but Felicity could at least give her tuition on a topic that interested her — and most of the other girls.

"Ahead of the next lesson," said Felicity, "I would like each of you to write a short letter inviting a male acquaintance to a shooting weekend. I shan't give you any more direction than that. Let's see what you can do."

Felicity hadn't written many — or any — such letters herself, though she'd received a number from potential suitors, none of whom had ever been worthy of the distraction from journalism. She smiled to herself as she remembered her tactful letters of decline.

"You shan't be disappointed, your ladyship," assured Dolores, standing up.

Felicity frowned, confused by Dolores rising from her seat, but footsteps and chatter in the corridor restored her composure. The lesson was over.

How had Felicity lost track of time?

The other girls stood up and filed out after Dolores.

"Thank you, your ladyship," said Gwendoline, who was the last to leave the classroom.

The damage done to Felicity's relationship with Gwendoline seemed to be healing, but there couldn't be any dawdling. The break time was already ticking away.

Exiting into the warmth and scent of the garden through the open French doors, Felicity put her hand in her pocket and touched the paper of Mrs Ogden's handwritten list. Behind a tall yew hedge full of chattering sparrows and out of sight of the school building, Felicity broke into a trot. She smiled to herself.

Alex had actually been rather clever to allow the groundsmen to imagine there might be romance between them. For Felicity to pop up and hand him a note wouldn't be odd.

However, there could be no getting lost if Felicity was to make it on time for her next class.

Following the sound of the trickling fountain, Felicity traced the meticulously memorised route to the rockery. After giving Alex the note, it would be a case of waiting. If the handwriting was confirmed as the spy's, it would make sense to dig further into Miss Petherick.

But if Mrs Ogden's handwriting wasn't a match, then—

Felicity's trot came to a sudden halt at the fountain.

Beside the water, her back as straight as a plumb line and in a dress of deep purple crepe, the headmistress of Liverton Ladies' Academy was thoughtfully smoking a cigarette.

"Miss Armstrong." If Felicity couldn't hide the surprise from her voice, she at least hid the disappointment.

To complete a return trip to the rockery, there was barely a moment to spare.

# Chapter Eighteen

Under the dappled shade of trees, the fountain's pool twinkled in the sunlight. A constant, gentle gush from the fountain's spouts blocked any background noise.

The headmistress turned towards Felicity. The wistful expression she'd been wearing lifted into a smile.

Having crossed paths in a relatively remote area of the garden, the oddness of the coincidence prevented them from merely exchanging a simple greeting.

"I suppose we all have corners we retreat to when things need to be thought through." Miss Armstrong put her cigarette out in a small portable ashtray and snapped the silver lid shut. "Does this also happen to be where you come for quiet contemplation, your ladyship?"

Felicity smiled politely and put her hands in her dress pockets. She touched the paper she needed to deliver to Alex. "I was taking a walk to refresh myself. I had no particular destination in mind."

Miss Armstrong gave a tight smile. She seemed mildly amused. Did she believe Felicity? "There's rather a lot to think about at the moment, isn't there?"

"I suppose there is," agreed Felicity, her stomach tense. Time was trickling by. How might she slip away from this encounter?

The headmistress stepped closer, the heels of her dark purple shoes crunching into the gravel. “May I confide in you?”

Felicity paused, her hand still on the paper in her pocket. Might this be worth the delay? “Of course.”

Folding her arms across her chest, Miss Armstrong watched the sparkling ripples in the fountain’s pool. “When I accept a girl as a pupil, I make a promise to her family. I promise the girl will be well cared for and prepared for a bright future. For a good marriage. So far, I’ve been able to deliver on my promises to all the mothers and fathers. This year, however, I fear things will be different.”

A wood pigeon fluttered clumsily through the branches above. The noise startled Felicity. She was more uneasy than she wished to be.

“What gives you that feeling?” enquired Felicity gently, trying to sound relaxed. Did Miss Armstrong have suspicions about Mrs Ogden or Miss Petherick? Or even about Felicity?

The headmistress watched as a few fallen leaves bobbed across the water’s surface. “You know, it was never my life’s aim to run a school like this. Certainly, I’ve strived to help people. To make a difference in the world. Sometimes I wonder if the academy is the right channel for these efforts.”

Miss Armstrong’s questioning of herself surprised Felicity. The headmistress appeared so steadfast. With their secret attic meeting, her loyal teachers had noticed the wavering of the headmistress’ resolution, though, hadn’t they?

Even without spies and murder, was the school somehow in trouble?

The silence was filled with the gentle cascade of the fountain.

“A person’s passing can prompt deep reflection,” offered Felicity. She was keen to dig deeper, to make delaying her visit to Alex count for something, but it couldn’t be rushed.

Miss Armstrong tilted her head slightly, confused. She narrowed her eyes, the penny having dropped. “You’re referring to Mrs Ogden. It’s funny, I hadn’t considered it.” A strange smile played on the headmistress' lips. "She died so peacefully. Compared to the men I cared for in the war, at least."

The comment sent a little shiver through Felicity. Not for the first time she considered the possibility that the headmistress had eliminated the needlework teacher, yet it hardly made sense. The risk posed to the school was significant.

Unless she'd been fully confident of avoiding any repercussions.

*Toot-toot!*

The sound of a motor horn broke through the fountain's peaceful trickle.

Miss Armstrong straightened, tugging on her dress to smooth it. "I suppose you must rush back. My apologies for interrupting your walk."

"Please, don't apologise." Had delaying her visit to Alex been worthwhile? Felicity had learned nothing tangible from the headmistress, and she needed to return to the house for her next lesson, but it was only an hour until another break. "I'm sorry I can't do more to help."

Miss Armstrong let out a sigh. "To have spoken such thoughts aloud already makes me feel better. Thank you."

"I'm pleased to hear that." It was always gratifying to help a person feel better, but the meaning behind what the headmistress had said remained elusive.

"Come," said Miss Armstrong. "I shall wave you off."

Felicity frowned. "Wave me off?"

"You're chaperoning the trip to Wickleigh, are you not?"

Felicity's stomach dropped like a stone.

The trip to Wickleigh. How could she have forgotten?

# Chapter Nineteen

The little shop felt far too small for the trio of girls who were tugging at dresses on hangers, rummaging through baskets of silk scarves, holding necklaces and earrings up in front of a mirror, and causing general mayhem.

"Darling, it's you. It's absolutely you."

"I can't choose. I'll have to take both."

As their chaperone, ought Felicity to have intervened? Dolores, Usha, and Jane weren't exactly reckless, but neither were they careful with the shop's stock.

"If I add this to my headpiece for the practice ball, then it's complete."

"Oh, darling. Yes. It's utterly complete."

Felicity remained watchful but, despite her impulses, didn't intercede, taking her cue from the shopkeeper.

A plump woman with shining curls set close to her head, the boutique's proprietress beamed as she watched the girls from behind the shop's counter. Wickleigh was a small market town on the edge of the moors. By all rights, such a glamorous shop had no right to exist there. The little business depended a great deal — perhaps even exclusively — on visits from the girls of Liverton Ladies' Academy, groups of whom visited the town on a rotating basis every week.

But while Felicity did nothing to interrupt the girls' frenzied approach to shopping, she kept a close eye on the time.

There was a regular schedule of outings from the school, from shopping trips to museum visits to society sporting events, and the trips were always tightly chaperoned and carried out with the rigidity of the school routine. The motors to take them back to Liverton would be waiting for them on Wickleigh's high street at four o'clock sharp.

On other occasions, Felicity might have been more relaxed about the time. She recognised the girls' need to have an occasional break from timetables and supervision. But there could be no such relaxation today.

The note in Mrs Ogden's handwriting continued to burn in Felicity's pocket like a hot coal. She had to get it to Alex.

"You must, darling. You simply must."

"Do you think so? Really? For the polo?"

Felicity wanted to give a look of apology to the little shop assistant, a thin, nervous girl with trembling hands, but she was too busy with her work to notice. Balanced on a stool, she held up a floor-length white gown with silver accents, draping it across the front of Usha's terracotta woollen coat as Usha twisted back and forth, looking at herself in a full length silver-framed mirror.

"It's stunning on you, darling. Really," said Dolores, barely looking at her friend as she continued to rifle through a rail of delicate shawls.

"Let's be mindful of the time, shall we, girls?" Felicity never enjoyed nagging or chastising, but she had to stay on top of things. It was worrying enough that she'd already forgotten it was her turn to chaperone the Wickleigh trip.

At Felicity's mention of the time, Jane hurried to the counter with fistfuls of beaded necklaces. "I can't decide now. I'll have to take them all. Yes. All of them."

The shop owner's eyes glinted. "Very good, your ladyship."

"I'll take it," said Usha of the white-and-silver dress to the relief of the little shop assistant, whose arms were flagging.

"I'm popping out for a breath of fresh air," said Dolores, who'd speedily completed the purchase of a glittering tasselled scarf. Felicity was relieved to have one less girl to chase outside towards the queue of Lanchesters.

"Ooh." A silver hair clasp caught Usha's eye, and she dropped out of the queue for the till.

Felicity withheld a gasp of frustration. "Lady Jane, Miss Ghatge, I'm going to wait outside. You have five minutes."

This seemed to alarm the shop owner more than it did the girls, and she set the little assistant to work packaging the purchases at twice the normal speed.

The shop's bell tinkled as Felicity stepped outside into the fresh air. Wickleigh's high street was sunny and pleasantly warm, and Felicity adjusted her straw musketeer's hat to shade her eyes. A light but steady stream of typically Devonian traffic meandered by. There were motor cars, delivery vans, the odd charabanc, and horse-drawn carts carrying goods or transporting farm labourers.

Three dark blue Lanchesters were parked in a neat row on the other side of the road, their uniformed drivers seated patiently behind the steering wheels.

Further along the pavement was Miss Eversley in a dark grey tweed jacket and skirt and a frumpy brown beret. There were always two teachers to chaperone every trip. Beside her in a plain black belted coat stood the maid who'd been tasked with clearing out Mrs Ogden's room. The maid's hands were full of shopping bags, but there wasn't a student in sight anywhere on the high street.

Felicity pressed her lips together as she moved along the pavement. She wouldn't stand for further delays.

"Miss Eversley, where are your girls?" asked Felicity as she approached.

The teacher looked mildly bewildered as she pointed through the leaded bay window of a tea shop.

On a broad shelf just behind the glass was an extravagant selection of cakes topped with white icing, bright red cherries, and glittering sugar. Beyond was a large round table crammed with girls from the year below Felicity's group. With streams of steaming tea still being poured into cups, and orders in the process of being placed with a black-and-white uniformed waitress, the girls clearly believed they had all the time in the world.

Under normal circumstances, Felicity begrudged no one a delicious pot of tea and a rich, moist bun.

"Have you told them we're due to leave?" she asked Miss Eversley.

The bespectacled teacher nodded. "I have."

*Have you really?* might have been Felicity's next question. Based on her experience on the tennis court, Miss Eversley was a proven liar. Had the maid not been in earshot, it would have been an opportune moment to challenge Miss Eversley about the incident.

"They don't seem in any hurry," said Felicity pointedly.

Again, Miss Eversley peered through the window at the girls in the tea shop. "They're in high spirits. Mrs Ogden used to chaperone this slot. I suppose they feel more at ease now she's gone."

Felicity tipped her head, her curiosity piqued. "Do you mean to say the girls weren't keen on Mrs Ogden?"

The maid carrying the shopping bags moved away from Felicity and Miss Eversley and towards the kerb, as though keen not to overhear.

Miss Eversley continued to peer through the tea shop window, though her attention had switched to the cakes. "Mrs Ogden got a girl expelled once."

Felicity's chest squeezed. She made every effort to appear unfazed. "Expelled?" Was such a thing even possible from Liverton Ladies' Academy? Miss Armstrong took such great care of the girls. "How did that come about?"

Miss Eversley sighed. "The girls will take risks sometimes."

"In what way?" asked Felicity, but could Miss Eversley's account of anything be believed?

The teacher turned away from the cakes and towards Felicity, her glasses glinting in the sun. "Mrs Ogden caught one of the girls with a young man."

Felicity frowned, her uneasiness growing. "When was this?" Had she gone too far in asking her students to write a letter to a gentleman friend?

"Oh," sighed Miss Eversley. "More than a year ago now. The risk wasn't just to the girl's own reputation. It was for the whole school." Miss Eversley's tone hinted at approval of the needlework teacher's actions. "The indiscretion might have appeared in the papers had there been a journalist nearby."

"Goodness," said Felicity. She couldn't hide her surprise. Expulsion from a prestigious school was surely extremely damaging for a girl's future. Grudges had been held against teachers over far less.

Miss Eversley turned fully towards Felicity. "You used to work for the papers, didn't you?" Her tone was accusatory.

Felicity drew in her chin. "I intend to go back to my post at the end of the term. The Western Daily News would never destroy a girl's reputation, in case that's what you were thinking," she added. Not that Felicity needed to defend herself or her family's newspaper to a peculiar character like Miss Eversley.

With the bag-carrying maid still out of earshot, Felicity seized her chance.

She stepped closer to the bespectacled teacher. "Actually, Miss Eversley, there's something I should like to ask you. When I came across you in the garden yesterday, you told me my services as an umpire had been requested. Yet when I arrived on the tennis court, that turned out not to be true. There had been no request made for me."

Miss Eversley pushed her glasses up her nose. "Oh." She sounded neither upset nor surprised by the confrontation.

"Why, may I ask, did you lie to me?" continued Felicity

Miss Eversley shook her head. "I didn't intend to lie."

Felicity squinted at the teacher. "You admit you lied, but you're saying you did so by accident?"

A flicker of something like pain passed over Miss Eversley's features. "Sometimes I say things because I think it's what people want to hear. It's an awful habit, but I can't shake it." Miss Eversley shrugged. "You're so popular with the girls. I thought it would make everyone happy."

Felicity stared at the household economics teacher. Could her explanation be believed, or was it another lie?

"We made it, Lady Felicity. We made it in time." Jane was galloping down the pavement, her arms overflowing with packages. "All purchases wrapped within the allotted time."

Usha trailed coolly in Jane's wake, a single slim box balanced elegantly in her hand, presumably containing the white-and-silver dress. "Lady Jane can be rather indecisive," she said with an amused smile, which quickly turned into wide-eyed panic as a box from the pile Jane was carrying toppled towards her.

As Usha side-stepped just in time, the maid dashed forward to help.

Miss Eversley used the commotion as cover to dive into the tea shop, where she encouraged the girls to leave their half-drunk tea and uneaten buns while also ordering an iced finger, which she carried from the premises in a paper bag.

It was difficult to grasp the inner workings of the bespectacled teacher. Was she completely harmless or utterly cunning?

With matters complicated enough, Felicity decided she would accept Miss Eversley's explanation of her lie about the tennis match. At least for now.

Far more significant was the news of Mrs Ogden's involvement in the expulsion of a girl. However, because this information came from Miss Eversley, it needed to be verified.

It was high time to get back to Liverton House.

With Felicity and Miss Eversley acting like shepherd and sheepdog, the girls made it across Wickleigh's high street and to the waiting Lanchesters, where the drivers stepped out to open the doors.

Miss Eversley counted the tea shop students back into the two vehicles in which they'd arrived. She gave Felicity a nod. "All present and correct."

Felicity nodded back. With the maid in the front seat, and Jane and Usha in the back, Felicity was about to climb into her designated motor.

She blinked.

There was a spare seat too many.

"Where's Miss Gastrell?"

"Dolly will be along any moment, your ladyship." Usha's tone was confident, though her dark eyes darted out the window and up the high street.

"Do you know where she is?" Felicity was cross at herself. How had she left it till the last minute to notice Dolores was missing? The end of the day was approaching. Alex might leave for Exeter before Felicity arrived back at Liverton.

"She'll be along presently, your ladyship." Usha didn't answer Felicity's question.

Straightening, Felicity stepped away from the motor. "Miss Eversley, please see that the girls remain seated in the vehicles. I need to locate Miss Gastrell."

Miss Eversley gave a firm nod.

"I'll find her, your ladyship." Usha began climbing out of the Lanchester.

"No," said Felicity firmly. "I'll go."

---

Wickleigh wasn't a big town, but its high street was rather long. The heels of Felicity's T-strap shoes tapped rapidly on the large paving slabs as she went to each shop front and peered inside.

Dolores was nowhere to be seen.

At the kerb beside the motors, Miss Eversley craned her neck anxiously, watching Felicity as she moved further away. The shops of the high street dwindled as the thoroughfare slipped over the brow of a small hill, where the buildings became residential.

The search was taking far too long.

Felicity was about to turn back to investigate the other end of the high street when the smooth rumble of an expensive engine caught her attention.

The echo of it came along a narrow alleyway that ran between two houses with stepped gables. In the shadows stood a young man and a young woman. They were engaged in an intimate conversation.

"Miss Gastrell." Felicity called out without pausing to think.

Dolores turned, surprise on her face.

The man's hand fell from Dolores'.

He retreated quickly along the alleyway without looking back, turning up the collar of his jacket as if to defend his neck from Felicity's gaze. He was tall with dark shining hair. A sporty gold-coloured motor had been left idling at the other end of the alleyway. He slipped into it and roared away.

Dolores' cheeks were pink and her eyes downcast as she joined Felicity on the high street pavement. There had been nothing except the touching of hands. At least not as far as Felicity had witnessed.

They walked in silence towards Miss Eversley and the waiting Lanchesters.

Surely, if anyone was in the wrong, it was Felicity. She'd been Dolores' chaperone, and a chaperone was supposed to prevent situations like this.

But was this the kind of risk Miss Eversley had spoken about? Might more have happened had Felicity not interrupted?

And what had Mrs Ogden seen that had resulted in the expulsion of a girl from the school? Had it been more or less than what Felicity had just witnessed?

There'd been no journalists creeping around Wickleigh that afternoon — Felicity would certainly have noticed — but a chaste meeting in an alleyway surely wasn't the untoward behaviour that could bring down a school. Was it?

Felicity and Dolores remained quiet as they climbed into the Lanchester. Usha gave Dolores a little smile, but Dolores didn't smile back as the motor pulled away into the meandering traffic of Wickleigh high street.

Soon, fields and hedges were rushing by. Felicity kept her eyes on the passing scenery. She would take matters one step at a time.

And the next step was Alex.

## Chapter Twenty

No one followed Felicity as she alighted from the Lanchester, claimed to feel a little queasy from the journey, and announced she would take a stroll in the fresh air of Liverton's grounds in the break before dinner.

Weaving quickly between tall hedges and along broad flower-lined paths, Felicity clutched the brim of her hat as the wind picked up, the silver leaves of a row of birches hissing like waves on a beach as the sun pressed lower in the sky.

Would she be too late? Groundsmen started and ended their working days earlier than most. Mrs Ogden's handwritten list had remained firmly tucked in Felicity's pocket all day. Might it begin its important onward journey that evening?

Felicity's heart lifted with relief as the sound of tools on rocks rose above the rustle of the leaves. Men's voices carried on the wind.

"That's about it for the day, lads."

"Looking forward to supper."

"Cheerio."

Felicity arrived at the rockery just in time. Men were downing spades, parking up empty wheelbarrows, and rinsing hands and faces in the cool flow of the ornamental waterfall. And Alex was among them.

He was dishevelled, his brown corduroy trousers flecked grey with stone dust, yet he glowed with energy, his muscular form pressing against the linen of his shirt.

Standing at the side of the rockery, in the shadow of towering fern fronds, Felicity swallowed. Was Alex enduring such hard physical labour just to be close to her?

Working at the rockery didn't give him access to the house or any of the teachers, although who knew what he was gleaning from the groundsmen. News travelled like a powerful river among servants on an estate, both inside and outside the main house.

And Alex always had his eye on a scoop.

He spotted Felicity, his dark blue gaze sparkling as he swept his hair back and adjusted his cap, the scar on his forehead clearly visible.

Felicity's instinct was to smile at him, but she fought it. She didn't want to be too flagrant in front of the other groundsmen.

She gave Alex a nod. He knew what it meant.

He went first along the path beside the waterfall. Felicity followed at a distance. She was glad when he passed the colonnaded seating area. They didn't need to be disturbed again. Crossing the open parkland with its shorn grass, the heat of the day radiated upwards from the ground as the wind blew gusts of cool air across the gentle slope.

Felicity stopped to sniff the sweet, creamy blooms of an elder, allowing the distance between herself and Alex to lengthen. He disappeared into a stand of hornbeams at the top of the rise. Their lower leaves had been nibbled away by grazing deer, but the shadow they cast was enough for privacy.

With a glance over her shoulder, Felicity ducked under a branch. The sun glowed gold through dappled leaves. Alex took off his cap and bowed as Felicity arrived.

"Your ladyship."

His tone was exaggerated and jocular. The social distance between them was far more pronounced now that he was in the dirty clothes of a labourer and she in the pristine hat, dress, and cardigan of an earl's daughter on a visit to a local town.

Felicity wanted to play along, to relax and joke with him. To indulge the tingling sensation she got whenever they were close and in high spirits together.

But it wasn't the time.

She delved into her pocket. "I found a handwriting sample." Though there was no one around, she spoke quietly.

Alex's eyebrows furrowed. His expression was suddenly serious. "Ogden?"

Felicity nodded.

He took the paper from her, their fingers grazing for a moment. He examined the writing briefly before folding it into his shirt pocket. "I'll pass this on." He saw the same similarities in the loops that Felicity did. "It'll take a couple of days."

"Then we'll know for certain." Felicity spoke eagerly, practically interrupting.

Alex nodded, any sense of fun having disappeared. "Then we'll know."

It was perhaps premature, but a feeling of relief washed over Felicity. Confirming the identity of the spy would be a major achievement. Apprehending Mrs Ogden's killer would be going too far, but Felicity would find out what she could about Miss Petherick, her lost sweetheart, and the cocoa. After that, it would be a matter for the authorities.

But what would it all mean for the school? For Miss Armstrong, her girls, and their reputations? Wouldn't headlines about a murdered war traitor be far worse than a girl caught *in flagrante* with her beau?

"Let's assume we get confirmation she was the spy," began Felicity, "and that she was done away with—"

The snap of branches underfoot caused both Felicity and Alex to look up sharply.

## Chapter Twenty-One

"Oh. Oh, dear," Gwendoline stammered. Her pale cheeks had turned bright red in the dappled light among the hornbeams.

Felicity's stomach churned. Alex couldn't hide his shock at being interrupted again and by the same girl.

"I didn't realise you weren't alone, your ladyship." Gwendoline had already begun her retreat. "I'm terribly sorry. Please, do excuse me."

Alex looked with concern at Felicity. His disbelief mirrored hers. Was there more to it than coincidence?

"It's all right, Miss Milligan," said Felicity, trying not to sound unsettled. Unless Gwendoline had been listening in, their covers hadn't been blown. Alex was known to the groundsmen as Felicity's romantic interest. That rumour had likely spread at least to the servants at the house by now. Perhaps even to the girls.

Gwendoline was in full retreat through the sinewy hornbeam trunks, but her flowing pale lilac skirt snagged on a gnawed down branch. Becoming flustered, she tugged at it. There came a ripping sound.

"Goodness!" Gwendoline's voice was shrill and trembling.

*Go.*

Felicity mouthed the word at Alex. He retreated from the scene as Felicity went to help Gwendoline with her dress. She hadn't said everything she'd wanted to say to him, but he at least had the handwriting sample.

"Don't pull. It'll be all right." Felicity spoke reassuringly as she crouched and fiddled with the fabric of Gwendoline's skirt. It was part of an outfit akin to a ballroom gown, as though Gwendoline had come from a dancing lesson.

"There." Felicity rose to her feet. "It's a little damaged, but nothing serious."

Gwendoline's cheeks were still flushed. Her pale blue eyes were glassy. Tears threatened. "Miss Vincent said you wouldn't mind me coming to you for advice. I saw you crossing the park. I didn't mean to interrupt anything, I promise. I can't apologise enough, your ladyship."

"You didn't interrupt anything," assured Felicity soothingly, her gaze straying briefly to watch Alex with his strong, graceful stride returning towards the rockery. "Tell me," continued Felicity, returning her attention to the Gwendoline, who seemed genuinely upset. "What advice do you need?"

Felicity was, in a way, touched that Gwendoline had sought her out. It was more how Miss Vincent had sent the girl to Felicity that didn't sit well. In the attic meeting, Felicity had declined to mentor Gwendoline. The other teachers were perhaps choosing to ignore that.

Gwendoline sniffed. "I've not made you angry with me?"

Felicity shook her head. "Not in the slightest."

The anxious pinch of Gwendoline's forehead softened. She reached into the bodice of her dress. "There's a letter I need to send. The topic is delicate. I understand if you don't want to look at it." Her hand trembled as she held out the letter.

The cream paper was thick. At the top, the initials *G. M.* were imprinted in an imposing gold-embossed script. The stationery seemed too austere to have been Gwendoline's own choice. It was easier to imagine a parent choosing for her.

In thin black ink, Gwendoline's handwriting was slanted, sharp, and, in places, uncertain.

"Shall we sit down and look together?" proposed Felicity.

Gwendoline bit her lip. She nodded.

There was a stone bench at the edge of the stand of trees that had been warmed by the sun. The letter glowed in the lowering light as the breeze whispered through the branches above. Gwendoline tucked her skirt underneath her and took a seat next to Felicity as she read the text.

The letter was addressed to 'a cherished friend'. It was elegantly worded, almost poetic, and highly polite. As the text progressed, its tone intensified. The 'cherished friend' was obviously a man, and Gwendoline wished to express her romantic interest in him. Not only express, but practically insist.

*...your virtues, intelligence, and fortitude are qualities that resonate deeply with me...*

*...I have found myself increasingly drawn to the thought of a future where our paths might not just run parallel but, indeed, merge...*

*...it is my sincerest hope that you will receive this letter with an open mind and a considerate heart...*

Felicity hadn't expected such forwardness when asking her class to write letters to male recipients.

Gwendoline's pale blue gaze was uneasy, her shoulders tense. The contrast between the physical meekness of the girl and her masterful, even forceful, use of words in the letter was unsettling.

As her teacher, Felicity had a duty to advise her correctly.

"Do you suspect the gentleman in question shares the same sentiments as you, Miss Milligan?"

Gwendoline looked at the ground. The breeze caught wisps of her pale hair. "He might do."

"You're uncertain?"

"Your ladyship." Gwendoline met Felicity's gaze. "The end of term is approaching. The debutantes' balls start in the autumn. I haven't any brothers. My father wants me to—" She broke off, frowning. Gwendoline didn't want to criticise her family.

She didn't have to. Felicity understood.

For the girls at Liverton, wealth, comfort, and prestige were rarely in short supply. Familial love and support were, however, sometimes overlooked.

Felicity lowered the letter to her lap. "Would you like to hear my honest opinion, Miss Milligan?"

Gwendoline nodded. "Very much so."

"The letter is bold, but you have expressed your desires with great civility. You open your heart without embarrassing yourself or the gentleman to whom you are writing. To keep such matters in private correspondence is the correct approach."

Gwendoline's lips twitched upwards with hope.

"I would, however," continued Felicity, "advise you to prepare yourself for the possibility of disappointment. While your appeal is polite and correct, it is something of a daring act, particularly from a young woman. Even in today's modern age. You are taking a risk."

Gwendoline nodded. "I've already considered what I might do should this attempt fail." A little smile quivered on her lips as she tucked her letter back into her dress' bodice and pressed it to her chest. "I'm so deeply grateful for your support, your ladyship."

Felicity returned the smile. "You're welcome, Miss Milligan." Communicating with gentlemen was in line with the school's goals, and letters to male friends would surely happen with or without review. Wasn't it preferable for a teacher to be engaged and give guidance?

"We're all so grateful to have you here at Liverton," continued Gwendoline, still smiling. "You've given us so much cheer and inspiration these past weeks. It's made all the difference."

"That's extremely kind of you to say." It was the type of ending about which Felicity barely dared dream, where everything was left in a better state than before her arrival at the school. "If I can help, then I'm satisfied," she added.

Gwendoline looked happier than Felicity had ever seen her. "We're so looking forward to your demonstration tomorrow, your ladyship."

Felicity was brought back down to earth with a thud. "My demonstration?"

# Chapter Twenty-Two

Preparation for and discussion of the practice ball had been ceaseless since Felicity's arrival at Liverton Ladies' Academy, yet the day of the event itself had somehow crept up on her.

And, to top it off, no one had thought to tell her about the demonstration.

Upon confirming what she'd heard from Gwendoline with the other teachers, Felicity had used the rest of her evening to rehearse dance steps in her stockinged feet in the privacy of her own room, keeping time under her breath.

*Tum-tee-tum. Tum-tee-tum.*

Felicity was proficient enough, but dancing never came naturally to her. When frustrated at making the same mistake in the waltz three times in a row, her ankles somehow tangling themselves on the carpet of her little room, Felicity huffed and dropped her hands to her side.

She could withdraw from the demonstration altogether. No one had actually invited her to take part. It had simply been presumed she would partake in the tradition with the rest of the teachers.

*No.*

The end of the term was approaching. After the summer holidays, the season would begin. It was a time of nerves and uncertainty. Felicity couldn't let the girls down.

So she continued to practise until after her bed time.

The next day, Felicity went willingly and slightly bleary-eyed to the teachers' common room, which had the air of a relaxed, feminine salon, with cushions in pale-yellow chintz and porcelain figurines positioned on side tables.

There, with a view through tall windows of grey clouds and Liverton's parterre rose garden, Felicity sat in a straight-backed wooden chair and allowed Miss Vincent, who was wearing a peach-coloured ballgown, to attend to her make-up and Miss Petherick, who had on a pewter-grey dress decorated with black lace, to work on her hair.

It wasn't remotely desirable to have a suspected murderess as one's hairdresser. Remaining undercover was paramount, however, and Felicity was extra vigilant.

On the far side of the room sat Miss Eversley. She was, for once, in a dress — a loose-fitting number in dark green velvet with silver sequins at the neckline — and over her lap lay layers of white tulle and taffeta, which she worked upon with a needle and thread, sealing a long gash in the fabric.

Miss Driver paced up and down before the window. Her satin gown was floor-length and robin's egg blue, featuring wide shoulder straps and a fitted waist. In her hand was a folded fan, which she smacked into her palm repeatedly with a belligerent rattle.

"The girls must have a good example to follow," she said, glowering slightly. "Especially this batch."

Miss Vincent tutted as she dabbed rouge on Felicity's cheeks, the chiffon of her sleeve rustling with her movements. "We've all taken care of the girls as we agreed, have we not?"

The French teacher's rebuttal of Miss Driver's concerns was gentle but still surprising. Was there tension between the teachers?

"We have," confirmed Miss Eversley without looking up from her sewing.

Felicity went to nod in agreement. It'd not been planned, but she had given Gwendoline special attention, hadn't she?

Miss Vincent caught Felicity's chin mid-nod and began adding mascara to her lashes, which felt immediately heavy and uncomfortable. Miss Petherick wasn't in view, but her comb was teasing through Felicity's auburn ringlets.

The door to the common room flew open without a knock. Miss Armstrong swept in, wearing a dusky red dress with flutters at the hem and cuffs and a sleek, straight silhouette that was not at all suitable for the foxtrot or quadrille.

"Finished?" The headmistress approached Miss Eversley without looking at the other teachers.

"Nearly." Miss Eversley took the thread between her teeth as she tied a neat knot, tucked her needle into a pin cushion, snipped off the excess thread, and lifted the layers of white fabric off her lap. It was one of the long, white dresses in which the girls practised their walking and court curtseys. Heavy with layers of skirts, beading, and ruffles, it was suitable to be worn at Queen Charlotte's Ball.

Miss Armstrong lifted the dress by the clothes hanger and inspected it. "Splendid work, Miss Eversley. We mustn't leave Lady Cecily waiting."

Felicity fought the urge to blink as Miss Vincent continued working on her lashes. "Did Lady Cecily damage her dress?" she asked. Gwendoline had ripped her skirt on a hornbeam just the day before. Carefulness regarding one's clothing was perhaps a lesson the girls needed to learn.

Miss Armstrong halted at the door. She stared coolly at Felicity. "Lady Cecily discovered the damage this morning." The headmistress tugged the door open. "The girls will, unfortunately, play tricks on one another." Exiting the common room, she drew the door sharply closed behind her.

"Hmm." Miss Vincent gave a small frustrated sigh as she took a step back and peered at Felicity's made-up face.

Felicity could no longer fight the urge to blink, though she suppressed a frown. To distract one another during singing practice or muddle the scores during a friendly game of bridge was all part of schoolgirl fun. But to slice through the rich silk of a unique and beautiful dress directly before an important event was not in the same spirit at all.

Miss Eversley stood up and went to a large mirror at the side of the room and began unravelling the brown bun at the back of her head. Miss Petherick — who had apparently finished with Felicity's auburn curls — picked up her small red-and-green paisley vanity case and went to assist her.

Felicity glanced at the other teachers, but they didn't appear surprised. "Is it common for the girls to sabotage one another's dresses?"

"Not common," replied Miss Driver, still rattling her fan, "but not unheard of."

Miss Vincent darted forward to add a final stroke of mascara. "There. *Fini.*" The French teacher smiled kindly at Felicity. "Go. Look in the mirror. You have never been so beautiful, your ladyship."

"What reasons would a girl have to do such a thing to a fellow student?" asked Felicity, as she eased herself out of the chair.

Miss Vincent sighed. "Oh, little things. Big things. You know what girls can be like."

Miss Eversley and Miss Petherick stood aside as Felicity approached the mirror.

"Do we know who it was?" she asked.

"Doubt we'll ever find out," said Miss Driver with a slap of her fan. "Can be hard to find witnesses willing to testify, so to speak."

Felicity drew in her chin, surprised by the teachers' lack of interest in finding the dress slasher. She turned towards her reflection.

And gasped.

The swooping neckline of Felicity's sleeveless dress in shimmering midnight-blue silk emphasised the elegance of her collarbones and shoulders. Gloves in the same dark silk reached above her elbows. Her ringlets had been gracefully swept away from her face and clasped with silver grips that sparkled like stars.

What made Felicity gasp, however, was the sight of her own face. Her make-up was so thick, she looked like a pantomime dame.

Miss Petherick stepped towards Felicity. "Turn to me, your ladyship," she commanded flatly.

Still reeling from what she'd seen in the mirror, Felicity did as she was told. The music teacher reached into her vanity case, from which she pulled a sponge, a series of brushes, and several tissues. The tools were quickly filled with excess rouge from Felicity's cheeks and lips.

"You don't think she looks beautiful?" Miss Vincent's forlorn question from the other side of the room went unanswered.

"Look down."

Felicity followed Miss Petherick's instruction, and the music teacher got to work on her eyelids. The vanity case was balanced on the music teacher's palm. Inside, in addition to brushes, sponges, and a comb, there was a pot of rouge, face powder, and a vial of pills.

Felicity read the label on the vial.

> *Each pill contains 0.1 grains of Digitalis Purpurea. Take one pill thrice daily before meals.*

Felicity felt suddenly rather queer.

"I'm finished, your ladyship."

Felicity looked up into the wistful, deep brown eyes of Miss Petherick.

Originating from foxglove, digitalis could be prescribed for heart conditions such as arrhythmia, but digitalis was also highly poisonous. The pills could be ground down and added to a drink. They could induce heart failure.

Yet the music teacher had not tried to conceal the pills' presence in her vanity case. If Miss Petherick were worried about being caught, wouldn't she have taken more precautions to hide the tablets?

"You may look again in the mirror, your ladyship," said Miss Petherick, returning her brushes to the vanity case and fastening the clasp.

Not wanting to give any indication she'd taken interest in Miss Petherick's pills, Felicity looked up promptly and turned towards the mirror, her heart pounding a little harder than usual.

She blinked at her reflection.

The make-up on her face was now hardly visible, yet there was clearly something different compared to Felicity's normal visage. Her hazel eyes sparkled and looked bigger. Her cheeks shone healthily, their structure more pronounced and delicate.

Felicity's lips had taken on the role of focal point in her face. Their sweet bow shape had always been there, but it was now somehow standing out in a subtle, charming way.

She'd not looked nearly as captivating on the occasion of her own debut.

With a snap of her fan, Miss Driver gave an affirmative nod in Felicity's direction. "That's the ticket."

"Yes," confirmed Miss Eversley. "Now, she looks beautiful."

"She does," said Miss Vincent, gracious in her defeat. "Indeed, she does."

Felicity turned back to Miss Petherick. The music teacher looked as sullen as ever.

"Thank you," said Felicity.

Miss Petherick gave a small nod and went back to work on Miss Eversley's hair.

Could someone so sensitive and creative really be capable of killing? From her own experience, Felicity knew murderers came in many forms.

There was a knock at the door. The butler entered. "Miss Armstrong requests you join her in the ballroom."

Miss Eversley gave a small squeak. "I'm not yet ready."

"Hold still," said Miss Petherick as her hands worked speedily on the bespectacled teacher's hair.

It was time for the teachers to put on a show, a task Felicity would have to juggle with watching Miss Petherick very closely indeed.

## Chapter Twenty-Three

The ballroom at Liverton House was a kaleidoscope of rich hues. There was the deep burgundy of the long damask curtains, which were drawn against the grey afternoon light, the royal blue of the walls, and the gilded mouldings that framed the ornate plaster ceiling.

Enormous crystal chandeliers dripping with cascades of sparkling pendants cast a soft, warm glow over the polished wooden floor. In the corner, a shining black grand piano would be the source of the music.

The rustle of silk and the gentle tapping of satin shoes mingled with whispers and giggles as the girls filed into the space under the watchful eye of Miss Armstrong. The headmistress stood with the other teachers, Felicity included, on a raised platform at the head of the dance floor beside the piano.

At the centre of the dance floor, the older girls formed neat rows while the younger students watched from seats at the side. Servants stood by, unobtrusive and ready to offer assistance.

Taking her place on the front row, with pearls at her neck and neat curls set into her sunshine-blonde hair, Cecily looked serene. Her shoulders were relaxed yet perfectly aligned, the last-minute mending carried out by Miss Eversley unnoticeable among the folds of her skirt.

Who might have done it? Was it really, as Miss Driver had implied, impossible to find out?

Miss Petherick, like Felicity, was in the row of teachers positioned alongside the headmistress. They were in full sight of everyone in the ballroom. Felicity used her vantage point on the platform to subtly scan the rows of girls forming on the ballroom floor.

Positioned behind Cecily, Gwendoline trembled, the white feathers in her headdress shivering. Jane stood next to her, the rouge on her cheeks overdone like a china doll's. She blinked hard, perhaps suffering from too much mascara.

In the row behind, Usha stood as elegantly as a lily, the white-and-silver dress purchased in Wickleigh looking as if it'd been hand-stitched by the finest dressmakers in Paris. Beside Usha stood Dolores. An effusive pink corsage on her shoulder echoed the coral tones of her delicately applied lipstick. A jewelled bracelet shimmered on her wrist as she brought her hand to her mouth to stifle a yawn.

Felicity recalled her own debut. She wasn't one for dresses and parties, but it had been an enjoyable affair. Rather underwhelming in terms of marriage prospects, but it was different then. The war had taken its toll.

As the last girl took her place on the dance floor, Miss Armstrong stepped forward. The flutters on the hems of her otherwise cigarette-straight dress quivered as she moved.

"Ladies of the final year."

The whispering and shuffling stopped. All eyes were on the headmistress.

"As students of Liverton Ladies' Academy, you may take pride in your accomplishments. You may look forward to opportunities. But remember one thing. Success in society requires more than attendance at balls and tea parties. It demands foresight, diplomacy, and determination."

Miss Driver leaned forward a little and looked along the line of teachers. She gave a little wink in approval of Miss Armstrong's words. Miss Eversley nodded. Miss Vincent smiled. Miss Petherick didn't react.

Miss Armstrong continued to address the ballroom, her voice ringing out coolly and clearly. "Your debut season isn't merely a series of social engagements to be enjoyed. You're not attending Queen Charlotte's Ball to partake in frivolity for its own sake. You are there to secure your future and to forge alliances that will benefit not only you but your family and their legacy."

Jane swallowed. Gwendoline's forehead furrowed. It was an awful amount of pressure. Was it enough to drive the girls to sabotage one another's chances?

"You are about to enter a world," continued Miss Armstrong, "where every smile, every word, every dance is a step towards your future. Do not squander these steps. Be judicious in your choices, be strategic in your friendships, and always, always aim to succeed."

The headmistress paused, surveying her troops.

"Girls, you may go to your seats."

The girls filed neatly to the sides of the room and sat down. Some who had looked relaxed now looked worried. Dolores was scowling. She whispered something to Usha as they sat down together. Gwendoline, Cecily, and Jane found seats close to the pair.

Was it plausible that the culprit who ruined Cecily's dress was a girl from Felicity's writing class? The group seemed to get on so well.

Miss Armstrong turned to the row of teachers behind her. "Miss Driver, you now have the floor." The headmistress left the platform, her heels tapping as she went to stand at the side of the room, her arms folded.

"Thank you, Miss Armstrong."

Miss Driver broke from the row of teachers. Using her folded fan, she indicated towards the piano. The instruction was picked up by Miss Petherick, who left the platform and went to sit before the keys.

It was a relief. As long as the music continued, Felicity didn't have to worry about watching Miss Petherick while dancing.

"Every year," began Miss Driver, her voice thundering through the ballroom, "our teachers give a demonstration." Looking at her fellow teachers, Miss Driver gestured with her fan towards the dance floor. "Ladies?"

Felicity took her lead from Miss Eversley and Miss Vincent, following them down onto the gleaming floorboards, casting a glance at the girls as she went. They seemed quite mesmerised by what was about to happen under the grand chandeliers.

Felicity wondered how useful watching women dance with other women would be for the girls, but she'd made her commitment. She wouldn't let the school down.

"In a line," hissed Miss Eversley to Felicity as she sought a partner among the teachers.

Felicity gave a little frown. "Are we not dancing together?"

"And every year," continued Miss Driver from the platform, "as is the Liverton tradition, we invite some rather unusual guests."

Felicity fell into line beside Miss Eversley. How could they dance without partners? What exactly was going on?

Miss Driver used her folded fan to gesture in the direction of the ballroom doors. "Mr Clark?"

The butler nodded and opened the doors.

"Our guests," announced Miss Driver, beginning a gentle applause. "Please give them a warm welcome."

As the clapping spread around the room, the guests filed in, and Felicity couldn't quite believe what she saw.

# Chapter Twenty-Four

Young men in dinner suits filed into the ballroom. All were around thirty or less. They were tall and upright, and each of them was recognisable. There was a footman, a couple of drivers, a groundsman, and Alex, dressed in a sharply cut dinner jacket that accentuated his broad shoulders and with his dark blond hair brilliantined smooth.

*Goodness.*

Felicity swallowed. It was quite the contrast to his dusty workman's outfit.

The gentle applause subsided as the men formed a row in front of the waiting teachers. Alex wasn't positioned before Felicity, but he caught her eye and gave her the subtlest of smiles.

Felicity felt warm. Extremely warm. The chandeliers' light was hopefully soft enough to hide the glow of her cheeks.

"The astute among you will recognise these men," boomed Miss Driver from the raised platform at the end of the dance floor. "They work below stairs and around the estate, but don't let their lowly positions fool you."

Alex pulled a little grimace. He seemed thoroughly amused. How was he so relaxed? Felicity was glad she'd at least practised a few steps, but would it be enough?

"These men are all accomplished dancers," continued Miss Driver, "either through hard work and practice, or through natural talent."

Whispering, giggling, and the rustle of taffeta spread around the sides of the room. Miss Armstrong's glares from her vantage point at the edge of the dance floor returned the girls to a hush.

"First, the teachers will perform so you can observe," bellowed Miss Driver, wielding her folded fan. "Then, girls, it will be your turn. The purpose? Miss Armstrong already told you. We're not here for frivolity. Liverton ladies are purposeful. We are strategic. Regardless of with whom we dance, we appear serene and elegant. Watch and learn."

Miss Driver descended from the raised platform and set about rearranging the couples. Several swaps were made. Alex was moved further down the row of teachers until he was paired with Miss Vincent, who smiled and batted her eyelashes at her new partner.

It was both a relief and a disappointment not to be matched with her friend. Felicity wasn't embarrassed to be associated with Alex. Far from it. But the demonstration had been sprung upon her. It would have been too much to have her first dance with Alex thrust upon her as well.

Felicity turned her focus to the tall footman she'd been paired with and smiled politely at him.

"Your ladyship," he said with a small bow. He looked only mildly uncomfortable in his single-button tuxedo jacket.

Miss Driver had taken another groundsman as her partner, a strapping fellow with a hulking frame who made Miss Driver look quite dainty.

"Ready, Miss Petherick?" asked the movement teacher.

From her seat at the piano, the music teacher gave a nod and put her fingers to the keys.

"Wait!" Miss Driver stepped away from her groundsman and stared at the couples on the dance floor. "I see it now." She marched up to the footman in front of Felicity. "You go here." With her hands on the lad's shoulders, she swapped him with a driver. "And you must go here." She brought the driver down to Miss Vincent. "And you—" she put a hand on Alex's shoulder "—must go here." Miss Driver deposited Alex in front of Felicity.

Her heart gave a little leap.

A smile formed on Alex's lips. "Your ladyship."

Felicity's cheeks glowed like coals. "Mr Cooper," she murmured. It was almost too much.

Miss Driver returned to her well-built dance partner. "Miss Petherick?"

The music started. A waltz. *Tum-tee-tum. Tum-tee-tum*. Felicity's back straightened. She couldn't allow her legs to turn to jelly. It was time to concentrate. It was time to dance. To put on a show.

The men all bowed deeply. Alex's dark blue gaze met Felicity's as he rose.

Her response was a deep curtsey, each of the teachers bobbing deeply in unison. It was hardly traditional for a titled lady to curtsey to the son of a greengrocer. Yet it felt more natural than any of the curtseys Felicity had given the men she'd danced with during her own debut season.

The dancers stepped closer to one another.

*Tum-tee-tum. Tum-tee-tum.*

Felicity hesitated.

"We don't have to do this," whispered Alex. "Not if you don't want to."

The piano's sound filled the ballroom. The girls watched from their seats.

Felicity put a hand on Alex's shoulder. "I want to." Her other hand slipped effortlessly into his outstretched palm. Through her glove, she felt his warmth. His other hand rested lightly on her back, just below her shoulder blade.

Again, Felicity hesitated. Which foot first?

"Shall I lead?" asked Alex.

Felicity frowned. "You don't imagine I—"

*Whoosh!*

They were away, twirling across the dance floor, the skirt of

Felicity's midnight-blue dress flying out behind her, joining the swirling, rhythmic movement of the other couples.

Felicity smiled. She even laughed. She was gliding smoothly, elegantly, and totally without thought. How was it possible?

Alex looked to be enjoying himself, his graceful movements effortless. "The other fellows have been practising, as I understand it."

The footman, driver, and male servants were indeed competent dancers. Even the bulky groundskeeper paired with Miss Driver had poise.

*Tum-tee-tum. Tum-tee-tum.*

Felicity's feet moved without her having to think about it. The guidance from Alex's hands was gentle but firm. Miss Petherick's piano playing was full of energy and emotion.

"They were asking if anyone knew how to dance," Alex continued. "I volunteered. Thought I'd get a look inside the place. They never said you'd be dancing, too."

"I only found out yesterday myself," said Felicity. As long as they kept their voices low, they wouldn't be overheard.

Alex's eyes twinkled. "You're so good at everything. No doubt they didn't find it necessary to warn you."

It was sometimes hard to tell when her friend was being sarcastic. "Dancing has never been my forte."

Alex frowned, still smiling. "You're joking, aren't you?"

As they twirled towards the edge of the floor, the faces of the watching girls shone with delight. The other couples were good, but Alex had flair. Dancing had never been so fun, so liberating.

"Where on Earth did you learn?"

Alex smiled. "I have three sisters, remember?"

The idea tickled Felicity. It was easy to imagine Alex at the whim of his siblings, helping them practise their dances. He was so patient, so caring.

Felicity gazed into his dark blue eyes. The light from the chandeliers caught the scar on his forehead, and something snapped taut within Felicity.

She wasn't there for frivolity.

"Did you pass on the handwriting sample?"

Alex nodded. "It'll be a few days before—" He manoeuvred to avoid Miss Driver and her groundskeeper partner, who came hurtling through the centre of the floor like a pair of cannonballs "—before we hear anything back. I made other calls, though. Got confirmation of the official cause of death, as logged by the doctor."

"And?" urged Felicity.

Alex frowned a little. "Natural causes. No further investigation."

It wasn't a surprise. Many poisons — including digitalis — were easy to overlook when no wrongdoing was suspected, as with Mrs Ogden.

Alex raised an eyebrow. "Are you keeping an eye on your suspect?"

"She's at the piano. She—"

*Crash!*

Felicity twisted to see what the commotion was. Somehow, Alex turned her sharp movement into part of the dance and kept them gliding across the floor. They twirled past a scene of thankfully innocent chaos.

Jane had been making her way to the exit when she'd knocked into a buffet beside the ballroom doors where serving staff had been preparing drinks. A whole tray of coupes had been knocked to the floor.

Wide-eyed and shaken, Jane crouched among yards of white chiffon and taffeta, attempting to help clear up the mess. "I'm so sorry," she sobbed. "I ought to be more careful. I'm so terribly sorry."

Her expression severe, Miss Armstrong briskly crossed the dance floor to reach the scene. One by one, the couples slowed, then ceased dancing. Though the music continued, even Felicity and Alex wound to a stop, their hands slowly slipping from each other's grasp.

Miss Driver huffed out a loud sigh and followed the headmistress.

"Poor Lady Jane," murmured Miss Vincent.

"It's always Lady Jane," said Miss Eversley a little too loudly.

Felicity cast a look over her shoulder. Miss Petherick was still seated at the piano, her hands in her lap, the music having stopped.

The girls remained seated around the edges of the room, but their fidgeting and whispering grew. Cecily had gone to assist Jane but had been turned away by Miss Armstrong. She returned to her seat next to Gwendoline, who, along with Usha and Dolores, watched Jane's struggle with pained expressions.

With a comforting arm around Jane's shoulders, Miss Armstrong said something stern to Miss Driver. The movement teacher nodded and went to the raised platform. The servants continued the clean-up as Miss Armstrong escorted Jane from the room.

"Thank you to our dancers," boomed Miss Driver from the platform. She took her folded fan from her belt and tapped it into her palm. It helped begin an enthusiastic round of applause, which focussed the room's attention back on the couples on the dance floor and away from Jane's sobs as the ballroom doors swung closed behind her and Miss Armstrong.

"As our headmistress wishes to watch your dancing, we shall pause before returning to the dance floor. While we wait for Miss Armstrong's return, we shall move onto the toast. Mr Clark?"

The butler looked up from where he was assisting two maids with the upset tray and broken glasses. The surprise of the toast having been brought forward registered only briefly on his face before Mr Clark swung into action.

Leaving one servant still picking up the broken glass, the butler went with the other maid to help hand out the glasses for the toast to the seated girls. The footman in his tuxedo also joined in the effort.

Miss Driver came down from the platform to help hand out the drinks. Miss Vincent and Miss Eversley also got involved. Cecily stood up again and went to assist. Dolores also sprang up. This encouraged more of the girls to leave their seats. The situation became rather chaotic.

Alex raised his eyebrows at Felicity. She folded her gloved arms over her dress. Dancing the waltz with Alex had been a distinctly unforgettable experience, but Felicity had to remain alert.

Miss Petherick was still seated at the piano, her forehead slightly creased, as though expecting the command to strike up a tune at any moment. Miss Driver brought a coupe of champagne to her.

The girls were quickly all furnished with drinks and stood mingling and chattering at the edge of the dance floor. Miss Vincent and Miss Eversley brought coupes over to the dancers. Felicity and Alex accepted theirs.

"A toast," thundered Miss Driver as she returned to the platform, drawing all attention back to her. "To you, the girls of Liverton Ladies' Academy." She held her coupe aloft. "I invite you to raise your glasses to your futures. To your success."

"To our futures. To our success." A gentle murmur of the toast echoed around the ballroom before sips were taken.

Alex turned to Felicity, his glass aloft. "To your future, to your success.".

Felicity smiled. "To yours," she said, and took a sip of the fizzy liquid. She desperately didn't want to be distracted, but she felt so happy in Alex's company. She always did.

*Smash!*

Alex straightened. Felicity twisted in the noise's direction. Not another accident, surely?

Cecily lunged forward onto the dance floor, her hand grabbing at the bodice of her ivory silk dress, her shattered coupe sparkling across the wooden floorboards.

"Oh, là, là." Miss Vincent was wide-eyed, her champagne spilling a little from her glass.

"What the..." Miss Driver started down from the platform.

Miss Petherick stood up from the piano.

Gwendoline chased after Cecily, her face as white as a ghost's. "Lady Cecily. Lady Cecily!" She caught her shoulder. "What's the matter? What's wrong with you?"

"I can't..." Cecily tugged away from Gwendoline, advancing towards the middle of the dance floor as she clawed at her chest, gasping. "I can't..."

Then Cecily collapsed.

The ballroom fell silent. Shocked faces ringed the dance floor.

The blood drained from Felicity's cheeks.

"Oh, dear," she whispered.

"Miss Vincent, fetch Miss Armstrong!" Miss Driver dashed to where Cecily was sprawled on the floor. "Miss Eversley, get your medical bag!"

"This is bad, isn't it?" said Alex quietly.

Felicity put a gloved hand to her neck.

It was bad. It was very bad indeed.

## Chapter Twenty-Five

If it weren't for the swift and competent actions of Miss Driver and Miss Eversley, would Cecily have survived?

As Miss Eversley administered first aid, Miss Driver fetched one of the school's Lanchesters to rush the girl to the hospital in Exeter, her old ambulance driving expertise coming into use. Miss Armstrong arrived from settling Jane in her room just in time to join Miss Driver, replacing Miss Eversley on the back seat of the motor with Cecily draped over her lap.

The male servants and estate workers who'd partaken in the dancing demonstration, including Alex, quickly departed from the ballroom. Felicity, Miss Petherick, and Miss Vincent helped guide the students back to their rooms. The girls were in an oddly giddy mood, chattering and giggling nervously about what they'd seen. None of them felt the full weight of the situation. None except those closest to Cecily.

"She complained of a pain in her chest. I urged her to take another sip of champagne."

Tears welled at the corners of Gwendoline's ice-blue eyes as Felicity escorted her into the final-year common room, a gentle hand at the girl's elbow.

"And then she fell forward," continued Gwendoline, turning

from Felicity to where Dolores and Usha were seated in silence on a red velvet chaise longue. Like Gwendoline, they were still in their silky white gowns, their faces grim. The common room's tall windows revealed a blanket of low grey cloud above the gardens.

"I don't understand what happened." A tear ran down Gwendoline's cheek. She looked up from the soft leather armchair into which Felicity had deposited her. "Will she be all right?"

"Lady Cecily is receiving the best possible care," assured Felicity. It was the only information she had. Felicity had questions of her own to put to the girls, but they were in a state of shock. Added to that, a group of first-year students further down the corridor had begun a pillow fight while still in their ballgowns, goose feathers flying everywhere. As a teacher, Felicity had a duty to intervene.

Miss Eversley, who had already changed back into her habitual tweeds, joined her in the effort.

With the first-year students wrangled back into their rooms and instructed to help one another in removing their gowns, Felicity paused in the corridor with Miss Eversley.

"Is there any news on Lady Cecily?" asked Felicity.

Miss Eversley nodded. "Her condition is stable. Miss Driver and Miss Armstrong will remain at her side." She shook her head a little. She still looked unsettled. "It was as if she were having a heart attack. I've never seen it in one so young."

Felicity bit her lip. She said nothing more. The symptoms of a heart attack could be brought on with digitalis. Yet Miss Petherick hadn't once moved from the piano.

What was going on?

Felicity considered telephoning Alex. He'd no doubt returned to his home in Exeter by now, but the phone booths were exceedingly busy, news of Cecily's collapse no doubt spreading to all corners of the land.

That night, after a subdued dinner, with many girls choosing to remain in their rooms, Felicity found it hard to sleep. A sliver of moonlight lit the plaster mouldings on the ceiling above her bed. Memories of the warmth of Alex's hands and the effortless twirling mingled with the panicked look on Cecily's face, her glass smashing over the ballroom floor. How she'd clutched at her bodice. Gwendoline's shocked expression. Miss Driver's booming voice calling for Miss Eversley to fetch her medical bag.

Was Cecily merely ill? Most of the school seemed to think so. After all, what link could be drawn between Mrs Ogden and Cecily? What reason would someone have for wanting to harm them both?

Unlike the needlework teacher, Cecily was too young to have had an active role during the war, yet she had at least one enemy. Her dress had been slashed. Had this petty act been the starting point for more drastic action?

If someone had slipped something into Cecily's drink, it certainly wasn't Miss Petherick. She hadn't moved from the piano for even a moment.

When Felicity awoke, the moonlight on her ceiling had been replaced by an angry orange, the sun still low in the sky.

She dressed in her dove-grey linen skirt and jacket, paired with a blouse in a soft shade of green, but feeling rather frazzled, she requested breakfast in her room. The maid who brought up her tray reported that Miss Armstrong and Miss Driver had returned to the school during the night. Cecily was safe, although very weak. She'd been transferred from the hospital to her family's nearby estate, where she was now receiving private care.

A summons to Miss Armstrong's office arrived directly after breakfast. Miss Petherick, Miss Eversley, Miss Driver, and Miss Vincent were also present in the headmistress' office. They all looked sombre.

Felicity mirrored their serious expressions.

On the surface, she was a teacher with a duty to help the school. Underneath, she wanted more than just to assist. Felicity needed answers.

The headmistress observed the teachers gathered on the other side of her wide oak desk, drizzle flecking the windows behind her. She wore a dark orange wool jacket and skirt with a cream silk blouse, her dark bob shining in the grey morning light, her jaw taut. She looked impeccable, yet in tending to Cecily, Miss Armstrong had no doubt slept even less than Felicity.

"Ladies, I shall come straight to the point." The headmistress tapped her fingertips together. "Lord Summervale has indicated that he wants the police involved."

Miss Driver leaned forward, gripping the armrests of her chair. "After everything we did? We saved his daughter's life."

"Why the police?" enquired Miss Eversley, her brow wrinkled with confusion.

Miss Armstrong paused. She met the gaze of each of the teachers seated before her. "It's not yet clear what caused Lady Cecily's illness. It appears she'll make a good recovery, but her heart has been affected. And news of the incident is travelling."

Miss Vincent shook her head. She had a lacy handkerchief gripped in one hand. "We did what we could. The girls were going quite wild. They get so very excited. We didn't think to close the phone booths."

"You did nothing wrong," said Miss Armstrong. "We cannot constrain young women like caged animals. Nevertheless, I understand Lord Summervale's concern. His daughter is of prime importance to him. He has no son. Her husband will be his heir. If word gets out that Lady Cecily has a weak heart or some other defect—"

"Is that what did for her?" enquired Miss Eversley. "A weak heart?"

Miss Vincent winced a little.

The idea of one so young with such a defect was tragic, but it would be a relief to discover Cecily's illness was just a coincidence.

Miss Armstrong looked sternly at Miss Eversley. "We don't know yet. I've spoken to Lord Summervale. I've requested him not to involve the police. At least not until Lady Cecily has been properly looked at by the right doctors and the precise cause of her illness has been confirmed. If Lady Cecily has a heart defect, then we don't want to waste the police's time. Equally, if the origin of her illness is related to the quality of our champagne or some other fault on the school's side, then I still see no need to involve the police. This is something we should be able to resolve privately."

Felicity remained quiet. She couldn't be the first to say it out loud, but was she really the only one among them who suspected something uglier than corked champagne?

Miss Petherick remained silent, her expression sullen. Was she still a credible suspect? Not for harming Cecily, she wasn't.

Miss Driver's fists tightened. "If the police get into it, then the papers get the story."

Miss Vincent shook her head and squeezed her handkerchief. "We cannot allow it. We must take every precaution."

Felicity edged forward in her seat. There was no reason for her to hide her expertise in this arena. "If it's the press we fear, we could consider a different approach. By going to the papers first, before they come to us, we take control of the story."

Miss Driver glared at Felicity. Miss Vincent looked rather surprised.

Miss Armstrong narrowed her eyes. There was a pause. "Let's say we go to the newspapers and tell them what happened. What if the whole thing turns out to be nothing at all?"

Miss Eversley adjusted her spectacles.

Felicity found it an unlikely outcome, but she kept the thought to herself. "Then you've set the record straight," she said. "You've been honest and open. That reflects well on the school."

"How does it reflect on Lady Cecily?" Miss Petherick spoke quietly and carefully.

Felicity considered the music teacher's point. "If Lady Cecily's father wishes to involve the police, he must know it would be tantamount to announcing it in the papers."

"No," said Miss Armstrong firmly. "No papers. No police. Not yet. I'll speak again to Lord Summervale. Everything is to carry on as normal. At least for the time being, until we know more. That's my request to you all. Classes shall continue according to schedule. Outings will continue as planned. We must do our best to behave as normal."

Normal? The sentiment behind the command was understandable. The girls were young and vulnerable. They relied on the school's protection.

But Miss Armstrong didn't know Felicity's real reason for being among her teachers. The headmistress didn't regard Mrs Ogden's passing as suspicious. She couldn't see Cecily's sudden, violent illness as a dangerous continuation of the pattern.

Felicity couldn't break her commitment to keeping her spy-hunting mission secret. Was there another way she might warn Miss Armstrong of the lurking danger?

With the meeting over, the teachers filed out of the headmistress' office, their heels tapping as they arrived on the stone flags of the corridor beyond. Miss Armstrong rose from her desk and lit a cigarette.

Felicity went to follow the other teachers, allowing them to go ahead, but when she arrived at the double doors of the headmistress' office, she stopped and turned.

"Miss Armstrong," she said. "Might I have a word with you in private?"

## Chapter Twenty-Six

Felicity retook her seat before the wide oak desk at the centre of the office. She was alone with the headmistress.

Miss Armstrong exhaled a plume of smoke and looked out over the gardens. "I do sometimes wonder if I'm suited to the role of headmistress," she said, without turning away from the drizzle-spattered window.

"If you haven't questioned yourself, you're perhaps not the right person for the job." Felicity had told herself this many times in relation to her career as a journalist.

Miss Armstrong turned towards Felicity, the faint flicker of a smile on her lips. "What is it you'd rather not say in front of your fellow teachers?"

Felicity was unperturbed by the headmistress' directness. "I should like to offer my assistance," she announced.

Miss Armstrong frowned. "Beyond your services as a teacher, for which I remain very grateful, I'm not sure what you could do." She stubbed out her cigarette in a crystal ashtray. Its bitter smell permeated the room. "As I already told you, I'm not interested in involving the newspapers. Perhaps your connections in that realm will become useful at some point. For obvious reasons, I hope not, but I shall for certain bear your position and that of your brother in mind."

"I didn't mean my assistance with reporting." Felicity was perched upright on the edge of the seat, her hands clasped in the lap of her grey linen skirt. She hadn't given herself an enormous amount of time to think this through, but something had to be done. "I would like to offer my help with investigating."

It was the first time Felicity had fully of her own accord offered her services purely as an investigator. She'd played the sleuth before, almost unthinkingly in certain situations, reluctantly in others. Yet here was an opportunity to make a difference.

"I've experience in carrying out discreet investigations," she continued. "Not only as a journalist, and with some level of success." It wasn't like Felicity to blow her own trumpet, but convincing Miss Armstrong of her ability to help meant she had to be bold.

The headmistress narrowed her eyes. "What makes you think an investigation is necessary?"

"Lord Summervale wants the incident with Lady Cecily investigated. What if you told him you had a private investigator on the case? He might reconsider his threat to involve the police."

Miss Armstrong folded her arms over her dark orange jacket. She had her doubts, but Felicity could tell she was interested.

"What might the activities of a private investigator include?"

"Talking to everyone who was there. Gathering a detailed picture of what happened that evening, and perhaps before that as well." The prospect was highly intriguing. Who knew what Felicity might find out? Just because a link between Mrs Ogden and Cecily wasn't obvious, it didn't mean there wasn't one.

Felicity went on. "Wasn't Lady Cecily's dress sabotaged the day of the practice ball?"

The headmistress' frown deepened. "What are you suggesting?"

Felicity had to tread carefully. Rivalries between the students seemed a sore point, but Miss Armstrong needed to see the fuller picture. "Is it possible Lady Cecily had enemies?"

Miss Armstrong's expression twisted as though she'd smelled something rotten. "You aren't seriously suggesting that one of the other students might be responsible for Lady Cecily's current state?"

"I'm not suggesting anything, Miss Armstrong." It wasn't Felicity's intention to anger the headmistress, but the seed of suspicion had to be planted. Until it was clear exactly what was going on — and Felicity was still practically chasing shadows, with Mrs Ogden's identity as the spy not even yet confirmed — it was possible whoever had wanted to do harm might strike again.

Felicity kept her tone calm. "I should simply like to look into the possibilities. Rule them out, if you like. So that even if the police are summoned, there are no surprises. Not for you."

Miss Armstrong's expression remained tinged with distaste, as though confronted by thoughts she had no wish to think.

There was a long pause. Rain continued to tap on the windows. Felicity sat poised on the edge of her seat.

"Very well," said the headmistress through pursed lips.

Felicity's heart gave a little leap. It was a small but important victory.

"Investigate and report your findings to me," continued Miss Armstrong. "No one else. I trust you to carry out your enquiries with the utmost discretion."

Felicity nodded solemnly. "I shan't let you down."

---

The air outside was still cool from the rain that had thankfully ceased as Felicity hurried across the grounds, leaving footprints in the wetness of the croquet lawn. She trotted past the fountain and along the path to the rockery. It was still early, but the groundsmen were all there already, wheelbarrows creaking, rocks darkened by the rainfall tumbling onto piles, the sound of metal tools scraping stone, the cliff face steadily taking shape.

A couple of the men tipped their caps to Felicity, but they hardly looked up from their work as a hint of milky sunshine burned through the clouds.

Where was Alex?

"Morning."

He was coming up the path behind her carrying a stone-laden wheelbarrow, his flat cap on the back of his head, the sleeves of his linen shirt shoved above his elbows.

Was this really the same man who had waltzed her so elegantly around the dance floor the day before? The same man who was a distinguished journalist and with whom Felicity—

There was no time for such thoughts.

"I need your help," she whispered.

Alex set his wheelbarrow down and adjusted his cap, quirking an eyebrow. "It's still too soon for the results of the letter analysis, if that's what you're after."

"Not that," said Felicity. "Something else."

# Chapter Twenty-Seven

The thunder of hooves. The grass churning into mud as the players dived for the ball, the long canes of their mallets swinging. *Thwack!* The ball sent spinning across the pitch.

The polo match was a warm-up and didn't count towards the winning of any trophy, but the young men on horseback were fired up and full of energy, their mounts switching direction quickly, hooves digging into the ground. Tumbling white-grey clouds occasionally allowed the sun to peek through and splash everything with brilliant warm light.

*Thwack!*

The long swing, combined with the horse's charge, sent the ball rocketing past the goal posts. Polite applause went up from spectators seated on folding chairs under parasols and gathered around the refreshments stands at the side of the pitch. The rich smell of freshly disturbed turf filled the air.

The ladies from Liverton House, including Felicity among the chaperones, were positioned towards the end of the field where the goal for the team from St Martin's Polo Club was currently located, but that would soon change. A blow from the referee's whistle indicated not just the end of the chukka, but also the midpoint break of the match between St Martin's and Bath Park Polo Club.

Usha, Dolores, and Jane — who had bounced back from her embarrassment at the practice ball — rose from their seats, clapping in earnest as the men retired, leading flagging horses away for a well-earned rest. The girls looked splendid in brightly coloured day dresses, chiffon scarfs, and broad-brimmed hats adorned with ribbons and feathers.

Miss Vincent was positioned next to Felicity. "It is quite the spectacle, is it not?" She seemed rather taken by the gentlemen on horseback. "In Belgium, we have nothing like this."

"Quite," agreed Felicity as she joined in with the applause. She watched the riders, too, but she also kept a close eye on the Liverton girls, ready to pick up on the subtlest of hints of something out of the ordinary.

Miss Driver applauded louder than anyone in the crowd. "Excellent play. Excellent play." She was among the first to go out to stomp the clods back into the ground, an activity in which women in more dainty footwear were not so interested in taking part.

Cecily wasn't at the event, for obvious reasons. Gwendoline wasn't present either, expressing a preference to remain in her room. Miss Eversley, in her capacity as a nurse, had been sent to check on her. Gwendoline wasn't ill, but she needed rest.

A full contingency of Liverton ladies was nevertheless present at the polo, both younger and older girls. Miss Armstrong had decreed that activities would carry on as usual, and her teachers were dedicated to enacting her wishes.

The approach made sense. Not just for the girls — most of whom were thrilled to be out and in the company of males of their own rank and age — but also for the school itself.

Word of Cecily's sudden and dramatic illness was spreading quickly via unofficial channels. Liverton's students continuing as normal contradicted the narrative that something terrible had happened. Indeed, from the girls' enjoyment of the polo match, it seemed as though they hadn't a care in the world.

Not that the girls weren't concerned about Cecily. Just that morning, the students had each been called upon to sign an enormous hand-decorated greeting card that was delivered to the Summervale residence. The card was accompanied by a display of flowers the size of a small forest and a box of chocolates with the dimensions of a travelling trunk, all to wish dear Cecily a speedy recovery.

The overwhelming sentiment at the school was that the incident was just a minor hiccough and not indicative of any wider problem, yet there had to be more to it. Felicity was convinced.

With the midpoint break underway, Jane, Dolores, and Usha hurried towards the horse enclosure, where the riders' multiple mounts — for no horse was used for more than a single chukka without rest — awaited their turn on the field.

The younger Liverton girls were moving towards the refreshments stand.

"You will join them, no?" Miss Vincent enquired of Felicity, nodding towards the group who had set off in the horse enclosure's direction. "Shall I fetch you a glass of lemonade?" the French teacher enquired, already moving after the younger girls.

Felicity's attention was split. She cast a glance towards the far side of the grounds, where rows of motors were parked and drivers idled with their caps tucked under their arms.

She returned her gaze to the French teacher. "Thank you, Miss Vincent. That would be most kind," Felicity added as she set off towards the horse enclosure, holding up her hand to shield her eyes from a sunburst from which the short brim of her grey cloche provided little protection.

In her role as investigator and chaperone, Felicity had to stay close to the girls. Until the practice ball, her focus had been on investigating the staff at Liverton Ladies' Academy. Had this been a mistake? Had Felicity underestimated the students?

In a salmon-pink cotton dress with a buttoned front and capped sleeves, Dolores moved faster than the other girls. She made a beeline for a group of young men in white jodhpurs, tall black boots, and collared shirts. One of the polo players, his foot on the wooden fence of the horse's enclosure, his unfastened helmet still on his head, seemed to attract Dolores' interest above the others.

She had absolutely no shyness in approaching him. Upon greeting one another, they briefly touched hands.

The girls couldn't be treated like children and made to ask permission before wandering off, but they also couldn't be left entirely to their own devices. There could be journalists at the polo match, not that Felicity had so far noticed any.

Still, one could never be too careful. Not in light of Miss Armstrong's fears about the press and what had happened to Cecily.

And not in light of what Felicity had seen on the shopping outing to Wickleigh.

Was Dolores talking to the same man she'd met in the alleyway? From his build, it was possible, but Felicity hadn't got a good enough look at him the first time to make a match.

As a chaperone, ought Felicity snatch Dolores away and reprimand her for inappropriate behaviour? Perhaps, but it wasn't Felicity's inclination, neither as a young woman not much older than the Liverton girls, nor as an investigator.

Felicity caught up with Usha and Jane, who'd stopped before reaching the group of polo players. In a cheerful though slightly garish dress with a blue-and-green floral print, Jane was standing at the fence, stroking the nose of a horse with a shining mahogany coat and bright, alert eyes. Usha leaned against the fence and watched Dolores from a distance, the flutter sleeves of her cream-and-gold voile frock catching in the breeze. Was there concern in the way she looked at her friend?

"Enjoying the match so far?" asked Felicity as she approached.

Jane didn't look away from the horse she was stroking. "What's not to enjoy about watching these beautiful creatures?"

Usha switched her gaze to Felicity. "It's entertaining enough." A little smile played on her lips. "But England is not the true home of the game."

"Of course," agreed Felicity. Polo had originated in India. Felicity supposed it was played differently there, but that wasn't the direction in which the conversation needed to be taken.

The polo player with whom Dolores was speaking had slipped off his helmet and tucked it under his arm. His hair was black and shining. His look was serious, but he said something that made Dolores smile.

It was rather brazen behaviour, wasn't it?

An older woman with curls set tight on her head under a prim little toque hat was making her way around the other side of the enclosure, notepad gripped tight, eyes roving over the horses. Felicity recognised her as a society reporter from a rival regional newspaper.

Fast and decisive action was needed.

"I say," said Felicity, her tone commanding. She was the girls' chaperone, after all. "Who's the gentleman with whom Miss Gastrell is speaking?"

"Lord Severin Carrothers, Earl of Westholm," said Jane, still without allowing her attention to leave the horse, who seemed just as enchanted with Jane.

Usha folded her arms and glared at Jane.

The name was vaguely familiar. To be so young and carrying the title earl meant Lord Severin was at least the son of a duke, and likely first in line to the dukedom.

If he didn't yet have a fiancée, then he was a highly eligible bachelor. He was also of distinct interest to the society pages.

But before the society reporter could reach her, Dolores waved a coquettish farewell to the earl and his friends and trotted towards Felicity, Usha, Jane, and Jane's new equine friend.

"May I enquire how Miss Gastrell knows the earl?" asked Felicity as Dolores approached them.

"I believe the Gastrells are quite close to the Carrothers," continued Jane. She was feeding the horse sugar lumps from her palm, which explained the animal's enchantment. "And to the Summervales."

Usha's eyes widened with disbelief at Jane. Her mouth fell open a little, but she said nothing.

"I imagine Dolores is offering her best wishes for dear Lady Cecily," continued Jane, "which I'm certain Lord Severin would happily pass on."

Usha practically shook her head at Jane.

"Is that correct, Miss Ghatge?" enquired Felicity.

Usha blinked rapidly. "Yes, your ladyship." Her tone was unusually deferential. "That's quite correct."

As far as Felicity could see, both at the edge of the horse enclosure and in the alleyway in Wickleigh, there was something more than merely polite exchanges going on between Dolores and the dark-haired man. But to what extent were Dolores' not-so-secret liaisons with her beau significant?

And there were other enquiries Felicity could make of the girls. Jane had left the room before the drinks were handed out, but Dolores and Usha had been present, right up to Cecily's sudden illness.

"What-ho." Dolores smiled at Felicity and her friends as she gave Jane's horse a pat on its muscular shoulder. Dolores looked pleased, even invigorated.

"May I remind you all," said Felicity in a mildly chastising tone, "that we're not to draw too much attention to ourselves."

Jane snatched her hand away from the horse's mouth, discreetly slipping the leftover sugar cubes into the pocket of her dress. "Of course, your ladyship," she said with an awkward little curtsey, but it wasn't the feeding of the polo ponies to which Felicity was referring.

The society reporter had reached Lord Severin and his teammates. Scribbling furiously in her notebook, she was interviewing the polo players.

"Oh, I know." With her hands clasped behind her back, Dolores smiled sweetly. She was an expert in getting her own way. "I was simply asking Lord Severin to pass on our well wishes to dear Lady Cecily."

Usha's shoulders dropped with relief. They'd all kept their stories straight.

"The Carrothers are dreadfully close to the Summervales," added Dolores.

Felicity folded her arms over her dove-grey jacket. "It is indeed quite terrible what happened to Lady Cecily."

"It certainly is," said Usha solemnly.

"Quite," agreed Dolores, though her tone was cool.

Jane sighed. "It must be terrible, being so young yet having a weak heart."

It was just as Lord Summervale feared. News of his daughter's perceived inadequacy was spreading.

It was, of course, still possible Cecily had a heart defect. It was also possible Mrs Ogden had passed because of natural causes, just as the doctor had decreed.

Equally possible was that something more sinister was going on.

If it wasn't Miss Petherick who'd poisoned Cecily, who was it? One of the girls standing beside Felicity at the horse enclosure?

Had someone with murderous intentions been sitting in Felicity's classroom, and she hadn't noticed?

Such extreme behaviour between school chums was still too hard to fathom. A prank gone wrong felt more likely, but that didn't explain what happened to Mrs Ogden.

The referee approached the teams. The players were pulling on their helmets and returning to their mounts.

Dolores lifted her chin. "Looks like there are refreshments waiting for us."

Tucking her arm through Usha's, Dolores ambled off back to where Miss Vincent had returned to the sidelines with the other girls, a serving boy carrying a large tray full of drinks close behind them. Jane followed, yelping when her foot found a pot hole as she hurried to keep up with the other girls.

Lord Severin was up in his saddle and back on the pitch, issuing instructions to his teammates. He didn't spare a glance in Dolores' direction, but then neither did she in his.

Had Felicity asked the right questions? Not to worry if she

hadn't. The investigation she'd promised Miss Armstrong was just getting started.

Felicity retook her seat at the side of the playing field among the Liverton ladies. The remaining chukkas followed without incident. Lemonade was sipped, polite applause was offered. The society journalist toddled over to ask the girls a few questions about the upcoming season, about how excited they were to debut, and to take notes about what they were wearing.

It was odd, acting so normal. Felicity itched to press the girls for more information, but not at the polo. She had to be subtle.

St Martin's, which was Lord Severin's team, won the match. The players shook hands as they left the field.

"Time to go home," announced Miss Driver in her sergeant major style, before any of the girls could break away and talk to the players or horses.

In an organised fashion, they went to the motors that were waiting to take them back to Liverton House. While Felicity helped the girls take their seats, she didn't join them.

"You're not coming back to Liverton?" Jane looked affronted as Felicity went to close the passenger door of the Lanchester in which Jane, Usha, Dolores, and a couple of first-year students were seated.

Felicity shook her head. "I've an appointment."

Usha frowned. "Where? In town?"

"Might we not accompany you?" proposed Dolores, ready to climb out of her seat.

"I shall see you all at dinner," said Felicity, closing the door firmly and indicating to the driver it was time to leave. The rest of the Liverton cavalcade departed promptly afterwards, the other teachers having been too busy with their own chaperoning duties to ask Felicity where she was going.

With the Lanchesters out of sight, she went to the farthest reaches of the field. In the shade of a row of trees, a dark blue Model T sat waiting. Its engine started as Felicity approached.

Tugging open the door, she slipped into the passenger seat.

"Where to, m'lady?" asked Alex with a playful smile. He was back in his habitual three-piece suit, a grey homburg sitting atop his dark blond smoothed-back hair.

A little shiver of excitement passed through Felicity. "Thank you for coming. You know where we're going."

## Chapter Twenty-Eight

The driveway through the centre of the Summervale estate was as straight as a pin and edged with neat rows of fastigiate poplars that shook in the breeze. Fluffy clouds chased above the green rolling landscape as Alex guided the Model T steadily along the drive, pulling the brim of his hat low to shield his eyes from the glare. Felicity squinted as the house came into view.

Like most of the families who sent their daughters into the care of Miss Armstrong, the Summervales had residences across England. This particular manor, built in creamy sandstone with symmetrical Georgian proportions, had been woken from its slumber to accommodate Cecily. While the hospital in Exeter was a fine establishment, it didn't offer the privacy and luxury a family like the Summervales expected.

The Model T drew to a halt on the gravel before the house's entrance. The scent of freshly cut grass met them as Felicity and Alex alighted from the motor. For the briefest of moments, they might have been on holiday together, without a care in the world. There was, however, work to do.

"And you're absolutely certain none of this is for the papers?" pressed Alex one more time as they began their ascent of the sweeping stone steps at the front of the house.

Felicity had used the journey to bring Alex up to date on everything that had happened at the polo, to discuss her suspicions with him, and to gather his reactions. Alex agreed it was possible for the combination of Mrs Ogden's passing and Cecily's illness to be a coincidence. But he also agreed it might not be.

In addition, Felicity had used the run over to the Summervales' residence to emphasise that there was no chance of reporting anything in the papers.

Felicity gave Alex a look to communicate her disapproval of his persistence on the topic.

He smiled. "Just checking. You realise I rather abruptly gave up a career in garden maintenance for this, don't you? Can't say I enjoyed the work, but the head groundsman seemed disappointed I was leaving."

"His loss is the investigation's gain," said Felicity, her heels tapping as she ascended the stone steps. She was mildly fearful about containing Alex's hunter-like instincts as a journalist, but she would rather have him at her side than be without him. "We need to tread carefully. We can't push this out in the paper. Not yet."

"Not yet," echoed Alex quietly.

A tall, thin butler came to meet them at the house's front entrance. "Lady Cecily awaits you, your ladyship." His gaze shifted to Alex. "The telephone call from the headmistress didn't mention a second guest."

Alex was about to speak, but Felicity reacted first.

"My apologies for the confusion," she said to the butler. "Mr Cooper is my assistant."

Alex's eyebrows shot upwards.

Felicity smiled serenely at him. He'd allowed the groundsmen at the rockery to imagine a romance between Felicity and himself. How was this any worse? There was still a chance Cecily would object to Alex's presence, but the butler couldn't refuse him entrance.

The servant bowed. "This way, please."

Following the butler's gesture to step through the grand doorway, Felicity and Alex passed through a cavernous entrance hall with black-

and-white tiles that echoed underfoot. Their progression was halted when an upright man with a barrel chest, bright white hair, and darting amber eyes came striding towards them.

"From the academy, are you? Come to speak to my daughter, have you?" The man shook with rage.

"Pleased to meet you, Lord Summervale," began Felicity, turning a little towards Alex. "May I introduce—"

"My Cecily almost died. Almost died, I tell you," boomed Lord Summervale, his livid gaze boring into Felicity.

Alex removed his hat. His forehead creased deeply, the scar there visible. He was about to intervene, but Felicity got there first.

"We are all deeply concerned about Lady Cecily's welfare," she said, remaining calm. "The wish of the school is to understand exactly what happened, so that we may—"

"I shall summon the police. I don't care if it's in all the papers. I'll have everyone know what happened. I sent my child to your school to prepare her for marriage. She was supposed to debut this year. How can she make the match she deserves, the match her family name deserves, if the doctor says she's not to stand up for more than five minutes? The very least a father expects is for his daughter to be safe."

"And you are utterly correct in that expectation, Lord Summervale. Miss Armstrong has the welfare of all her girls—"

Lord Summervale stepped closer. Felicity remained deadly still, as though face-to-face with a wild animal.

"If you don't find out what happened," growled Lord Summervale, "I will."

Alex gripped his hat tightly to his chest. Felicity prayed he wouldn't intervene.

The butler blinked, apparently surprised by his master's behaviour.

"And when I do, heads shall roll, I tell you. Heads shall roll." Lord Summervale stormed off, his footsteps echoing through the entrance hall.

Felicity took in a deep breath.

Lord Summervale had continued to make threats to call the

police but hadn't done so yet. Was he more bark than bite? He was clearly upset, and when powerful emotions were involved, people became unpredictable.

Alex continued to stare along the corridor down which Lord Summervale had disappeared. Even after they set off again, following the butler, Alex continued to look over his shoulder. He was usually cool-headed, but something about Cecily's father had got under his skin.

"What is it?" hissed Felicity as the butler pulled ahead of them on a sweeping, carpeted staircase.

"I've seen Lord Summervale before," whispered Alex. "The name somehow escaped me, but I never forget a face."

The butler stood to wait at the top of the stairs, allowing Felicity and Alex to catch up. "It's just along here, your ladyship."

Felicity nodded her acknowledgement. As the servant turned to lead them along a corridor, Felicity slowed again. "Seen him before where?" she hissed.

Alex's brow drew low. "In the war."

Felicity's stomach squeezed.

Might Lord Summervale be the link between Cecily and Mrs Ogden?

It was far-fetched. There was barely a man in the country above a certain age without some kind of involvement in the war.

The butler knocked on a panelled door and turned the brass door knob, disappearing inside.

Alex pressed his lips together, deep in thought.

After a brief exchange within the room, the butler reappeared. "Lady Cecily will see you now, your ladyship." The butler stepped aside to allow Felicity to enter the room.

Alex hesitated.

"Mr Cooper, too?" enquired Felicity.

The butler nodded and gestured towards the open door.

# Chapter Twenty-Nine

Tall windows surrounded by heavy red curtains framed views over a rigidly striped lawn. The lowering sun cast shadows from dark green topiary pyramids over the grass.

Inside, deep chairs and a wide sofa upholstered in plush ivory chintz gave the room a welcoming feel. Warm-hued paintings, family photographs, and mementos from far-flung travels hung on the walls, stood on side tables, and decorated the mantelpiece. Cards and colourful bouquets from well-wishers had been squeezed onto all available surfaces. The zesty scent of freesias lightly perfumed the air.

At the centre of the room, her feet in elegant burgundy slippers resting on a footstool, Lady Cecily Summervale was seated on a cushioned sofa, a thick cashmere blanket draped over her knees. Her dark blue dress with a broad sash resembled a kimono. Her sunshine-blonde hair was loosely scraped back with a gold clasp. A delicate, pale blue silk scarf hung limply around her neck.

Although her skin had lost some of its vivid, healthy glow, Cecily's smile was warm.

"I should like to stand up to greet you, only I'm on doctor's orders not to move around. And, well..." She looked down.

On her right, beside an open book placed pages-down, lay a floppy-eared Springer Spaniel with liver-and-white fur. The dog had its chin on Cecily's lap, moving only its eyes to watch Felicity and Alex enter the room.

The guests declined the offer of refreshments.

"We shall keep our visit short so as not to tire you," said Felicity as the butler withdrew. "I appreciate your agreeing to see me."

Cecily gently stroked the faithful canine's head. "Oh, I'm quite out of the woods. Just a little tired, that's all."

Felicity and Alex each took a chair opposite the sofa. Holding his hat, Alex made no move for the notebook he always carried in his inside jacket pocket. He looked to Felicity to lead the conversation.

With no time to waste, Felicity came straight to the point. "Have you any news about what caused your collapse?"

Cecily sighed. "The doctors say there's nothing wrong with me. And there's been a few of them, because father wanted second, third, and fourth opinions."

Felicity glanced at Alex. He returned a grave look. Weakness or illness originating with Cecily had been firmly ruled out.

"Rather a freak occurrence, by all accounts," continued Cecily, looking down at the dog on her lap. "They're repeating some tests, just to be sure. We should have the results soon, but on the surface, the doctors can't see anything wrong with me."

"Might you know when exactly you'll have the results?" asked Felicity, doing her best to sound relaxed.

The spaniel's ears twitched.

Cecily frowned a little. "Is there something the matter?"

"We should like to understand what exactly happened to you," assured Felicity. "That's all. Might you be able to recount what you remember?"

Cecily's brow wrinkled. "It started with a tightness in my chest. Then a terrible pain. It was as if I couldn't breathe. I must admit I panicked. I've never felt so ill so suddenly."

Alex shifted in his seat. He no doubt had questions, but he was leaving everything to Felicity. She had the gentle touch needed for this situation.

"And just before you were ill," continued Felicity, "do you recall exactly what it was you were doing?"

Cecily's brow wrinkled further. "I was sitting with the girls and watching the waltz." She flashed a glance at Alex. "You and your partner are sublime dancers."

Alex's mouth pulled into a smile. "Thank you, your ladyship."

Felicity's smile was more awkward. She hadn't expected Cecily to recognise Alex from the dance floor, but then he was strikingly handsome. What exactly might Cecily imagine the nature of Felicity's relationship with her 'assistant' to be? It didn't matter. Not now.

"Do you remember the toast?" asked Felicity.

Cecily nodded. "I took a sip or two of champagne. We all did. But if the drink was bad, then wouldn't the whole school be ill?"

Felicity nodded. "One would expect so, yes."

Cecily's expression changed, her eyebrows drawing low. She stroked the spaniel's head more firmly. "You believe something was wrong with just my drink?"

Alex's smile had disappeared, replaced with tension in his jaw.

"We're looking at all the possibilities," said Felicity gently. "In the same way that your father is desperate to know what happened to you, Miss Armstrong is also looking for answers. If the doctors say there's nothing wrong with you, then..." Felicity left the statement hanging in the air for a moment. "Do you remember who gave you the drink?"

"I took it from a tray. The tray was offered to me by one of the maids. No, by Miss Eversley." The lines on Cecily's forehead deepened. "Or perhaps one of the other teachers." Her testimony on this point was sadly unreliable.

"Who was with you when you received your drink? Do you remember anything odd about the occasion?"

"Jane had left us, of course. Dolores, Usha, and Gwen were all close by.

"Do you remember the seating arrangement?"

Cecily blinked. "I was between Dolores and Gwen. Usha was next to Dolores." She shook her head. "Are you saying one of them wanted to hurt me?"

Felicity cast a glance at Alex. He continued to look sombre, his grip a little too tight on his homburg.

Their investigation had the potential to set things right. If carried out clumsily, however, Felicity's sleuthing posed a risk to everyone involved.

Felicity spoke softly. "I understand your dress was sabotaged ahead of the practice ball."

Cecily shifted uncomfortably. The spaniel whined and looked up at her. "I thought it was an accident. Miss Armstrong said..." Cecily trailed off.

Felicity waited. It was a terrible thought, a school friend planning and carrying out such hurtful actions. If Cecily was considering the possibility for the first time, she needed room to come to terms with it.

"These are just ideas, you understand," said Felicity. "We're looking at all possibilities. Discretion is a priority, of course. We don't want to place blame where there is none."

Cecily nodded eagerly. That there may be no one to blame was reassuring to her.

"The girls all wish you well," continued Felicity. "I believe you've received their messages by now."

Cecily's eyes scanned the cards and flowers that filled the room. She swallowed and nodded.

Had Dolores' message via the young earl reached Cecily? Or had sending Cecily a message been just a ruse for spending time with the dark-haired polo player?

Felicity paused. She wouldn't single out Dolores in Cecily's mind. Not yet.

"Can you think of any reason anyone at the school would want to cause you embarrassment?" Embarrassment was easier to consider than physical harm.

Cecily blinked. Her mouth was down turned. She was so well-liked, so supportive of the other girls. Not that she expected repayment, but Cecily had perhaps never imagined herself to have enemies.

"I only told one person." Cecily's voice trembled slightly.

Alex straightened.

Felicity remained still. "You only told one person what?"

Over-reacting wouldn't encourage Cecily to open up, but they were onto something.

Cecily looked down at her spaniel. The white-and-liver dog lifted his eyes towards her as she stroked the top of his shiny head. "About the engagement."

"You're engaged to be married?" Felicity couldn't erase all trace of surprise from her voice.

A smile crept over Cecily's lips. "We didn't want to tell anyone, at least until I'd finished at the academy. It seemed so premature. It happened rather quickly, you see." Cecily sounded truly happy, though she was trying to tamp it down. "Father's very pleased, but he's cautious. He wants to make sure we won't change our minds. We won't, of course, but he's very protective."

While she didn't count Alex among them, Felicity knew what it was like to manoeuvre around overly protective men. It wasn't the time for digging into that topic, however.

Felicity offered a gentle smile. "Might you be able to tell us who the lucky fellow is?"

Cecily beamed. "Of course. I trust you're both able to keep the details of a liaison to yourselves."

Alex nodded. "Naturally," he said, having done enormously well to have kept quiet as long as he had.

*Tap-tap.*

There was a knock at the door.

The butler had returned. "Terribly sorry to interrupt, your ladyship, but it's time for your cocoa. Do you wish to take it here in the salon, or would you like it delivered to your room?"

*Cocoa?*

Felicity and Alex exchanged glances. The knot in Felicity's stomach tightened.

"In my room, please." Cecily gave the servant a pleasant smile. "I'm under doctor's orders to retire to bed after my guests have departed."

The butler acknowledged the command and withdrew

"Now," said Cecily. "Where were we?" She sounded practically cheery, her light brown eyes flashing.

"Do you take cocoa every evening?" asked Felicity innocently, as though the question was a natural part of polite conversation, even though they were supposed to be anxiously awaiting the revelation of Cecily's fiancé.

Yet Felicity had to ask. She had to grasp and pull on the thread.

Cecily nodded, a little confused. "Usually yes. I find I sleep better with it."

*Did you also take cocoa on the evening Mrs Ogden met her end?*

It was the next enquiry on Felicity's mind, but she hesitated. The detail could be checked with the servants at Liverton House. Cecily had been pushed far enough into the dark realm of Felicity's suspicions, and an unnatural end for Mrs Ogden was uncomfortably close to the secret spy-hunting mission that had brought Felicity to Liverton Ladies' Academy.

Alex quirked an eyebrow. "You were about to tell us about your fiancé, your ladyship," he said, steering the conversation onto safer ground.

"Yes," agreed Felicity, with a pleasant smile, her hands neatly folded on her grey linen skirt. "We can certainly keep a secret. Do tell."

A cloud passed before the sun. The room darkened.

Cecily met the gaze of the spaniel in her lap as she played with a soft ear. "It's Lord Severin. Lord Carrothers' son."

The revelation hit like a thunderbolt. Felicity opened her mouth to react, but no sound came out.

Lord Severin was Dolores' dark-haired polo player. He'd been in the alleyway with her in Wickleigh. Yet Cecily was engaged to him?

Alex looked questioningly at Felicity. She'd not thought to

mention the name of Dolores' beau to him. She hadn't understood the significance.

Felicity cleared her throat. "And you say you told only one other person at the school?"

Cecily nodded. "One week ago, Severin and I both agreed we would tell one other person. It was becoming simply too much to keep to just our families."

"Who did you tell?" pressed Felicity.

Cecily hesitated. "I don't see why she'd be jealous." She looked outside at the sombre sky. "And she certainly wouldn't wish to hurt me. She wouldn't wish harm on anyone."

"Who was it?" Alex sat forward in his chair. He didn't have all the details, but he understood the gravity of the situation.

The sternness in his voice brought Cecily's attention back into the room.

She bit her lip.

## Chapter Thirty

Alex left Felicity at the steps of Liverton House's front entrance and motored promptly away. The wind had picked up, spreading long, thin clouds like ribs across the sky. With the sun setting, the pattern was lit gold-orange on a dramatic backdrop of purple-tinted pink.

In the entrance hall, the soft evening light filtered through the tall windows and lit the marble-effect columns and the polished wooden staircase that led up to the students' apartments. Girls giggled as they passed Felicity in the first-floor corridor, still in high spirits from the polo match.

Felicity struggled to return their smiles. Her mood was anything but high.

Alex had also come away from the Summervale's residence somewhat troubled. Keen to gather more information on Lord Summervale's movements during the war, he would return to his digs in Exeter and place calls to his contacts at the War Office. He also promised to inform Felicity straight away of any update on the handwriting analysis.

Would Alex's research lead to a connection between Cecily and Mrs Ogden? Was there more to connect them than cocoa?

Not that the evening ritual they shared was insignificant. What if

Cecily had been the primary target all along, and Mrs Ogden's untimely demise had been accidental?

But if Mrs Ogden had been poisoned by mistake, where did that leave the investigation into the spy? The idea that the needlework teacher had been deliberately killed had shored up Felicity's suspicions about her. If Mrs Ogden wasn't the wartime traitor hiding at the school, then who was it?

One thing was now certain. Cecily had confided in only one girl at the school. Had jealousy of Cecily's engagement to Lord Severin triggered the drama that now posed a threat to the academy's existence?

Felicity arrived at the apartment door. As her first move, she might have interviewed the servants about the cocoa. Was it possible Mrs Ogden's cocoa had been mistaken for Cecily's?

But engaging with the girls felt more urgent. If the academy's students were involved — and how could they not be? — then it wasn't simply a case of proving who did wrong. The girls had their whole lives ahead of them. They needed to be guided back onto the proper path.

Felicity knocked firmly at the door.

"Just a moment," came a voice from within.

Then the door opened.

"Lady Felicity." Gwendoline's eyes were wide. Her white-blonde hair sat in a thin braid on her shoulder. Her hand clutched the lapel of her blush-pink silken robe, the hem of which reached pink velvet slippers.

Perhaps Gwendoline had been expecting a friend or a servant. She'd definitely not been expecting Felicity. But then Felicity hadn't expected to be paying Gwendoline a visit.

When Cecily announced she'd only told Gwendoline about her engagement to Lord Severin, it had been a surprise. More shy and private than the other girls, Gwendoline seemed to be the perfect keeper of Cecily's secret, while allowing Cecily to rid herself of the dreadful urge to tell at least one of her friends.

Had Gwendoline kept the information to herself? Was there a chance she'd even acted upon it?

"Miss Milligan." Felicity's tone was matter-of-fact. "In light of your missing the polo, I wanted to check on you. Are you feeling better?"

Gwendoline nodded. "I am, thank you."

"Glad to hear it." Felicity's smile was tight. "May I come in?"

"Certainly." Gwendoline stepped aside.

Each girl's apartment comprised a sitting room, a bedroom, and a private bathroom with a small dressing room attached. The space was at least twice that of the accommodation provided to Liverton's teachers.

With stints at the school lasting up to three years, some girls made efforts to stamp their identity on their living spaces, bringing furniture, haberdashery, and artworks down from London or importing them from abroad.

In Gwendoline's sitting room, there were no works of art on the muted sage-green walls, no shining damask pillows, and no chaise longue. There was only the standard set of furniture upholstered in mustard-yellow velvet that was provided with the rooms, which was of good quality but not particularly elegant. The room's scent was the faint smell of furniture polish.

A tall stack of books on a side table added a dash of character. Beside the pile stood a little wooden box like a carriage clock with a handle atop. It was a battery-powered lamp, likely used for reading in the dark.

"Please, your ladyship."

Gwendoline gestured for Felicity to sit in a straight-backed chair beside the fireplace and set about clearing the chair opposite, which was occupied by a pile of dress boxes. The boxes bore the names of London's most exclusive dressmakers, but their lids remained tightly in place, as though never opened.

As Gwendoline sat down, she gave Felicity a faint smile. Outside, the dramatic sunset had turned the sky an angry red, and the light slanting in through the window gave Gwendoline's cheeks an odd-looking glow.

Was Felicity alone with a murderess?

Surely a jealous classmate would only harm Cecily with the intention of undermining her engagement to one of England's most desirable bachelors. The intention wouldn't have been to kill, would it?

Taking precautions against the possibility of her own naivety, Felicity noted that though her seat was close to Gwendoline's, the fireplace tools — including a rather hefty poker — were closest to Felicity. She was also nearer the door than Gwendoline and would certainly not accept any offer of refreshments.

"How can I be of help, your ladyship?" Gwendoline continued to smile weakly.

Felicity perched on the edge of her seat, her hands folded in her lap. "I will come straight to the point, Miss Milligan. I should like to create a clear picture of what happened when Lady Cecily was taken ill. You were seated next to her at the practice ball, were you not?"

Gwendoline's smile fell. She looked confused for a moment, then nodded. "I was."

"Who else was seated with you?"

"Dolores. Usha. Jane." Gwendoline attempted a smile, but it wavered. "The usual gang."

"Do you remember the details of what happened when Lady Cecily became ill?"

Gwendoline's lower lip trembled. "I tried to help. It was horrible."

Gwendoline had chased after Cecily as she lunged out onto the dance floor. Was she cunning enough to have staged an attempt to help?

"Do you recall what happened in the lead up to the incident?" asked Felicity.

Gwendoline sat up straighter. Another flicker of a smile passed over her lips. "I remember watching you dance, your ladyship. You danced so beautifully."

"Thank you." Felicity's voice was taut. She'd enjoyed dancing with Alex immensely, but it had caused her to become distracted. What had Felicity missed? "When the dancing paused, do you remember the circumstances?"

Gwendoline's forehead creased. "Poor Jane. She only wished to powder her nose ahead of being called to dance. She was so nervous. I didn't see exactly what happened. Knocked into the buffet, I expect. All those glasses were in pieces all over the floor. She was devastated, poor thing. Miss Armstrong escorted her from the room, didn't she?"

Felicity nodded. If Jane tampered with the drinks before leaving the room, then the poisoning would have been practically at random. If someone had intended to harm Cecily, a person who had been close to her was to blame.

"Do you recall what happened after Lady Jane left the room?"

Gwendoline frowned, her fingers fidgeting with the belt of her pink gown. "It was the toast, wasn't it? We each received a coupe."

"Who handed you and Lady Cecily your drinks?"

Gwendoline swallowed. Her expression was suddenly serious. She understood the nature of Felicity's enquiry. "We were out of our seats and moving about. Dolly handed me my glass. I didn't see who gave Cecily hers."

Felicity paused.

*Dolores.*

"As students here at Liverton," continued Felicity, "there's a certain camaraderie, is there not?"

Gwendoline gave her head a little shake. "Of course."

"But there can also be a degree of..." Felicity moderated her tone to sound understanding but also mildly disapproving. "Competition. Perhaps even envy."

The corners of Gwendoline's mouth twitched downwards. She said nothing. The red glow of the sunset was fading. Gwendoline's cheeks were returning to ghostly pale.

Felicity leaned forward, her fingers interlaced on her dove-grey skirt. "I understand Lady Cecily confided in you. About a certain matter very private to her."

Gwendoline's eyes widened, but her voice remained steady. "That's right. She did."

"She told you about her engagement, didn't she?"

Gwendoline hesitated. "Yes, she did."

Felicity would keep pushing, but she had to be gentle. "I believe you have goodness in your heart, Miss Milligan. I don't believe you wish harm on anyone."

Gwendoline shook her head vigorously. "Of course not."

"I believe that of every girl at this school," continued Felicity. "You are all brilliant and young, with full lives ahead of you. But that doesn't make you immune to mistakes. We all make mistakes."

A little tear appeared in the corner of Gwendoline's eye. She wiped it away with a knuckle. "I'm not perfect, your ladyship. I'm really very far from being perfect."

It was perhaps better to rip off the bandage. "After Lady Cecily told you her secret, what did you do?"

A tear rolled down Gwendoline's cheek. She dropped her gaze to her lap and sniffed. "I do my best to fit in, but I'm never quite there. I'm never truly one of the gang. The other girls tolerate me rather than like me. I don't want to be disliked, your ladyship. I want to have friends. I really do, but it's so hard."

It was impossible not to have sympathy for Gwendoline. Felicity was supposed to have taken the girl under her wing, yet here she was, making her cry, when Gwendoline's only crime had been the sharing of gossip. Who could say they'd never been guilty of that?

Felicity offered a handkerchief from her jacket pocket, which Gwendoline accepted and used to dab her eyes.

"Who did you tell about Lady Cecily's engagement?"

Gwendoline sniffed. "It can be so difficult to get them to like me."

"I know, Miss Milligan," said Felicity with genuine pity. "Who did you tell?"

Gwendoline squeezed the handkerchief. "I told Dolly."

Felicity nodded. It was as she expected, yet the confirmation of her suspicion felt nothing like a victory, because the picture coming to light was sadly quite grim.

Dolores had designs on Lord Severin. That much was obvious. To sabotage the competition was brutal but also logical. It wasn't about love. It was a question of familial duty and social advancement. Cecily was already the daughter of an earl, while Dolores was merely the daughter of a viscount. A match with Lord Carrothers' eldest son was worth more to Dolores than to her classmate.

Gwendoline wiped a tear from her cheek. "I presume she told Usha. She might also have told Jane. I suppose everyone knows by now. Oh, I know I shouldn't have. It was so very wrong of me."

"We've all made mistakes," said Felicity.

An odd little smile came through Gwendoline's tears. "You're too kind to me, your ladyship."

*Bang-bang-bang!*

The knock was violent. The door flew open without further pause or warning.

Miss Armstrong stood in the doorway in her sharply cut jacket and skirt in dark orange wool. She lifted her chin, her dark eyes burning with rage and fear.

Felicity's heart lurched. Something was terribly wrong.

Gwendoline gasped. "A-am I being expelled?"

"Miss Armstrong," said Felicity. "Whatever's the matter?"

"Come with me, please," intoned the headmistress.

Gwendoline went to rise, her whole body trembling.

"Miss Armstrong," began Felicity. "I'm sure we can—"

"Not you, Miss Milligan." The headmistress spoke sharply. "Lady Felicity. You're needed downstairs. Urgently."

# Chapter Thirty-One

Felicity dashed across the main entrance hall, doing her best to keep up with Miss Armstrong as she strode between the marble-effect columns, the dramatic red sunset having faded to inky grey beyond the windows.

The headmistress stopped to speak to a passing maid. "Tell Mr Clark to come and wait by the drawing room door. And to be discreet."

The maid curtseyed and hurried off.

Felicity caught up with Miss Armstrong. "May I ask why my presence is required so urgently?" She was as curious as she was concerned about what lay ahead. "I believed I was getting somewhere with Miss Milligan."

The headmistress kept walking, her eyes ahead. "An acquaintance of yours is here."

"An acquaintance?" echoed Felicity.

Miss Armstrong stopped before the drawing room door. There was a fierce glint in the headmistress' eye but also a dash of fear. "Our hope of settling things peacefully is dwindling." She opened the drawing room door. "After you, your ladyship."

She had no time to prepare herself, but Felicity wouldn't back down. It was far too late to disentangle herself from matters at Liverton.

With a little tug to straighten the linen of her jacket, Felicity entered the room, where a familiar face greeted her.

"Lady Felicity Quick."

Chief Inspector Luscombe rose from a winged armchair at the centre of the powder-blue formal drawing room. The uniformed officer at his side also stood, his helmet under his arm.

Felicity smiled and politely greeted the police officers. "Always a pleasure to see you, Chief Inspector."

The headmistress had done what she could to hold them off, to convince Lord Summervale not to involve the police. Whether or not the constabulary wanted it, the newspapers would no doubt follow them, and soon all eyes would be on Liverton Ladies' Academy.

For what was more titillating than the business of young, beautiful debutantes?

Had Felicity made a mistake in insisting Alex hold back on reporting? Their chance of being the first out with the story and setting the tone for the whole affair was slipping away. Journalists from across the country would descend on the school like wolves. Any hope of subtle investigations — into wartime spies or otherwise — would be completely dashed.

Calmly and with poise, Felicity and Miss Armstrong seated themselves on the sofa opposite the policemen.

"I hear you're a teacher now, your ladyship," said the detective as he retook his seat. He had on a tan overcoat and held a brown trilby on his knee, his balding head shining under delicate crystal lamps.

"Temporarily, yes," confirmed Felicity.

Chief Inspector Luscombe huffed. "Even as a teacher, you're somehow able to end up in the most unpleasant of situations the Devon County Constabulary has the unfortunate task of handling."

Felicity quirked an eyebrow. She was, by now, immune to the attitude of the police towards her.

"Does my school strike you as an 'unpleasant' establishment, Chief Inspector?"

Miss Armstrong's hands were gripped into fists on her dark orange skirt. The police had every right to carry out an investigation, but that wouldn't prevent the lioness protecting her cubs.

The uniformed police officer looked at his colleague, alarm evident on his clean-shaven face. He looked young for his rank and perhaps held the school in higher regard than the Exeter-based detective.

"Err, no, Miss Armstrong," confirmed the chief inspector, switching his gaze uneasily between his colleague and the headmistress. "As I understand from Sergeant Wilcox here from the station over in Wickleigh, the activities of your school are utterly above board. He's never had a report from you."

"Never had a report," echoed the sergeant with a firm shake of his head.

"But you've received a report now?" asked Felicity. Had she been wrong to imagine Lord Summervale was bluffing?

The detective shifted in his armchair, glancing warily at the headmistress. "I was about to explain the situation to Miss Armstrong when she bade me stop and wait while she went to fetch you, your ladyship."

Miss Armstrong sat straight and unflinching. She concealed any sign of fear from the police.

The detective reached into his coat pocket and withdrew a notebook. He flicked past a couple of pages. "The teacher who passed on here a few days back."

"Mrs Ogden," confirmed Miss Armstrong stiffly.

The detective swished past another few pages and squinted at the notebook. "Mrs Johanna Ogden. No known next of kin. Or so it was thought." Chief Inspector Luscombe raised an eyebrow at Sergeant Wilcox.

"Mr Andrews, the parish clerk," began the uniformed officer, the light from the crystal lamps shining on his brilliantined hair. "He did the research. Made a few telephone calls, and before you know it, he'd found a cousin over in Canada."

Miss Armstrong turned briefly to Felicity. "I ask all my teachers for their particulars. Mrs Ogden never informed me of a next of kin."

"The cousin in question had never met Mrs Ogden," continued the sergeant. "She was pleased to learn about the possibility of a small inheritance, naturally, but what she was unhappy about was the cause of death."

Felicity's brow furrowed. It made little sense. "How so?"

"Heart trouble," said Chief Inspector Luscombe with a satisfied tone. "The doctor who saw Ogden put it down to heart trouble."

Miss Armstrong shook her dark bob. "I don't follow."

"Mrs Ogden's cousin wouldn't hear of it," continued Sergeant Wilcox. "Said their family's never had a heart issue. Insisted it must be something else. Well, Mr Andrews told me of his exchange with the woman, and I told Doctor Underwood. Doctor Underwood said he had no objection to a second opinion, so we called in the coroner."

"And after he did his tests, the coroner telephoned me," said Chief Inspector Luscombe, tapping the trilby on his lap impatiently. "And that's why I'm here talking to you."

"I still don't..." Miss Armstrong's voice trailed off. She swallowed. The realisation was dawning on her.

"Mrs Ogden's death wasn't from natural causes." The detective looked very grave. "She was poisoned."

The blood drained from Miss Armstrong's cheeks. "Poisoned?"

"What sort of poison?"

While Felicity wasn't as shocked as the headteacher, it was surprising that Alex hadn't come through with the information before the police. It was also a surprise that Lord Summervale hadn't sent the police to the school.

But what did it change to know Mrs Ogden had been poisoned?

Confirming the poisoning a day or two ago would have solidified Mrs Ogden's identity as the secret spy. However, following Cecily's sudden illness and everything Felicity had discovered since, Mrs Ogden's — or anyone else's — status as a wartime traitor seemed disconnected from the deadly events at Liverton House.

Chief Inspector Luscombe flicked past another couple of pages in his notebook. "Digitalis. Rather a common substance, of course. Highly deadly, however. According to Ogden's medical records, she'd never been prescribed or used the stuff."

Miss Armstrong was still reeling. "So it wasn't Lord—"

Felicity quickly cut in before the police were given another avenue to explore. "And that's why you're here, Chief Inspector?" It was a foolish remark, but under pressure, it was the best she could do.

The detective frowned. "A poisoning is a matter for the police, your ladyship. As you well know."

Felicity fired a sharp glance at the headmistress. Had Miss Armstrong realised now? If Lord Summervale hadn't called in the police, then they only knew about Mrs Ogden. They didn't yet know about Cecily.

There was still a chance. A chance to unravel matters quietly, to unmask the culprit without a scandal.

Miss Armstrong narrowed her eyes slightly at Felicity, then she turned a piercing gaze on the two policemen. "You are, I hope, aware of the calibre of student we have at this establishment."

The local sergeant nodded admiringly. "Of course, ma'am."

The detective blinked slowly. "Enlighten me."

"We educate the daughters of high-ranking officers from the armed forces. Of dukes. Of chiefs of industry."

The sergeant nodded along. The detective looked unmoved.

The headmistress continued. "We've even the daughters of politicians. Of the Home Secretary."

A slight flinch passed over the detective's features. The Home Office oversaw law and order in the United Kingdom. Miss Armstrong had leverage.

"In short, gentlemen, we have some extremely important young women here at Liverton. These girls are the best and brightest in the country. But they are also in need of guidance and protection. That's why they're sent to me. And put in my care."

The local sergeant looked thoroughly cowed. Even the detective was sinking into his seat. The lioness was preparing to roar.

"I cannot allow their peace and their privacy to be rudely

disrupted. And before you object, Chief Inspector—" the detective had opened his mouth "—I would never, ever stand in the way of a policeman's duty. All I ask is that we're allowed one day—"

Miss Armstrong threw the briefest of glances in Felicity's direction. It was all the headmistress could demand. It was — if it were granted — all Felicity would have to work with.

Felicity gave a discreet nod.

"—one day," the headmistress continued, "to prepare our establishment and our girls to receive the police for the enquiry into a poisoning."

One day to unravel matters in a peaceful, gentle manner, without scandal and damaging gossip. One day to uncover what had really happened. To save the girls from consequences they had never considered. Could the school be saved from ruin?

Chief Inspector Luscombe frowned. He looked to the local sergeant for support, but the uniformed officer was staring in awe at Miss Armstrong. He was ready to lay down his life for the headmistress and her girls.

The chief inspector cleared his throat. "You're an intelligent woman, Miss Armstrong. Surely, you understand. There'll be an inquest. This could be murder. We can't give prior warning ahead of collecting evidence. That could jeopardise our chances of finding the culprit."

There was a slight quiver in the headmistress' bottom lip. The mention of 'murder' had given the detective the upper hand.

"Perhaps you haven't fully understood what Miss Armstrong has attempted to explain to you, Chief Inspector Luscombe."

The detective's head swivelled slowly in Felicity's direction.

Felicity continued confidently. "I can assure you, you've never met anyone of the quality and background like these girls. They are quite beyond even myself. It's a combination not only of family but also of position. The wealth and power they wield is quite unparalleled. They can make or break a person's career—" Felicity snapped her fingers "—as easily as that."

The detective narrowed his eyes. There was a flicker of

uncertainty in his gaze. How many years had it taken him to reach the rank of chief inspector?

Felicity held his gaze. Was she going too far, making veiled threats and keeping quiet about what happened to Cecily? It was risky, but the stakes were high. It wasn't the reputation of one or two people on the line. The whole school was in danger.

"We all know that time is crucial in a murder enquiry," she continued. "But days have already passed. What difference would one more day make? Preparing the girls and the school doesn't mean informing them that the police are coming. Does it, Miss Armstrong?"

The headmistress sat as straight as an arrow. "We shall be extremely discreet."

"It's a case of setting the right tone," continued Felicity before the detective could object. "We want to avoid big shocks. The girls' families will be thankful to the police for being so understanding of the vulnerability of their daughters."

"Of course," said Sergeant Wilcox deferentially.

Chief Inspector Luscombe gasped with exasperation. "Sergeant, really. We—"

"Can you give us that, Chief Inspector?" pressed Felicity. "Just one day?"

## Chapter Thirty-Two

"Poisoned by whom? And why?"

With the police departed — smuggled discreetly out of a side door by the dependable Mr Clark — Miss Armstrong paced up and down before the Calacatta marble fireplace in the pale blue drawing room, smoke curling upwards from the cigarette holder in her hand. With no servant besides the butler having been allowed access to the room to avoid news of the police's presence spreading, the drawing room curtains still stood open. Beyond the dim reflection of the room's interior, a thin sliver of bright white moon hung high in the sky.

Felicity remained on the edge of her seat, her insides as taut as a coiled spring. "I don't believe it was anyone's intention to do real harm."

The police had given the school one day. One day to prepare itself for their investigation, before men in uniform came to ask uncomfortable questions and search through trunks, hat boxes, and frock pockets.

"Not to that degree," Felicity added.

One day wasn't long, but neither was it insignificant. As far as police procedure went, it was highly unusual. Chief Inspector Luscombe and Sergeant Wilcox clearly felt they could trust both Miss

Armstrong — whose brave endeavours during the war were well known — and Felicity, who, for all the police might think of her, was at least considered capable of discretion.

Felicity and Miss Armstrong had sworn to keep the upcoming investigation secret from the rest of the house. But how might they make best use of the time?

Miss Armstrong stopped pacing. She drew hard on her cigarette. "What do you intend to do?"

Felicity straightened. The way ahead was a narrow and difficult path, but for a gentle outcome, it was the only option.

"I have a firm idea of the perpetrator's identity," she said. "I shall talk to the person. Have them understand the gravity of the situation they've created, both for themselves and for the school. If she approaches the police with a confession before they come back for their investigation, then—"

"She?" Miss Armstrong's eyes were wide with alarm. "You mean to say it's one of my girls?"

Felicity grimaced. She didn't like it either. "The ending shan't be pretty. But it's the best of all options."

When the butler returned to report on the policemen's departure — the motor they'd arrived in thankfully had no police markings — Miss Armstrong requested a stiff drink and lit another cigarette. Citing the lateness of the hour and the ticking clock of the time pressure they were under, Felicity excused herself from the drawing room and went to the phone booths. It was late enough that Felicity was the only person wishing to use the telephone. Thankfully, the local exchange was still open, but the operator reported no answer from Alex's Exeter residence.

If he was following up with contacts at the War Office regarding Lord Summervale, might he be at the newspaper's offices?

"Mr Cooper's not here, your ladyship," reported the night watchman after checking the smoke-fugged room where journalists could be found typing up their stories late into the night.

Felicity left a message requesting Alex to come to Liverton House as soon as he was able. It wasn't just a race against the police's return to the school. A rival newspaper might get hold of the coroner's report, and the news could be splashed about the place before Alex had time to even scribble down a word.

"I shall deliver the message to Mr Cooper as soon as I see him, your ladyship," assured the night porter. "I'll make sure he knows to come as quickly as he can."

Felicity returned the receiver to its hook and remained seated on the little cane-work stool in the booth.

Telephoning Jasper wasn't an option. He had a tendency to over-react when it came to Felicity putting herself at risk. Alex could be relied upon to remain level-headed and keep his focus where it was needed.

When Alex reappeared at Liverton as a journalist, how might it be received that a reporter from Felicity's brother's newspaper had been working undercover as a groundsman at the school? Miss Armstrong was rather dependent on Felicity now. When press coverage of the goings-on at the school began, the headmistress would come to rely on Alex as well.

Felicity had to hope he received her message in time.

Might she write a piece for the paper herself? The idea was somehow odd. Since arriving at the school, Felicity had put her reporter's instinct on hold.

It hadn't stopped her from investigating, however. And she wasn't done yet.

## Chapter Thirty-Three

It was quiet, too early even for breakfast trays to be brought upstairs, when Felicity rose from a fitful night's sleep and dressed in a forest-green pinafore over a cream silk blouse with a Peter Pan collar. Birds sung as the sun broke over a bank of clouds beyond the trees at the bottom of Liverton's main lawn.

Treading lightly in brown suede one-strap shoes down staircases and along corridors, Felicity moved swiftly with the twin goals of being uninterrupted and unexpected.

She'd considered making her move the evening before, but a night's sleep and some extra time to think had bolstered Felicity's position.

In a deserted corridor, she stopped before a door and took a deep breath. She had one shot to get this right. One shot to save the school and the girls from the chaos and embarrassment of a full investigation and ruinous newspaper coverage.

Felicity knocked on the door.

Silence.

She knocked again, more insistently this time.

There was movement. Movement and whispered voices.

"Come in."

Felicity twisted the shining brass knob.

Lavender silk drapes covered the sitting room walls. Emerald-green damask had been chosen to upholster curved Rococo furniture. There were elaborate vases dripping with flowers, tasselled lamps, and marble busts, all glowing in the early morning sun, which filtered through the partially open gold-trimmed curtains.

The design was playful and creative. Even ironic. The combination ought not to have worked, but it somehow did.

If Dolores had overseen the decoration herself, then she had talent.

In a flowing pair of satin pyjamas decorated with a repetitive print of swooping green parrots, Dolores leaned back on a chaise longue, a dressing gown in dark blue velvet draped around her. Her eyes were red and puffy, her wavy chocolate-brown bob a little wild.

On a nearby fauteuil, Usha was curled into a thick bank of cushions. She had a sketchbook on her lap, a pencil in her hand, and an ivory satin nightgown that covered her down to her ankles. A delicate lace-trimmed shawl lay around her shoulders. Her dark brown eyes were more awake and alert than her friend's.

Both girls looked surprised to see Felicity. They sat up straighter as she entered the room. Usha closed her book, her pencil still inside it. Dolores frowned.

"May I?" enquired Felicity, gesturing to a Rococo armchair.

"By all means," said Dolores coolly.

An uneasy silence followed.

Dolores held her chin high. There was defiance but also anxiousness in her gaze. She had designs on Lord Severin. Felicity had seen the evidence herself. Had learning of his engagement driven her to poison Cecily, accidentally doing away with Mrs Ogden in the process?

Yet the girls at Liverton had practically everything. Why risk it all? Or was it precisely this abundance that had warped Dolores' perception to the point where getting what she wanted was all that mattered?

"Do you often sleep over together?" The question was for both

Dolores and Usha. Felicity had counted on finding Dolores alone. Did it help or hinder to have Usha present?

Careful conduct was required. It was an urgent interrogation, but it mustn't seem so.

"Most nights," confirmed Usha. "Especially since..." Her words trailed off.

Dolores glared at her friend.

Felicity nodded. "Much has happened here recently. Unfortunately, not all of it pleasant. I should like to know how you are both faring."

Usha looked at her friend. She would follow Dolores' lead from now on.

Dolores rolled her gaze over to Felicity. There was a weariness about her that went beyond irritation at the early hour of Felicity's visit. "What have you come to talk to us about, exactly, your ladyship?"

Felicity had planned to ease into the most delicate of topics, but adaptability had served her well in the past. If too much beating around the bush risked riling her suspect, then she needed a different approach.

"As you are aware, Lady Cecily was suddenly taken ill at the practice ball. Might you know anything about what caused her illness, Miss Gastrell?"

Usha's eyes widened as she looked at her friend. Felicity's question was exceptionally direct.

Dolores drew in her chin. She was surprised but not stunned by the enquiry. "I'm not a doctor, your ladyship."

"Prior to the practice ball," continued Felicity, "a large and deliberate slash was made in the skirt of the dress Lady Cecily planned to wear for the occasion. Might you know anything about that?"

Dolores' brow lowered. "Why ask me this? How the deuce should I know?"

Felicity had failed to avoid irritating Dolores. Perhaps it had always been inevitable. Quickly bringing matters to a head was now the priority. Dolores mustn't become so angry she couldn't be reasoned with.

Felicity forged ahead. "You're acquainted with Lord Severin Carrothers, are you not?"

Dolores' mouth hung open for a moment. "What if I am?"

Usha frowned. "Dolly."

"I saw you with him," said Felicity. "When we were out in Wickleigh. Is that not correct?"

Dolores fumed, her nostrils flaring.

Usha scrambled forward in her seat. "It's not at all what you think, your ladyship."

"You know that Lord Severin is already betrothed, don't you?" continued Felicity.

Dolores' cheeks were reddening. She fixed Felicity with a hard stare.

"Dolly." Usha clutched at the ivory satin covering her knees. "Dolly. This has to stop. Just tell her, will you? It's getting out of hand."

"Tell me what?" Felicity looked at Usha and Dolores.

Usha stared hard at Dolores, but Dolores wouldn't look at her.

"Fine." Usha was becoming agitated herself. "If you won't say it, I will. Lord Severin—"

"Lord Severin is a pal." Dolores spoke over Usha. "Nothing more." She continued to scowl. "We've known one another since childhood."

Felicity blinked. Had the gestures between Dolores and Lord Severin been that of childhood friends and not lovers? She was unconvinced. "Knowing a man since childhood isn't a reason not to wish to marry him."

Usha was on the edge of her seat. "Dolly, please."

Dolores turned her scowl on Usha.

"Please," urged Usha gently. "Tell her."

Dolores returned her scowl to Felicity. "I have no interest in Severin or his engagement to Cecily." Her face softened slightly. "I have a beau of my own."

Usha slumped back in her chair. "Finally," she sighed.

Felicity's forehead creased. "You do?"

"Can you be discreet, your ladyship?" Dolores hadn't yet dropped her air of hostility towards Felicity.

Felicity had been nothing but discreet since her arrival at the school, but Dolores wasn't to know that. "Of course."

Dolores hesitated, still unconvinced.

Usha huffed. "You're being exceedingly tiresome. Do you want me to tell your story?"

Dolores snapped at her friend. "Don't mother me." She returned her scowl to Felicity. "Ralph's a racing driver. We met through Severin. They were pilots together in the war. We get little opportunity to see one another. Severin's kind enough to pass notes." Dolores' countenance softened only slightly as she spoke about her beau. "My father wouldn't approve, of course. Ralph's not from any significant stock." She squared her shoulders defiantly. "But the heart's desire cannot always be tamed."

Felicity blinked. "Ralph?"

Had she got it all wrong?

If Dolores had no interest in Lord Severin, Felicity's theory of what happened to Cecily crumbled. The chances of resolving matters in a calm and orderly fashion were disappearing.

Dolores sighed and leaned back on her chaise longue, adjusting the lapels of her velvet robe. "Ralph Wills. You can read about him in the paper. He wins every race he enters." Looking out the window, she focused on the treetops in the distance. "I'll sit through the end of this school year. I'll make my debut. I'll go to the balls. I'll appear to be the very best daughter anyone could possibly want. But after that whole rigmarole is done with, I'm marrying Ralph. And if pater and mater refuse to approve, we'll elope." Dolores gave Felicity a steely stare. "Papa can cut me off, and frankly, I don't care. Ralph and I will be happy, regardless."

A little smile passed across Usha's face. "Dolly is rather hopelessly in love, your ladyship."

Dolores glared crossly at her friend. "There's nothing remotely hopeless about it. We're thoroughly dedicated to one another."

"I'm... I'm happy you've found a love match." An uneasy feeling spread from the pit of Felicity's stomach. "I hope Mr Wills is worth your efforts."

Dolores held her chin high. "You don't need to worry about me, your ladyship. But I promise you, I have no interest in Severin." She pulled a grimace. "Not in that way."

"Indeed," agreed Felicity. "I see that now." She'd gone to Dolores' apartment convinced of the girl's guilt, but there'd been a fundamental error in Felicity's calculations. And time was ticking.

"Did you speak to Gwen already?" enquired Usha.

Felicity nodded. "I did, yes."

"That sly little fox." Dolores shook her head and gave a wry smile. "I suppose she informed you she told me about Cecily's engagement. And that's what brought you here."

Felicity narrowed her eyes, mildly affronted that her investigative skills were being called into question. "I had seen you with Lord Severin myself, Miss Gastrell."

Dolores tipped her head reprovingly. "You might have asked me about the relationship before jumping to conclusions."

Felicity had indeed made a mistake. "You're quite right, Miss Gastrell. I apologise." How could she fix it? Was there time enough to fix things?

"It's Gwen you need to speak to about the damage to Cecily's clothing, your ladyship." Usha spoke matter-of-factly.

Felicity cocked her head. "Are you saying Miss Milligan slashed Lady Cecily's dress?"

Dolores piped up. "We don't know for certain, but she would be our first suspect."

Felicity's mind flew back over all her interactions with Gwendoline. What was her motive? There hadn't been a hint of animosity towards any of her fellow students, but Felicity had clearly overlooked a thing or two.

"May I ask why Miss Milligan would do such a thing?"

Dolores frowned. "It's not a pleasant matter to speak about." She looked at her friend.

"But Lady Felicity ought to know." Usha leaned forward in her fauteuil. "Gwen is her family's last hope, your ladyship. They had no sons, and her older sister has been disgraced."

Dolores nodded. "Her father needs a son-in-law to whom he can entrust his estate."

"Gwen has spoken of her interest — or rather her family's interest — in Lord Severin." Usha sounded concerned. "She mentioned it a few times, actually. This was before Cecily shared the news of her engagement."

"Gwen stopped speaking about him after that," said Dolores.

"But she did once ask if an engagement might be undone, and if so, how." Usha looked at her friend.

A chill swept through Felicity. "And how did you answer her?"

There was silence as Dolores and Usha looked at one another.

"We didn't take it seriously," said Usha. "But we told her that the degradation of a person's reputation might cause the cancellation of an engagement."

Felicity's stomach sank like a stone.

Gwendoline. It was Gwendoline who had to be convinced to confess to the police, not Dolores. It had been Gwendoline all along.

But there was still time. Time to make it all right.

## Chapter Thirty-Four

The distance between Dolores' apartment and Gwendoline's was short. Gwendoline would likely be in bed or not long out of it. It was still rather early, the golden orb of the sun barely visible above the treetops at the edge of the gardens.

Felicity moved swiftly and quietly along the wood-panelled corridors before coming to an abrupt stop.

Jane was standing outside Gwendoline's door in tennis whites, her caramel-brown hair tightly scraped back. She looked dismayed.

"You're out of bed rather early, Lady Jane." Felicity approached the willowy girl. "Are you here to see Miss Milligan?"

Jane pouted. "Gwen said she'd help me with a letter, but she's not answering her door. I only have a few minutes. Miss Driver expects me on the court."

"Did you knock?"

Jane nodded vigorously. "Several times. I've never had a problem knocking her up early before."

"Perhaps she's still asleep?" Felicity tapped firmly on Gwendoline's door. *Please, let her still be in bed.*

Jane huffed out a sigh. "Gwen's a light sleeper, your ladyship, and I really need to send my letter this morning."

Felicity's dread grew as she knocked again, this time with more force.

She glanced at Jane. "Perhaps you might go to Miss Driver and seek Miss Milligan's advice on your letter later in the day?"

Jane shook her head. "Mavis is expecting my news. I really need to send it this morning."

It wasn't the moment for an argument.

Felicity pressed her ear to the door. There was no sound from within, only the distant cacophony of birds twittering in the gardens.

The clock was ticking, counting down to the police's return to the school. Decisive action was needed.

Felicity put her hand on the polished brass knob and found the door unlocked. There was a gentle creak as it swung open.

Jane's deep green eyes widened with surprise at the gesture.

Felicity entered the room. "Miss Milligan?"

Jane followed gingerly after her. "Gwen?"

The prim sitting room with its plain, sensible furniture was empty. The bedroom was empty, too, the bed neatly made, golden sunlight on the counterpane. The little bathroom and adjoining dressing room were also devoid of life.

There was no trace of Gwendoline.

Felicity felt a shiver run down her spine. "I must find Miss Milligan."

Jane blinked. "She told me to come to her room, but I suppose she might have gone down to breakfast?"

Jane was right. There was no need to panic. Not yet. Still, Felicity's heartbeat quickened as she hurried downstairs to the conservatory, losing Jane along the way.

"The usual, your ladyship?" enquired the butler as Felicity stood in the doorway, the blood draining from her face.

The conservatory was empty.

"Mr Clark, have you seen Miss Milligan this morning?"

"I haven't, your ladyship." The butler's brow drew low. "Is something the matter?"

"No, no," said Felicity with a tight smile as she retreated from the conservatory doorway.

*Think. Where might Gwendoline be?*

Felicity moved instinctively towards the marble-effect pillars of the house's grand entrance hall and the big oak doors that lead out onto the porticoed entrance and the sweeping gravel drive.

The grounds of Liverton House were vast. One woman alone couldn't find a girl intent on not being found. But Felicity had to try.

A sob echoed through the entrance hall.

Felicity stopped before reaching the doors that lead outside.

The sobbing continued.

"Miss Milligan?"

In a floor-length charcoal-coloured gown, Miss Petherick appeared from behind a column. Her gaunt cheeks were wet with tears. In one hand, she held a black handkerchief. In the other, a folded newspaper.

Felicity frowned. "Miss Petherick. Whatever's the matter?"

The music teacher squeezed her handkerchief, her knuckles white. "The school's finished."

Felicity swallowed. "What do you mean, 'finished'? How?"

Miss Petherick held the newspaper out for Felicity. "It can't be true, can it?"

It was that day's early edition of the Empire Examiner. The front page's headline read: *Teacher poisoned at exclusive girl's school*.

Felicity's stomach dropped like a lead weight.

"Goodness."

She had sorely underestimated the time it had taken for the coroner's report to reach the press.

"Mrs Ogden wasn't murdered, was she?" Tears ran down Miss Petherick's cheeks. She was supposed to leave at the end of the term, yet her strong affection for the school was obvious. "Not that it matters. True or not, that headline's the end of us."

Felicity went to speak, but the words caught in her throat.

She'd miscalculated.

Felicity had misread the situation with Dolores. She'd been wrong not to allow Alex to report while they still had the upper hand. And to top it off, she'd overestimated her own ability to resolve matters.

What could be done? How might Felicity fix her mistakes?

She took a deep, steadying breath. "Is Miss Armstrong aware?"

Miss Petherick nodded, swallowing down her sobs. "I just came from her office."

Felicity touched the teacher's arm. "Try not to panic. The school isn't completely powerless in this situation. Go upstairs to your room, have a pot of tea sent up and calm yourself. Let's not worry about things that haven't happened yet."

*There's enough that's already happened to worry about*, thought Felicity but kept it to herself.

The music teacher dabbed her eyes. "I shall try," she said, sniffling as she moved towards the stairs.

Felicity kept the newspaper — there was no point in Miss Petherick dwelling on the news and upsetting herself further — and took it with her as she strode across the entrance hall and knocked on the door to Miss Armstrong's office.

Without waiting to be invited inside, Felicity entered. Swift, decisive action was more important than the norms of polite behaviour.

In a plum-coloured jacket with a wide, pointed collar, Miss Armstrong was sitting behind her desk, setting the telephone receiver back in its cradle. Her dark eyes flicked up towards Felicity, surprise registering momentarily. She remained seated. "Lady Felicity."

Felicity didn't sit down. "I apologise for the impertinence of bursting in unannounced, but I must speak to you urgently. About both Miss Gwendoline Milligan and the front page of the Empire Examiner."

Miss Armstrong folded her arms as she regarded Felicity from behind her desk. "That was Chief Inspector Luscombe. He and his men are leaving Exeter this minute."

"But he gave us a day." Even as Felicity said it, she knew the situation was hopeless. There was too much at stake for both the police and the school.

"I asked the chief inspector about the front page of the Empire Examiner." The headmistress spoke calmly, her jaw tense. "He said it was out of his control. He said newspapers have paid informants all about the place."

"We must get our story out," pressed Felicity. "It's not too late to take control of the narrative. The press hasn't yet heard about what happened at the practice ball, but it's only a matter of time. Lord Summervale—"

The headmistress cut Felicity off. "It was a mistake to imagine we'd be able to keep things under wraps. We were never in control. We'll cooperate fully with the police. What will be, shall be."

Was Miss Armstrong resigned to defeat?

"There's still time to make a difference," countered Felicity. "Jasper will run our side of the story in the next edition. I can write the piece myself." Should Felicity not have done so the night before upon failing to reach Alex? The regret made her stomach twist, but she had to focus on what she could do now, not on missed opportunities.

Miss Armstrong narrowed her gaze. "What did you want to tell me about Miss Gwendoline Milligan?" The headmistress seemed keen to move away from Felicity's suggestions. From Miss Armstrong's point of view, Felicity had her shot at fixing things and made a mess of it. The idea stung, but there was more at stake than Felicity's pride.

"Miss Gwendoline Milligan is missing," she told the headmistress. "She's not in her room. She's not been seen at breakfast. And I've reason to believe she's played a role in this. In everything that's happened."

A flicker of distress passed over Miss Armstrong's stoic expression. "You think Miss Milligan is the guilty party?"

Felicity wasn't willing to commit an answer to this question. She'd been proved wrong too many times already.

"I should like to speak to Miss Milligan rather urgently," continued Felicity. "Before the police get here." If she could convince Gwendoline to come forward with her story, to confess and go along quietly, there was still a chance they could minimise the damage to the school's reputation.

Miss Armstrong gave Felicity a stern look. "Hard work and determination have made this school what it is. But it's possible I've taken risks I ought not to have taken."

Felicity gave her head a little shake. *Please. Not more revelations.* "Whatever do you mean?"

The headmistress stood up from the desk. She went to the window overlooking the garden and folded her arms. "Miss Milligan's sister attended Liverton Ladies' Academy. It had never happened before, and it's never happened since, but Miss Milligan's sister was sent away before she could complete her studies here."

As she recalled what she'd learned from Miss Eversley in Wickleigh, Felicity wished she'd sat down. She felt a little unsteady. "Did Mrs Ogden have something to do with that?"

Miss Armstrong gave Felicity a hard stare. "It's a topic I would prefer not to discuss."

The picture was now complete. It was even worse than Felicity had imagined.

*Tap-tap-tap!*

"Come in," called the headmistress.

A footman entered. "Telephone for Lady Felicity. At the phone booths. A Mr Alexander Cooper."

*Alex.*

There was a glimmer of light at the end of the long, dark tunnel.

---

"You've seen the Empire Examiner this morning?" Alex's voice crackled over the line from the office in Exeter.

They'd dispensed with pleasantries. Alex had explained that he'd indeed been busy with war-related contacts the evening before. Nothing of any grand significance had so far been uncovered about Lord Summervale, other than his deployment at a command post near Ypres, which was how Alex recognised him.

Felicity's grip was tight on the receiver. "You were absolutely right. I should have pushed for earlier exposure in the News. It would have been better for everyone, and you would have got your scoop."

"Don't worry about me." Though tinged with concern, Alex's deep voice was reassuring. "What's the situation like there?"

Felicity updated Alex on the revelations from Gwendoline and Dolores, and Gwendoline's status as missing. There was no one in the other phone booths to overhear, although discretion at this stage was somewhat unnecessary.

"Gwendoline's sister attended Liverton and got expelled," said Felicity. "Mrs Ogden was responsible for sending her away. I fear Gwendoline might have done something silly. I'd like to find her before the police get here, but that headline in the Examiner. It can't be left unanswered."

"I'm jotting down notes as we speak. I'll submit a piece right away."

Felicity's shoulders loosened with relief. Alex always prioritised his work as a journalist. They quickly discussed what should be in the first Western Daily News article.

"Then you'll come here?" asked Felicity. "I'm certain I can convince Miss Armstrong to allow you to report from the scene."

"I'll be in my motor as soon as I get the story off my typewriter. Oh." There was a rustling of papers. "One more thing. The handwriting sample."

"Do you have the result?" said Felicity with a touch of apprehension. Her original motive for being at the school had been almost completely pushed aside.

There was a pause. The line crackled. "It's not a match."

Mrs Ogden wasn't the spy.

"Oh, goodness."

It was a double blow. In terms of her secret assignment, Felicity was back to square one, but for Gwendoline's guilt, it was further confirmation.

Felicity straightened. "I'll hold the fort till you get here. We must do what we can to save the school."

## Chapter Thirty-Five

The police arrived at Liverton House shortly after Felicity got off the telephone to Alex, which undermined Felicity's plan to venture out into the pale morning sunshine to search for Gwendoline in the grounds.

Chief Inspector Luscombe looked extremely sombre as Felicity sat across from him in the powder-blue drawing room and recounted everything she'd found out regarding Gwendoline and her possible motives. Felicity also told the detective about the evening cocoas and her suspicions about the digitalis, which had perhaps been pilfered from the music teacher.

The chief inspector slapped his pencil flat on his notebook. "Why didn't you tell me about Lady Cecily when I was here yesterday?"

Felicity gave a little shrug. "I'd hoped we might settle matters quietly. I imagined I might deliver the culprit to you with a full confession."

Chief Inspector Luscombe's brow drew low. "For as polite and well-bred as you are, your ladyship, you are rather a risk-taker."

Felicity couldn't disagree. But neither could she spare the time to consider how she might correct her behaviour. "I should still like to find Miss Milligan. With all due respect, Chief Inspector, it might be beneficial to approach her with more gentleness than your men can provide."

The detective's eyebrows shot up. "My men are quite capable of carrying out a search for a missing person, your ladyship."

Her interview with the detective abruptly over, Felicity attempted to go outside. On a paved terrace at the side of the house, having sneaked out of a service door, Felicity was met by a uniformed police officer.

"I've instructions to ask everyone to remain indoors, your ladyship. At least till we can locate the missing girl."

Felicity was about to object when the hum of a motor caught her attention.

A dark blue Model T drew up on the gravel at the front of the house. Alex stepped out, dapper and graceful in a grey three-piece suit.

Deftly slipping past the police officer, Felicity went to meet Alex. It was time for another audience with Miss Armstrong. The power of the press would be wielded in defence of the school's reputation.

"Message from Jasper," said Alex as he and Felicity moved briskly in lock-step up the stone steps of Liverton's main entrance. "He said we're to do whatever it takes to protect the school's standing."

"He really said that?" Jasper held Miss Armstrong in high regard, but he was usually hesitant about Felicity getting involved in any drama.

Alex nodded sombrely. He lowered his voice. "I suspect he feels rather guilty about the whole secret mission thing. So do I, as a matter of fact."

"Yet this isn't about the spy, is it?" hissed Felicity.

*And after my failures, I'm the one who should feel guilty.*

Felicity kept the thought to herself. It was time for action, not self-pity.

Upon passing into Liverton's grand entrance hall, however, the plan to speak with Miss Armstrong looked doubtful.

The news that Mrs Ogden had been poisoned had spread through the school. A mass of teachers and students swelled unhappily outside the firmly closed doors of Miss Armstrong's office. A belligerent-looking Miss Driver was positioned beside the office's entrance.

Felicity and Alex would have to elbow their way through a crowd ten-deep to reach the headmistress, and even then, she might not receive them.

"Quiet, girls. Quiet, please," boomed the movement teacher. "Miss Armstrong is on the line to some extremely important people."

Not far from Miss Driver, Miss Eversley, and Miss Vincent were delivering what reassurance they could to girls who were particularly upset, although both teachers looked rather stunned themselves.

"It's all right, my dear," said Miss Eversley somewhat awkwardly to a first-year student in floods of tears.

"Miss Armstrong is doing her best to look after all of us," Miss Vincent assured an irate-looking final-year student.

From the general clamour echoing around the entrance hall, there were worries for the school and the continuation of educations and careers. There were concerns for reputations and anger that the police had begun searching private rooms. Some even feared for their lives. There was, after all, a poisoner in their midst, wasn't there?

Alex had withdrawn his notebook from his inside jacket pocket but wasn't yet approaching anyone for comment. He waited for Felicity's signal.

Dolores, Usha, and Jane were amidst the girls surging among the entrance hall's pillars and clamouring to see the headmistress.

"We wish to help find Gwen, but those ogres in uniform won't let us," said Dolores, her arms folded, her scowl directed at the front doors and the uniformed policemen out under the portico.

"Do they imagine Gwen to be a poisoner?" Usha's brow was creased with concern. "She might have cut Cecily's dress, but she did nothing more than that."

"Gwen committing any act of violence is unthinkable," said Jane, shaking her head adamantly. "Utterly unthinkable."

Alex gave Felicity a questioning look.

Felicity wanted to believe it, too. She wanted to agree with Jane and Usha that, of course, Gwendoline was essentially innocent. She wanted to assure them that the whole situation was just a huge muddle and that normal life would be restored forthwith.

But she couldn't.

All signs pointed to Gwendoline being deeply involved in the drama that had struck Liverton Ladies' Academy, and her disappearance was only making matters worse.

With his notebook clutched at his side, Alex scanned the gathering outside the headmistress' office. His dark blue gaze was focussed and calculating, perhaps already planning who he might interview. "Miss Armstrong didn't exactly forbid us from reporting, did she?"

Felicity bit her lip. "She didn't exactly give us her blessing."

Chief Inspector Luscombe appeared in his trilby and tan overcoat, his expression very grave as he paced purposefully towards the large oak doors that led outside.

Felicity overheard his discussion with the policeman under the porticoed entrance.

"Seen anything?"

"Not yet, sir."

The chief inspector grumbled. "We've swept the whole gardens and not found a trace. We're widening the net."

A little firework of an idea went off inside Felicity.

She turned to Dolores. "Miss Gastrell, are you familiar with the location of Lord Severin Carrothers' residence? Does his family live far from here?"

Dolores shook her head a little, confused. "Not far. Why?"

Felicity flashed a glance at Alex. His dark blue eyes twinkled. He'd understood immediately.

"Might you be able to tell us the way?" enquired Felicity.

Alex readied his notebook.

"May I enquire what you're up to, your ladyship?" Chief Inspector Luscombe's approach had been as fast and stealthy as a cat's.

Felicity could have kicked herself. She'd been too eager. She could easily have waited till the detective had departed the entrance hall.

The detective turned to Alex. "I say. You're a journalist, aren't you?"

Alex held up his hands with a little smile. "Guilty as charged, though I haven't written a word yet."

The policeman returned his unfriendly stare to Felicity. "And I thought you were keen on keeping matters out of the papers. At least that's the reason you gave for withholding so much information from the police."

Dolores, Usha, and Jane looked rather surprised. This was not a conversation Felicity wished for them to overhear, and there was no time to explain the subtle machinations of the press to the chief inspector.

Felicity cleared her throat. "I was wondering if anyone had considered expanding the search to the nearby Carrothers residence?"

The detective blinked, confused.

"If Miss Milligan was fixated on Lord Severin," continued Felicity, "is there a chance she might have gone to him?"

The girls still looked stunned. The detective regained his composure, and the wary expression with which he regarded Felicity returned.

Alex also watched Felicity carefully, his notebook still at the ready.

Felicity went on. "And even if Miss Milligan isn't there, is it possible Lord Severin might provide information to help us find her?"

Dolores looked at Usha and Jane. "It's possible," she said, agreeing with Felicity.

Chief Inspector Luscombe's eyes sparkled with curiosity for a moment before narrowing. "I shall send an officer to the Carrothers' residence straight away." Felicity's idea was clearly an excellent one, but he wouldn't give her the credit of explicitly acknowledging it as such.

The detective went to walk away. Felicity pursued him.

"I should quite like to speak to Lord Severin myself," she said solemnly. *And reach Gwendoline before your officers do.*

The detective sighed as though rather tired. "This is a police matter, your ladyship. I shall speak with the man myself."

*Bang!*

The doors to the headmistress' office flew open. Moving with the determination of a hunter fixed on its prey, Miss Armstrong cut through the crowd, her eyes on the chief inspector. Upon noticing Felicity at his side, she stood even straighter.

"I've had Miss Milligan's father on the telephone." Her arms folded, Miss Armstrong spoke to the detective in a commanding tone no doubt used at her field hospital. "She's to be treated with kid gloves, not collected by a policeman in uniform—" she gave Alex a glare "—and not harassed by journalists."

Alex held up his hands apologetically. Had Miss Armstrong known he was a journalist all along? Perhaps his association with Felicity and Jasper had prevented the headmistress from having Alex escorted from the premises.

Miss Armstrong returned her gaze to the detective. "If you're to expand the search beyond Liverton's grounds, then your men must be accompanied by one of my teachers. Lady Felicity?"

"Yes, Miss Armstrong?" Felicity spoke as though reporting for duty.

The detective frowned. Alex gave a half-smile. Dolores, Usha, and Jane continued to watch, somewhat awestruck.

Felicity was still in the game. There was still a chance for her to make a difference.

## Chapter Thirty-Six

Foxridge Manor was just a brief ride from Liverton House. Pink and white roses scrambled up its grey granite walls, which were studded with deeply set leaded windows and topped with sloping slate roofs.

A butler with a long, sharp nose greeted Felicity and Chief Inspector Luscombe at the entrance. He reassured them that Foxridge's staff had been put to work searching for Gwendoline soon after the telephone call that had announced Felicity and the detective's visit.

"You'll be most discreet should you find her, I trust?" enquired Felicity.

"Certainly, your ladyship," confirmed the butler in a nasal tone. "As mentioned on the telephone, the duke himself is in London. His lordship's eldest son is in residence. However, Lord Severin has friends staying for the weekend, and they've gone for a hack across the grounds."

The detective's brow drew low. "When might he be back?"

"Difficult to say, sir."

"We'll wait," said Chief Inspector Luscombe, glancing at a pocket watch. "At least for a short while."

"Very well, sir," said the butler with a bow.

Felicity and Chief Inspector Luscombe were shown to a bright, airy drawing room where they were served tea and cakes. The silence was awkward as they sipped the Earl Grey, neither of them touching the cakes.

It was better this way, wasn't it? For Felicity to work in tandem with the official investigation. Her own enquiries had gone rather off the rails, but if Gwendoline were discovered at the Carrothers' residence, Felicity might make all the difference. A familiar face could help convince her to come fully clean with the police as quickly as possible, rather than needlessly dragging things out.

Felicity's initial goals had been far grander than simply offering a comforting presence, of course. She'd wanted to reveal the spy and uncover a poisoner, all while keeping the school's reputation intact. Looking back, it had been dizzyingly ambitious.

Felicity continued to sip her tea.

Alex had likely swung into reporting from Liverton House in her absence, interviewing students, teachers, and staff. He didn't have the same obligations Felicity felt towards the headmistress and her school. Perhaps that enabled him to see matters more clearly.

When pressing for earlier coverage in the newspaper, he'd not been driven purely by his desire for the scoop, had he? It would have been better if Felicity had followed Alex's advice at an earlier stage, yet he didn't gloat. He never did.

"Awfully sorry to keep you waiting."

Lord Severin Carrothers strode into the drawing room, his sleek black hair and leather riding boots shining in the sunlight from the leaded windows. His tweed breeches and jacket were flecked with mud, and his chiselled cheeks were red from outdoor activity. He was full of energy, but his presence was also steady and grounded.

Close at his heels, tail wagging, was a liver-and-white Springer Spaniel. It was almost identical to the dog with its head in Cecily's lap during Felicity's visit.

After a round of greetings and introductions, Lord Severin seated himself on the edge of a sofa opposite Felicity and Chief Inspector Luscombe. As he rested his elbows on his knees, the dog jumped onto the sofa and curled next to him. The dog's pose was one of rest, but its dark eyes watched the visitors intently.

As they retook their seats, the detective gave Felicity a stern look.

*Don't even think about muscling in on this.*

That seemed to be Chief Inspector Luscombe's message, which was absolutely fine. Felicity had no intention of interviewing Lord Severin. She was working with the authorities, not against them.

Severin's blue gaze was warm with a hard edge. "Have you news of Lady Cecily?"

The detective frowned, caught off-guard by Severin's opening gambit. The young earl's concern and care for his betrothed was clear.

"Not exactly, your lordship," said the policeman. "Although I hear she's recovering at a tremendous rate. I also understand the two of you are engaged to be married?"

The young earl gave a firm nod. "Suppose the cat's rather out of the bag now. We were hoping for Cecily to have something of a normal debut season, so to speak. Didn't want anyone thinking we were rushing into things in a foolhardy manner."

Severin's sincerity was touching. Felicity regretted having jumped to conclusions about what she'd seen between him and Dolores.

"Love is love, though, is it not?" she offered.

The young lord smiled reluctantly. "It is." His face became once again serious. "Gwen Milligan's gone missing. Is that right?"

"That's correct." The detective readied his notebook. "Already acquainted with Miss Milligan, are you, your lordship?"

"Our fathers have business ties. Their relationship goes back a long way. I've known Gwen since we were children."

The detective glanced up. "Anything more to the relationship than that?"

A flicker of doubt passed over Severin's clear features. "I'm not quite sure what you mean."

"Miss Milligan was in the habit of sending you correspondence, was she not?" asked Felicity, remembering the letter she'd discussed with Gwendoline in the parkland by the colonnade. The letter in which Gwendoline politely yet — in retrospect — desperately revealed her intentions towards a male suitor.

The detective shot Felicity a look of mild disapproval, which Felicity disregarded. If there was an opportunity to help things go more smoothly, why not assist where she could?

Severin clasped his hands tightly before him. "That's correct." He was becoming uneasy.

"What was in these letters, your lordship?" continued the detective.

The spaniel's ears pricked.

The young earl frowned. "Perhaps it's more appropriate for Gwen to explain matters once she is found." He was doing his best to protect the girl. It was an honourable gesture.

"She had romantic aspirations, didn't she?" Felicity spoke gently. "Romantic aspirations that weren't reciprocated."

Severin dropped his gaze to the drawing room carpet. "I feel rather sorry for her, you know. We all do. What happened to her sister wasn't Gwen's fault. But such associations can cast a long shadow. It put her under rather a lot of pressure. She wasn't quite herself, you know. Not the girl I knew when we were children."

"Might you be aware of what caused Miss Milligan's sister to face expulsion?" asked Felicity.

Severin shook his head. His expression was pained. "I think it's better if you ask such questions of the Milligan family, your ladyship."

"Did you keep the letters?" enquired Chief Inspector Luscombe. "Might I take them with me?"

Severin whipped his gaze towards the detective. "I say, what's this all about? Is Gwen under investigation?"

"Lord Severin," said the policeman, impatiently. "We're trying to get a picture of Miss Milligan's frame of mind. We're looking for any clues that might help us locate her." Chief Inspector Luscombe at least had the decency not to bring up the prospect of Gwendoline's guilt.

"We're awfully desperate to find her," added Felicity.

The detective scowled. He was tired of Felicity's interruptions, but he couldn't say anything to silence her. She rarely leaned on such discrepancies in class, but Felicity was the daughter of an earl speaking to the son of a duke. Short of an urgent threat, it was hard for someone outside of the aristocracy to intervene.

The spaniel looked up at his master.

"I destroyed the letters," said Severin. "Burned them, in fact. Couldn't bear the idea of anyone finding them. There wasn't only Cecily to think about, but Gwen, too. She was... She was embarrassing herself. She wasn't in her right mind."

"How did you respond?" asked Felicity.

"I didn't. Ever. It was such a shock when I received the first one last year. She was quite forward, even though we'd had no kind of interaction to suggest any inkling of romance between us." His brow creased. "But they kept coming. And the last one..." He trailed off.

The detective was about to speak, but Felicity got in first. She knew more about this than he did.

"It was a declaration of firm affection, was it not?" Felicity vividly recalled discussing the letter's content with Gwendoline. "With Miss Milligan laying her emotions bare in the hope you might reciprocate." Felicity had informed Gwendoline that her letter was bold. Had the lack of response to a desperate attempt pushed the girl over the edge?

Severin looked momentarily confused. "No. Not that one. I got a note while I was at the polo match. Tucked into my jacket pocket."

"I say," began Chief Inspector Luscombe. "What's all this letters business about, exactly?" He was having difficulty keeping up.

Felicity's skin tingled. She tilted her head. "A note from Miss Dolores Gastrell?" Had the whole affair been a double bluff?

Severin cleared his throat. He appeared to be a gentle, honourable fellow, and Felicity regretted having to mention Dolores. But she needed to be sure.

"No, not from Dolly. That's quite, ah... That's something else altogether." He adjusted his elbows on his knees, his hands still clasped. "The note I found in my pocket wasn't signed, and it was typed rather than handwritten. It was tucked into my jacket while it was hung up by the horse enclosure, while I was out on the field. But it can only have been from Gwen."

A chill passed through Felicity. Gwendoline hadn't been at the polo.

"Do you have that note?" The detective dived in with the question.

"I told you. I burned all of them. As much for Gwen as for myself."

"What did the note say?" pressed Felicity.

Severin put a hand on his dog's head and stroked its silky ears. "I don't remember exactly. I only read it once. I was so... So... The letter upset me. It upset me a great deal."

"Do you recall anything that was written within it, your lordship?" The detective was beginning to understand the significance of the written correspondence.

Severin shook his head. "The queerest of things. It made me think Gwen had quite lost her mind." He paused, his face twisted with displeasure.

Chief Inspector Luscombe was about to speak again, but Felicity shot the detective a hard glance.

*Give the fellow space.*

The detective closed his mouth.

Severin continued to stroke his dog's ears. "'Cruel blood'."

"'Cruel blood'?" repeated Felicity.

Severin met Felicity's gaze. He looked rather haunted. "Gwendoline had never gone that far before. Never even mentioned Cecily in her other letters. But in the note I found in my jacket, she told me to beware of Cecily's 'cruel blood'. She said Cecily's family had death and guilt on their hands that would never be washed clean."

Felicity's insides had turned to ice. "What do you suppose the letter writer was referring to, exactly?"

Severin shook his head. "I don't know. I can't remember the wording. I'd never read anything like it. And I never wish to read anything like it again."

Gwendoline had to be found. She had to be found right away.

Felicity turned to Chief Inspector Luscombe. "We need to get back to the school. Now."

# Chapter Thirty-Seven

Felicity was seated in the back of the black Austin 12/4 with Chief Inspector Luscombe in the front passenger seat as a uniformed officer chauffeured them back to Liverton House. The ride was quick, tall hedges and bright green fields whizzing past in the sunshine. As they neared the school, the police driver had to squeeze carefully past Rolls-Royces and other chauffeured limousines waiting in the lane.

The policemen standing at the school's gates allowed the motor carrying Felicity and Chief Inspector Luscombe through, much to the disgruntlement of the drivers waiting in the luxury vehicles sent by concerned families to collect their girls.

Thankfully, there were no family members there to make a scene. Miss Armstrong no doubt had them on the telephone, however.

The chief inspector praised the work of his officers at the gates. "Hold the line, lads. We're not letting anyone leave till we've interviewed them all. And certainly not till we've found this missing girl."

The police driver drew the Austin to a stop before Liverton House's grand porticoed entrance. Felicity alighted, turned her back on the school, and hurried towards the formal gardens. Updating Alex would have to wait.

Chief Inspector Luscombe attempted to follow Felicity as she headed into the grounds. "Don't you think we ought to—"

Felicity turned sharply towards the trilby-wearing detective. Their discussions in the Austin can't have counted for nothing. "We agreed you wouldn't follow me, or can you not be held to your word?"

The chief inspector raised his palms. "We did agree." His forehead creased deeply. Felicity's methods weren't always to his liking, but he'd commended her results in the past. "You must come to me directly and personally. Is that understood?"

Felicity nodded firmly. "I promise."

Following the familiar route past the trickling fountain and along the avenue lined with horse chestnuts, Felicity arrived at the rockery. It was, as expected, deserted. Everyone was engaged in the hunt for Gwendoline across the many acres of Liverton's grounds. The only movement was the gentle wave of the ferns in the breeze and the steady gush of the ornamental waterfall.

Passing the sparkle of the water as it tumbled over slick, jagged stones, Felicity exited the rockery and arrived at the colonnaded seating area, which was also empty. No doubt the search party had already passed through the area.

Thankful for the coolness of the shade after hurrying in the sun, Felicity took in a deep, steadying breath. The air was sweetly scented by the jasmine that curled around the stone pillars. Across the open parkland was the stand of trees where Gwendoline had interrupted Felicity and Alex for a second time. The breeze made the leaves shiver and hiss.

Might Felicity have provided Gwendoline with better advice? Could she make up for the error of judgement?

At the back of the seating area, between the two long stone benches that stretched along the wall, was a small door. Though painted the same sandstone-yellow as the pillars and benches, there was nothing hidden or subtle about it. No doubt whatever lay beyond it had already been searched. Chief Inspector Luscombe's men may not have been subtle, but they were thorough.

Felicity put her hand on the cool metal of the lever handle. Unlocked, the door swung open.

Cold, damp air rushed out of the space. Water could be heard rushing along, as could the rhythmic churn of a pump. It was the machine room for the waterfall in the rockery.

Aside from the light cast from the open doorway — which wasn't much, the colonnaded seating area being shaded from the sun — the room beyond was in darkness.

Felicity stepped inside. She gave her eyes a few moments to adjust to the darkness.

"Miss Milligan?" she called out.

There came no response. Only the sound of the water and the gentle rhythm of the electric pump.

Felicity closed the door gently behind her. She was fully in darkness now. Blinking, she saw nothing at all. The steady movement of the water through pipes was soothing, as was the pump's rhythm.

Felicity stepped forward into the darkness.

The first time Gwendoline had interrupted Felicity and Alex, she'd had a book with her, but she'd also been carrying a little wooden box. Felicity hadn't recognised it at first, but when she spoke to Gwendoline in her apartment, she'd seen the box again. It was a battery-operated lamp.

Gwendoline might have had the light with her because she intended to stay out reading until it got dark, but Felicity didn't think so. That would have involved sneaking back into the house after hours, and the rules on bedtime were strict.

Gwendoline didn't relish risk. She preferred peace.

"Miss Milligan?" Felicity raised her voice above the sound of the water and the pump but kept her tone gentle. "If you're here, I should very much like to speak to you. You're not in any trouble. I promise you that."

Felicity waited, blinking in the darkness, the water gushing, the pump keeping its rhythm.

It started as a faint glow, then grew to a warm light filling the room. Walls built from roughly hewn stone and rows of neatly arranged water pipes were lit with a soft orange hue.

In the far corner, with a blanket over her knees and a book on the floor beside her, Gwendoline was seated on the floor.

She blinked up at Felicity with ice-blue eyes. "I didn't think anyone would find me."

Slowly, Felicity advanced towards the girl. "I'm glad I did." She crouched to Gwendoline's level. "Are you all right?"

Gwendoline looked shaken but unharmed. "I'm ashamed of myself."

"Don't be," said Felicity. "We all make mistakes."

"I lied to you."

"I forgive you for doing so."

"You suspected me of harming Cecily, didn't you?"

Felicity hesitated. "I admit I did think that, but not anymore."

Gwendoline looked simultaneously relieved and thoroughly depressed. She sniffed. "I've let my family down."

Felicity paused. "We cannot always live up to the expectations others put upon us."

Gwendoline blinked at Felicity. Though still sad, her expression softened. Was Felicity getting through to her?

She pulled on a lock of her white-blonde hair. "My father so desperately wanted me to make a match with Lord Severin. I could barely focus on anything else." She looked at the ground, her shoulders hunched.

"The letter you showed me. You sent it to Lord Severin, didn't you?"

Gwendoline nodded. "I did my best. He never replied, and I kept writing to him. It was so foolish of me. But I had to try, even though I felt so ashamed. After I heard he was engaged, well..." She trailed off.

"You felt rather desperate, did you not?" Felicity spoke carefully, injecting her voice with as much sympathy as she could muster. "Is that what led you to cut Lady Cecily's dress?"

Gwendoline nodded without looking up. "It was so silly and childish. And utterly futile. Cecily was disappointed, but she took it so well. As soon as I'd done it, I hated myself." She met Felicity's gaze. "Cecily is truly lovely, and I've been simply beastly. I'd never say a bad thing about her, and I certainly didn't hurt her. I'd never hurt anyone."

"I know," said Felicity, confident there was no need to question Gwendoline about the note warning Lord Severin about Cecily's 'cruel blood'. Gwendoline hadn't sent it.

"Lord Severin and Cecily truly deserve one another," continued Gwendoline. "They are both wonderful people. When I learned of their engagement, I ought to have stopped. I see that now. I was so very wrong. I was looking at it all like some kind of game, like it was possible to out-manoeuvre the other players. Only it's not a game, is it?"

If there was a game being played at the school, it was a much more sinister endeavour than rivalries over potential husbands. And as misguided as Gwendoline's actions had been, they hadn't been truly harmful.

Tenderly, Felicity tucked a lock of Gwendoline's pale blonde hair behind the girl's ear. "Everyone's extremely worried about you."

"They shouldn't be." She hugged the blanket over her knees. "They should forget about me. I'm a terrible person."

"No one is perfect. The pressure you've been under has been immense. You have an older sister, don't you? That hasn't been able to find a match?"

Gwendoline frowned. "Lydia, you mean?"

Felicity nodded gently. "She attended Liverton and was expelled. Is that correct?"

Gwendoline continued to frown. "Yes, but according to Lydia, it's the best thing that ever happened to her. She's in Paris, having the time of her life as a bohemian."

Felicity resisted the urge to smile. A stroke of bad luck could sometimes turn out to be a blessing in disguise. And Gwendoline's sister's happiness quite destroyed any suspicion that Gwendoline might have sought revenge on Mrs Ogden for the expulsion. She had, however, probably gone to hide in the pump room before news of the poisoning began spreading through the school.

"I'm pleased to hear your sister's doing well. But her departure put an awful lot of pressure on you, didn't it? In terms of finding a good match for your family's expectations."

Gwendoline's expression turned thoughtful. "I've not looked at it like that before."

After reassuring Gwendoline she wasn't a ghastly person and promising her it would be a weight off everyone's mind to know she was safe, Felicity coaxed the girl into leaving the pump room. The suggestion of tea and scones also helped, as Gwendoline was rather famished.

Draping the blanket around Gwendoline's shoulders, Felicity allowed her to lean on her arm as they made their way through the deserted rockery, past the fountain, and back towards the house, its tall symmetrical windows sparkling in the sunshine.

But Felicity's work wasn't over yet.

## Chapter Thirty-Eight

A small group had gathered on the front steps of Liverton House to greet Felicity and Gwendoline.

"Gwen!" Dolores, Usha, and Jane flew down onto the gravel. They hugged Gwendoline and brushed her hair back from her face. Gwendoline even smiled a little.

"Come on, we have to get you ready."

"Let me do your hair."

"No, I'll do her hair. You can do her make-up."

"I should rather like some tea first."

A hint of warmth glowed within Felicity. When camaraderie between women flourished, it was a powerful force for good.

Chief Inspector Luscombe descended the steps, his hands in the pockets of his tan overcoat.

"Ladies," he said, addressing the girls. "I'm afraid you'll have to wait. I need to speak with Miss Milligan first."

Felicity had already explained to Gwendoline that she would need to talk to the police but that she shouldn't fear trouble.

Hugging her book to her chest, the battery-powered lamp hanging from her fingers, Gwendoline gave a little nod. "Of course."

Two uniformed officers who'd been waiting under the porticoed entryway escorted the girls inside.

The detective approached Felicity. "Is it as you suspected?"

During the ride between Foxridge Manor and Liverton House, Felicity had explained to Chief Inspector Luscombe how Gwendoline hadn't been at the polo match to place the note in Lord Severin's pocket. Nor did she have the influence to have someone else do it for her. There was also the shock and remorse on Gwendoline's face as she chased Cecily onto the ballroom floor as she collapsed.

Felicity nodded. "Miss Milligan has confessed to damaging Lady Cecily's clothing but nothing further."

Gwendoline already regretted slashing Cecily's dress. Even though she hadn't caused her illness, seeing Cecily so suddenly and violently sick made Gwendoline's regret even more acute.

"Well, we still need to talk to her." The detective put his fists on his hips and shook his head. "If only we had that blasted typed note Lord Severin received. We might have more of an indication of what we're looking for here."

Felicity looked up at Liverton House's orderly facade, its red-brick walls and white stone trims brilliant against the bright blue sky. It was the picture of propriety and quiet power. Yet within dwelt someone with the answers to all their questions. Someone who wasn't afraid of going to extremes.

*Beware of her cruel blood.*

Certain avenues of possibility had been closed off, but there were countless that still stood open.

Who was the culprit? How might they be lured into the open?

Felicity turned to the detective. "Would you be able to tell me where I might find Mr Cooper?"

---

Passing girls in evening gowns, teachers carrying boxes of decorations, and uniformed police officers trailing after them, Felicity found Alex in one of Liverton's phone booths, reading from his notebook as he spoke rapidly into the receiver.

His eyes lighting up upon seeing Felicity, he quickly finished his telephone call, tucked his notebook into his inside jacket pocket, and exited the booth.

"You found her?"

Felicity nodded. "Gwendoline was here in the grounds the whole time."

"So it's over?"

Felicity shook her head. She informed Alex of the 'cruel blood' note received by Lord Severin.

"That wasn't Gwendoline," said Felicity. "Someone else is targeting Cecily."

Sergeant Wilcox, the local policeman who'd held Miss Armstrong in such high regard, dashed past waving his notebook, chasing through the telephone room after two giggling girls wearing paper crowns.

Alex winced, the scar on his forehead emphasised by his creased brow. "Do you think the police are on top of things?"

Felicity had to hope they were. "Did you find out anything further about Lord Summervale? Until we know what 'cruel blood' means, it's rather difficult to imagine a motive for someone wanting to harm Cecily."

Alex stepped aside as a tangle of girls tumbled out of a telephone booth. One of them was weeping while the other two were laughing.

The school was on the brink of chaos.

"Nothing other than a rather standard stint as a brigadier-general on the Western Front, although my source at the War Office said he'd dig deeper." Alex pressed his hands into his pockets. "I'll ring him up and chivvy him along, but it might take a day or two."

Felicity bit her lip. It was too long to wait. There was a killer at the school and a wartime spy. Or were they one and the same?

Music wafted along the corridor. A jaunty foxtrot played rather too loudly on a crackling gramophone.

"What on Earth..."

Alex shrugged. "Fiddling as Rome burns, I suppose. Or playing on as the ship sinks. Something along those lines."

Felicity threw a perplexed look at Alex.

He tucked his chin. "You didn't hear about the party?"

"What party?"

"All classes have been cancelled. The term's ended early. It's not even clear if there'll be a next term, so the girls are doing the only logical thing. They're throwing a party."

Felicity frowned deeply. Then her forehead cleared. She raised an eyebrow.

"Just a moment," said Alex. "I know that look."

"What look?"

He smiled, looking pleased with himself. "You have a plan, don't you?"

Alex's ability to read Felicity's thoughts used to be a source of frustration, but she'd grown to take pleasure in their alignment.

"You're right," she said. "I do."

# Chapter Thirty-Nine

For the first time in rather a long while, everything went more smoothly than expected. As a dramatic sunset streaked pink and orange above the treetops at the edges of Liverton's gardens, everything was in place.

With the news of Mrs Ogden's poisoning and Cecily's sudden illness running riot in the papers, and with parents demanding their daughters be immediately transported away from the school, Miss Armstrong had announced the term was over.

Few of the girls were pleased by this news, as they were loath to leave the camaraderie of their peers. The headmistress was nonetheless adamant.

Upon being pressed about when lessons would start up again, Miss Armstrong answered that it was a matter for review only after the police had finished with their duties. The uncertainty greatly worried students, teachers, and servants alike.

Despite the queue of chauffeured motors at the school gates, none of the girls had actually left. Chief Inspector Luscombe had insisted upon this.

His men continued with interviews and rooms searches, although the situation wasn't fully under control. The police couldn't risk reports of the girls being manhandled, so a certain amount of drama had to be tolerated.

Making use of his exclusive position as the only journalist at the school, Alex sent regular reports to the Western Daily News, but less salubrious publications had already hooked their claws into the story. Coverage of Cecily's unfortunate episode had been published, as well as the suggestion that she, too, was the victim of poisoning. News of her engagement to Lord Severin was also spreading.

The telephone booths were constantly busy. It was certainly how the scandal rags got their gossip. Was someone at the school deliberately notifying the papers? Or was the information passing via osmosis, as girls telephoned friends and sisters to keep them abreast of the happenings at the school? In any case, the genie couldn't be returned to its bottle.

Thankfully, no mention of the hunted spy or Felicity's undercover mission had made it into the press. It was a small comfort, however. The chaos at the school made further investigation into the matter practically impossible. Felicity's original mission was as good as failed.

But all was not lost.

While Miss Armstrong remained shut up in her office, fielding telephone calls from worried parents and making whatever plans she could for the future of the school, preparations for an impromptu end-of-term ball got underway.

Paper garlands and ribbon streamers in bright blues, reds, and yellows were slung over the ballroom's chandeliers. Freshly plucked wild flowers mixed in with the odd bloom stolen from the rose garden were arranged into riotous, scented bouquets in mismatched vases in the middle of each table.

Velvet curtains and colourful bedspreads had been slung over tables and chairs and hung on the walls to create a cosy, dishevelled look. Table lamps with fabric shades of all patterns and sizes had been gathered from across the girls' apartments, their soft, colourful glow giving the space an intimate feel.

A gramophone had been brought in and popular show tunes were playing. Long gowns swept the polished wooden floor boards. Beaded tassels sparkled in the lamp light. Some of the party's attendees were even in fancy dress, with cat ears adorning headbands, flowers painted on cheeks, and butterfly wings fashioned from wire and coloured tissue paper. Perfumes applied more liberally than normally encouraged scented the air with floral, musk, and citrus fragrances.

Girls danced with one another and talked at tables while servants brought a steady and incongruous stream of food and drinks. From succulent veal chops to fragrant fish curry to colourful layered trifle, the cook was clearly eager to run down the food that had been stocked for the term that was now ending so abruptly.

*Fizz! Crackle!*

Gasps and then applause went up around the dance floor as sparkling silver and gold fountains of indoor fireworks went off on the raised platform at the end of the room. A metallic gunpowder-like smell hung in the air.

It was a stark contrast to the rehearsed orderliness of the practice ball.

The teachers were present as guests of the girls rather than in any position of authority. Gathering everyone in a single room had, however, been approved by Chief Inspector Luscombe. He'd had to strike a bargain with the girls, which hadn't been easy.

Dressed in an eye-catching ruby-red dress with a straight silhouette and layers of beaded gold fringing, Dolores had been the detective's counterparty in the negotiations. Usha, Jane, and Gwendoline, also attired in sparkling party dresses as if their demands for a celebration were a foregone conclusion, stood alongside Dolores like a gang of glamorous heavies.

Dolores insisted that a ceremony of some kind was required in order for the students to accept that their time together at Liverton was suddenly over. The girls had already decided that a mad hatter's tea party held in the ballroom was the appropriate ceremony.

The chief inspector cast a wary glance at Felicity before agreeing to the ball. *I hope you know what you're doing*, his look seemed to say.

It was agreed that the party shouldn't run too long into the night. In the morning, Chief Inspector Luscombe and his men would carry out interviews with each of the girls, a feat the police had so far only patchily been able to accomplish. After each girl had been spoken to, they would be free to leave the school.

But would the interviews still be necessary by the end of the evening?

Felicity stood at the side of the ballroom and watched the merriment. Her long pale-grey satin gloves were folded over a sparkling silver-grey dress, which had a dropped waist and a decorative bow on one shoulder.

It was miraculous the girls weren't more worried about a killer at the school. Did the threat of danger only heighten their excitement and abandonment? Now was not the time to burst any bubbles. The party was at the core of Felicity's plan.

The other teachers were dotted around the ballroom, trying to help where they could. Unlike Felicity, they hadn't changed out of their usual teaching attire for the occasion, although the girls had given them feathered headbands and bejewelled tiaras, which they dutifully wore.

Miss Driver and Miss Vincent were on high alert as layers of colourful taffeta and tulle swept past the smouldering remnants of fireworks. Any strong cocktails requested from the servants were quickly spotted by the teachers and sent back to the butler's pantry.

Somehow Miss Eversley had been coaxed onto the dance floor and was being taught some of the latest steps by a gaggle of first-year students. Miss Petherick couldn't be coaxed, however. She remained seated in a corner by herself. She looked less distraught than earlier, but she still seemed on the edge of tears and wasn't in a fit state to play the piano.

No police were inside the ballroom for the duration of the party. That had been one of Dolores' conditions. Miss Armstrong was also absent from the proceedings. Was she doing what she could to save the school? Or had she given up?

Aside from the serving staff, Alex was the only man present. Just as at ease in the role of society journalist as in his normal post as a hard-nosed crime reporter, he took down quotes from the girls about how happy they'd been at Liverton, how sad they were about what happened to poor Mrs Ogden, about how certain they were it was all a big mix-up, and how much they were looking forward to their debut seasons, regardless.

Alex had fetched his camera from his motor and set up the tripod in the corner. He took photos of girls dressed as fairies, medieval princesses, and even a caterpillar, yards of bed linen having been sacrificed for that particular outfit. Such images wouldn't help reinforce the notion that the young women at the academy remained swan-like and graceful through desperate times. But even if the photos couldn't all be used in the newspaper, Alex continued to take the pictures, promising to share copies with the girls who were desperate to always remember their Liverton chums.

"Will you dance with us, your ladyship?" Gwendoline swept up to Felicity in a pale mint-green satin dress with a floor-grazing hem. Powder with a silver lustre sparkled on her cheeks and she wore a filigree headband positioned at the centre of her forehead, her white-blonde hair styled in curls set tightly against her head.

Out on the dance floor, Dolores, Usha, and Jane beckoned to Felicity, all glittering and smiling as the gramophone played on.

"Thank you, Miss Milligan," smiled Felicity. "But this is your special night, not mine. I've had my time on the dance floor." She cast a glance at Alex, who was still busy behind his camera. "I shall remain on the sidelines, if you don't mind," she added, returning her gaze to Gwendoline.

Felicity couldn't be distracted. Not this time.

As Gwendoline returned to her friends for a waltz, the butler approached Felicity.

He spoke in low tones. "Your guests are here, your ladyship."

Felicity shivered a little. It was time.

"Thank you, Mr Clark. I shall make the announcement."

"Very good, your ladyship."

Standing beside the ballroom doors, and using the back of a knife against a glass — and after persisting for rather a long time, Miss Driver adding long, sharp shushes to the effort — Felicity quietened the room and attracted all attention towards herself.

She stood tall before the crowd.

Alex's gaze was steady. He gave Felicity a subtle nod. They were the only ones who knew what was coming next.

"Is it time for speeches?" asked Dolores, cutting in before Felicity could speak.

"No, Miss Gastrell." Felicity raised her voice. "My apologies for the interruption to this important celebration, but we have guests."

The ballroom was filled with the twittering of excited, nervous chatter. Eyes widened. Some gazes were full of delight, some concerned.

Felicity nodded to the butler.

As Mr Clark opened the ballroom doors, Felicity watched the room extremely carefully.

# Chapter Forty

In a tiered chiffon skirt in emerald green, a gold sequinned bodice, and a jewelled tiara nestled into her sunshine-blonde hair, Lady Cecily Summervale was radiant.

Only her small, uneasy steps into the ballroom gave any sign that days ago she'd received a dose of poison that might have done for her.

She leaned on the arm of Lord Severin Carrothers, who looked dashing in a black bow tie and tuxedo jacket with peaked lapels, his slick, dark hair shining under the light from the chandeliers.

His smile was less easy than Cecily's. He was watching the room almost as carefully as Felicity.

"Cecily!"

Gasps went up when the girls saw her. The teachers were equally surprised. Felicity had kept her plans very close to her chest.

Gwendoline dashed towards Cecily, took her hand, and practically kneeled in front of her, the pale green satin of her dress spreading over the floor like water.

Alex looked over at Felicity for her reaction to Gwendoline's approach. Felicity raised an eyebrow but maintained her position beside her ballroom doors. She wouldn't miss anything. Not this time.

"Can you forgive me, Cecily?" sobbed Gwendoline. "Can you ever forgive me?"

Cecily and Severin looked upon Gwendoline with sadness. She'd made mistakes, but she wasn't the worst of the bunch. Far from it.

"It's all right," said Cecily gently. "None of this is your fault." She smiled at the pale-haired girl. "All is forgiven."

Gwendoline kissed Cecily's hand. "I'll never do anything like it ever again. I promise. I've been so silly, and I love you both dearly. Really, I do."

"We know, Gwen," assured Severin. With his free hand, he helped Gwendoline to her feet. "We know."

*Ting-ting-ting!*

Dolores tapped a knife on her glass, and all eyes went to her, except for Felicity's. She couldn't afford to drop her watch over the room for a moment.

"Lady Cecily Summervale." Dolores approached Cecily and Severin, the beaded tassels of her ruby-red dress gently clattering. "It's an unexpected honour to have you with us for our last hurrah at Liverton. You are beautiful, brave, and so very kind. You are a quintessential Liverton lady. We are all so very happy for you and Lord Severin." Dolores turned to the crowd. "Aren't we, girls?"

The applause took off immediately. There was even stamping and whooping.

Cecily clutched Severin's arm and smiled up at him. He looked at her lovingly and put a large hand over her dainty one.

Felicity caught Alex's gaze from across the room, and they smiled at each other. Dolores' speech wasn't part of the plan, but was difficult not to be swept up in the enthusiasm.

Yet though it was not clear who, someone in the room was faking their adoration of Cecily. Someone who had wished her genuine harm.

Cecily smiled bashfully and brought a hand to her chest, still leaning on Severin. "Dolly, you're too kind."

Dolores winked at Cecily. "I propose a toast," she said, raising her glass. "To the happy couple."

Felicity's pulse quickened. The toast hadn't been planned, but it was a scenario for which she was prepared.

Not everyone had drinks. The footmen were busy clearing plates of food. There was a lone, nervous-looking maid beside the large mahogany buffet at the side of the room. The butler joined her as she began pouring champagne.

The poisoner had tried once and failed. Would they dare try again?

The girls started swarming to collect their drinks.

Alex widened his eyes at Felicity. This was her chance, but she couldn't rush in. Subtlety was everything.

Miss Driver, Miss Eversley, and Miss Vincent helped hand out the glasses being filled by the maid and the butler. Without hurrying too urgently, Felicity hastened towards the buffet as though keen to help.

"There you go," said Miss Vincent.

"Don't quaff it all at once," warned Miss Driver.

Drinks were changing hands at a rapid rate.

Overwhelmed, the maid fumbled with the big champagne bottle and knocked a glass over. It smashed on the countertop.

Miss Eversley tutted and caught the spilled champagne with a napkin, but the service had to continue.

Reaching the buffet, Felicity joined in the effort to hand out the coupes while still keeping watch. Or trying to.

The area around the buffet was a sea of hands reaching for glasses of fizzing liquid, corks popping from bottles, tulle skirts, sparkling armbands, and laughter.

It was difficult to stay on top of everything.

*Poof!*

Alex had manoeuvred his camera closer to Cecily and Severin. The flash went off as he took a picture of the couple posing with Dolores and Usha. Cecily looked tired but happy.

"How much have you drunk already this evening?" Miss Driver challenged one of the girls.

Miss Vincent smiled warmly and handed the girl a drink. "Come now, Miss Driver. It's the last night, is it not? They may let their hair down, just for tonight."

Miss Petherick had drifted over to the buffet, a handkerchief still clasped in her hand. She appeared to lack the energy to participate in distributing glasses.

*Poof!*

Another picture of the happy couple, this time with Gwendoline and Jane also in the frame.

Alex glanced over his shoulder at Felicity. He was closely monitoring Cecily, just as Severin undoubtedly was.

Felicity handed champagne to a pair of first-year girls wearing dresses adorned with feathers in a kaleidoscope of colours.

"There you go," said Felicity with a little smile, while inside, her heart pounded.

What if nothing happened? Or, even worse — what if she missed it?

The preparations for the toast were so sudden and chaotic, and she was only one person trying to keep watch over it all. Had she taken risks with other people's safety, only to—

Then she saw it.

The small trail of tiny bubbles was distinct from the normal bubbles that shimmered upwards through the pale golden champagne and clung to the glass of the coupe.

Something had been added to one of the glasses.

And the hand that had done it was just retreating.

Felicity swiftly reached out. She grabbed the wrist and held it tightly.

She met the poisoner's gaze.

# Chapter Forty-One

*Crash!*

There was a scream like a wild animal's as the remaining coupes on the buffet were swept onto the ballroom floor, glass and champagne sparkling everywhere. Those nearby stepped back in shock.

Miss Vincent had torn herself free from Felicity's grip, swiped everything onto the floor with an almighty howl, and now stood facing Felicity, a broken champagne stem held out like a dagger, the pale pink voile of her blouse's sleeve shaking.

The French teacher snarled like a trapped beast.

"You!" she cried, her nostrils flaring, her brown eyes burning with rage directed at Felicity.

Felicity hadn't expected the culprit to be the gentle, encouraging Miss Vincent, who'd lost her family to the war in her native Belgium. Indeed, Felicity hadn't known who to expect. But she couldn't allow herself to reel with shock. She had to concentrate. It was time to bring an end to it all.

Teachers, pupils, and servants all backed away from the scene, clinging to one another with fear. Felicity stood her ground, her chest heaving under her sparkling silver-grey dress.

Alex had left his camera and was slowly approaching the stand-off. Apart from the crunch of broken glass under his shoes, the room had fallen silent.

"You," growled Miss Vincent, eyes wide and wild, the sharp point of the coupe's broken stem glinting in her hand. "*Sale traîtresse*."

Might the police rush in at any moment? That they hadn't done so already was a surprise. They were positioned just on the other side of the ballroom doors. Felicity had requested she be allowed time to speak to the wrongdoer should their identity be revealed, but she hadn't expected the police to give into this demand. Chief Inspector Luscombe had already agreed to so much.

Felicity held up the palms of her satin gloves. "No one wants to see this end badly, Miss Vincent."

Miss Vincent's face creased as she fought back tears. With her free hand, she clutched at the fabric of her skirt. "There is no other ending. It will be bad. It is bad. My brother remains unavenged, and not one of you has learned any kind of lesson." Her voice was becoming shrill, tears rolling down her cheeks. "And I will be punished for what I have done!"

Alex had come to a stop a short distance from Felicity and Miss Vincent. The rest of the room had backed far enough away to be out of harm's reach. Severin had his arms tightly around Cecily, his fiancée clasped close to him.

Felicity could raise her voice and call for the police. They would burst into the ballroom and wrestle Miss Vincent to the ground, and she would howl and rant as she was taken away.

Was that how matters should end?

With her gloved hands still raised, and with a glance at Alex to tell him to hold steady, Felicity took a small step forwards. "Miss Vincent, please. Tell us about your brother."

The French teacher blinked with surprise. She gave her head a little shake, though her expression remained an anguished grimace. "While one family goes from desperation to ruin, another goes from riches and power to even greater wealth and influence. Where is the justice? I could not stand it. It isn't right. It simply isn't right."

Felicity took another step forward. She gently brought down her palms in a gesture of appeasement. "Please, Miss Vincent. We are eager to learn from you. You mentioned your brother. You lost him in the war, didn't you?"

A conflict between anger and profound sadness played out on Miss Vincent's face. "Paul died here in England. On the streets. He died a pauper, and an addict of drink."

Felicity brought a hand to her chest. "I'm very sorry to hear that," she said with genuine sadness. It was a tragic way for any life to end. If the person had already fled from war, it was even more harrowing.

Miss Vincent's laughter started low in her throat. A disturbed combination of pain and glee, it broke out loudly across the silence of the ballroom. "You don't actually care," she said, wiping her eyes with her knuckle. "No one cared for Paul except me."

"You still do care about him, if I'm not mistaken." *Far too much.* Felicity fired an apologetic glance in Cecily's direction. "Is there some connection between your brother and Lady Cecily?"

Miss Vincent snarled, an angry wounded animal once more. "We had just arrived in England, and Paul worked as a hall boy. He was so happy and proud, so pleased to wear his uniform. So grateful to be safe and away from the guns and the explosions. Until he was accused of stealing. Stealing! Can you imagine?"

Felicity spoke calmly. "But your brother was not a thief?"

"Of course not!" cried Miss Vincent, her tears flowing. "He was simply the newest member of staff, and only sixteen years of age. The police were never even called. He was just sent away. Without a reference."

Felicity furrowed her brow. Alex's expression was grave.

A servant without a reference struggled to find work, meaning poverty and destitution weren't far away. One had to be extremely sure of wrongdoing before taking such a step. If the police hadn't been summoned to investigate, it seemed certainty had been lacking.

Felicity could guess at the connection to Cecily, but Miss Vincent wasn't yet in a stable enough state to be pressed for the details.

"That must have been most difficult for your brother," said Felicity gently.

Miss Vincent nodded. The hand in which she held the broken glass drooped. "Paul was the sweetest boy. He never stood up for himself, and he never recovered. He couldn't find another job. I tried to help him, but he sank further and further into his sadness and memories. Our mother and father both lost. Everything we left behind." Miss Vincent let the weapon fall to her side. "We had already been through so much. We thought we'd survived."

The ballroom was silent. All eyes were on Miss Vincent and Felicity. Someone sniffed. It was an ugly situation. Miss Vincent had been tormented to the edge of madness by the loss of her brother.

Were there lessons to be learned from it all? Perhaps, but it wasn't yet the moment for deep reflection.

Felicity took a careful step towards Miss Vincent. "It sounds as though you did your best for your brother." Might she get close enough to slip the broken glass stem from her hand? "Paul is surely at peace now."

"No thanks to her!" Miss Vincent swung wildly. There were gasps as the French teacher trained her broken-glass weapon on Cecily.

Although a safe distance away, Cecily's eyes widened with fear.

Severin clasped her tighter to his chest. "You'll not harm a hair on her," he growled.

Felicity swallowed. She had to change tack.

She cast another brief look of apology at Cecily. "Did your brother work for the Summervales, Miss Vincent?"

Miss Vincent's gaze flickered towards Felicity. She bared her teeth at Cecily. "They have cruelty in their veins. They deserve to pay for what they did to Paul."

Felicity recalled what Severin had shared about the type-written note received at the polo match. *Beware her cruel blood*.

"You must know that Lady Cecily would have been no older than your brother when he worked for her family," said Felicity. "She would hardly have been involved in household decisions."

"I-I never even knew there'd been any sort of theft," said Cecily, looking to Severin for comfort.

"Is that justice, Miss Vincent?" pressed Felicity. "Lady Cecily might have died."

The French teacher gnashed her teeth and sobbed.

"And Mrs Ogden perished at your hand, didn't she?

"That was a mistake!" shrieked Miss Vincent.

"Yet it didn't stop you from continuing your deadly mission. You've told us that your brother was a tender soul, Miss Vincent. What might Paul say about what you've done?"

Miss Vincent howled with pain. The hand holding the broken glass fell to her side. "I didn't come to the school planning to do this. I wanted Lord Summervale to pay. I had always dreamed of making him pay." She shot a rage-filled glance at Cecily. "Then I saw my chance."

*Thunk!*

The broken stem dropped to the floor beside Miss Vincent. "But that chance has gone. There is no other way to end this." She pulled up the sleeve of her blouse. Held in place by rubber bands on the inside of Miss Vincent's wrist was a tiny vial of white powder.

"No!" Felicity dashed forward as Miss Vincent grabbed for the vial.

# Chapter Forty-Two

It was Alex who called out for the police.

Uniformed officers poured into the ballroom, Chief Inspector Luscombe leading the way.

Felicity had grasped Miss Vincent's hand in time to prevent her from swallowing the vial's contents. The local sergeant and his men had raced to assist her.

"We'll take it from here, your ladyship."

Chief Inspector Luscombe put his hands on his hips and looked Miss Vincent up and down, but there was no surprise in his gaze. The capacity for destruction in such a petite, sweet-looking woman might have been alarming. The chief inspector was, however, a seasoned detective.

"This our woman, is it?" he asked without recognition of Felicity's actions, but that was perfectly fine. She didn't need acknowledgment. The fact the police let Felicity execute her plan was enough.

Felicity gave a nod. "Miss Vincent has a vial of powdered digitalis secreted under her sleeve."

Felicity's instinct had been to protect Miss Vincent from harm, but now the French teacher looked at her with desperate despair. Miss Vincent's fate had been snatched from her own hands.

"We heard your confession," said the detective, addressing the French teacher. "In fact, I saw everything that happened through a chink in the service doors. I'm afraid I have no choice but to place you under arrest. You'll accompany us to the police station at Exeter for further questioning."

Her cheeks still wet from weeping, Miss Vincent looked numb and remained silent as she was handcuffed and led away by two police officers, Chief Inspector Luscombe following close behind them.

Whispers grew around the ballroom. Severin kissed the top of Cecily's head and held her close. Everyone seemed relieved.

Felicity felt suddenly exhausted. It was over. A killer had been apprehended, but while it was a victory of sorts, there was no sense of glory about it.

Alex approached. "You all right?"

"I am," she said with a brief nod. "Looking forward to a cup of tea and a sit down."

Alex smiled. "Sometimes I think your talents are wasted as a journalist." He was reaching for the notepad in his jacket's inside pocket, preparing to report. "And as a teacher."

Felicity drew in her chin, about to respond, when Miss Vincent tugged on the arms of the officers as she reached the ballroom doors.

"Steady on," said Chief Inspector Luscombe warningly.

Miss Armstrong had appeared. She stood with her arms folded in the doorway, her hard, dark-eyed gaze tinged with sadness.

As Miss Vincent looked up at the headmistress, her tears flowed again. "*Je suis vraiment désolée.*"

The headmistress looked down at the French teacher. She said nothing as the policeman continued to lead Miss Vincent away.

With the culprit gone, the room came alive with chatter. There was even nervous laughter. With the approval of the policemen that remained in the ballroom, the servants began clearing up the broken glass. The policemen produced notebooks and began taking statements from witnesses. The case against Miss Vincent was clear, but proper procedure must be followed.

Still leaning heavily on Severin's arm, Cecily approached Felicity. Dolores, Usha, Jane, and Gwendoline followed.

"Thank you, Lady Felicity." Cecily was tearful but smiling. "I feared we might never find the wrongdoer."

"I'm the one who is grateful to you both," said Felicity, addressing Cecily and her betrothed. "You weren't obliged to help with my plan, especially after everything you'd already been through."

Cecily frowned. "But I wasn't in any danger. You'd already informed me not to allow any food or drink to pass my lips, no matter who gave it to me. And I had Severin with me." She smiled up at her fiancé.

Severin stroked Cecily's hand. "You've been extremely brave, my darling."

Jane piped up. "But who would have guessed at Miss Vincent?"

Usha shook her head. "She always seemed so kind."

Dolores narrowed her eyes, her arms folded over the tassels of her dress. "If Lady Felicity hadn't dared to lure her into the open, she might never have been detected."

Alex was busy writing in his notebook but paused to raise his eyebrows at Felicity. *I told you so*, his look seemed to say.

Felicity ignored it.

"Miss Vincent would not have been able to stay hidden forever," she assured the girls. "The police don't draw their conclusions on appearances alone."

But Dolores had a point. If Miss Vincent had presented herself well in the police interviews planned for the following morning, and if she'd been free to leave the school pending further investigations, she might have disappeared. Now, at least, she would face justice.

Gwendoline stepped forward. "We owe so much to you, Lady Felicity. Your courage and kindness have delivered us from a much worse fate."

"We do indeed owe much to Lady Felicity."

The girls stood aside as Miss Armstrong appeared at the front of the gathering, her arms folded over her dark purple jacket. "I don't quite know what brought you to us in our hour of need, your ladyship. But I'm thankful you stuck with us."

Felicity winced a little at the praise and the possibility that Miss Armstrong had her doubts about Felicity's real reasons for being at the school. Still, she reacted graciously. "My time at the academy has given me so much."

Alex smiled broadly, expressing a mix of pride at Felicity's achievements and amusement at her discomfort.

He stepped forward, notebook in hand. "Would you be willing to say a few words for the Western Daily News, Miss Armstrong?"

"Certainly, Mr Cooper," said the headmistress without hesitation, her attitude towards the press clearly having changed.

"Three cheers for Lady Felicity!" Dolores had sprung onto the raised platform at the end of the room. "Hip hip!"

"Hurray!"

Someone put the gramophone back on. The police looked baffled but were powerless to prevent the girls from flooding back onto the dance floor.

Felicity sat at the side of the room, a pot of tea having been brought to her by Mr Clark. As she sipped her Ceylon, she watched the merriment but declined invitations to take part, saying she felt rather tired, which she did.

In truth, however, it didn't feel right to celebrate. Felicity wasn't wholly satisfied. What chance remained to unmask the spy that had betrayed the Allies in the war?

Alex had taken Miss Armstrong to a quieter part of the ballroom. It wasn't possible to hear the interview above the hubbub on the dance floor — with Cecily watching from a seat on the sidelines, Severin still close at her side — but the headmistress was shaking her head as she spoke. Alex pushed with another question, and she shook her head even more firmly.

Felicity smiled. Miss Armstrong no doubt regretted giving Alex the go-ahead to interview her, although her mind would change once she read his articles. He was a first-class journalist, and even if his questions were difficult, he had the best interests of the school and the girls at heart.

"Well, if that wasn't a shocker of an ending, I don't know what was." Miss Driver looked rather wan as she marched towards Felicity, with Miss Eversley and Miss Petherick in her wake. "How long had you known Miss Vincent was behind it all?"

Felicity set her teacup and saucer on the table beside her and shook her head, only mildly discombobulated by Miss Driver's brisk and direct approach. "I didn't. All I knew was that someone passionately wished harm on Lady Cecily."

"But you weren't surprised, were you?" asked Miss Eversley, eyeing Felicity with suspicion. "You didn't look surprised."

Felicity gave a little smile. She was still watching Alex. Miss Armstrong looked ready to snatch his notebook and tear it up.

Miss Petherick picked up what Miss Eversley had been asking. "You didn't suspect Miss Vincent, yet you were not surprised it was her. Is that it, your ladyship?"

"In a sense, Miss Petherick, yes." Despite everything Felicity had so far witnessed as a crime reporter and sleuth, she could still be shocked by the dark depths of human nature.

During the act of apprehending Miss Vincent, however, she'd remained in control of herself.

"I take my hat off to you, your ladyship," continued Miss Driver. "Things might have been a good deal messier for all of us if this matter hadn't been cleared up so neatly and quickly. Of course, there'll be the trial and all that, but the police have their culprit and their confession. It won't drag out for too long. Not that it makes too much difference for us." Miss Driver turned to Miss Eversley. "Miss Armstrong has already advised us to look for other posts. The academy is done for."

"Goodness," said Felicity, her stomach squeezing a little. Saving the school had been too much to expect along with everything else. "I'm terribly sorry to hear that."

Miss Petherick looked uncomfortable. As announced at the attic meeting, she already had another position lined up. "I shall put a good word in for you with the family for whom I'll be working," she promised her colleagues. "I'm sure they have good connections."

Miss Eversley frowned, as though confused by the idea.

Miss Driver laughed. "I'm afraid Eversley and I aren't the governessing sort. We'll figure something out, though. Won't we, Eversley?"

"What'll you do next, Lady Felicity?" enquired Miss Eversley, her eyes blinking rapidly behind the lenses of her glasses.

Alex had moved on from the headmistress. After some furious scribbling in his notebook, he'd cornered Severin and Cecily for an interview.

"I'm actually not quite sure," said Felicity in a deliberately vague manner.

Not that Felicity didn't know what she wanted to do. She just couldn't talk about it.

Might there still be a chance, however slim?

# Chapter Forty-Three

Stars twinkled in the inky sky above Liverton House. Wearing a big-collared coat in dark blue wool velour over her silver-grey party dress, Felicity stood on the front steps, saying farewell to Cecily and Severin, the smooth lines of Severin's gold Hispano Suiza waiting for them on the gravel drive.

With Miss Vincent on her way with Chief Inspector Luscombe to the Devon County Constabulary's headquarters, the girls had been given permission to leave the school. Only none of them particularly wanted to go. Not directly. They remained in the ballroom, dancing, gossiping, and laughing together, reluctant to admit their time at Liverton was over.

The ending had been too abrupt. Too unexpected.

But as the night wore on, and as yawns could no longer be stifled, the girls began slipping away to the chauffeured vehicles waiting to whisk them off into the night and onto the next phase of their young lives.

As the ballroom emptied, Felicity had stepped through the heavy oak double doors of Liverton's front entrance seeking fresh air and space to think. Shouldn't she, too, accept that this was the end?

But she ought to have chosen a side door, as the constant flow of farewells was quite a distraction — albeit a welcome one — that didn't allow for quiet reflection and delicate planning.

Cecily clutched both of Felicity's hands, her amber eyes sparkling in the dim light. "Thank you again. You've been a marvel."

"Please," said Felicity, smiling dismissively. "You were the marvel of this evening. Without your bravery, we would never have unravelled matters."

Severin shook Felicity's hand. His grip was strong and gentle. "We sincerely hope to see you at our wedding."

It was a delightful prospect. Cecily and Severin's union was a fairytale ending of sorts.

"I shall certainly be there," promised Felicity.

With the clatter of beads and the rustle of taffeta, Dolores, Usha, Gwendoline, and Jane tumbled out onto the steps.

Dolores stood with her hands on the hips of her ruby-red dress, a flush on her elegant cheeks. "Did you think you could sneak off without saying goodbye?" she said, reprimanding Cecily with a mocking tone.

"So this is where Lady Felicity has been hiding," said Jane, imitating Dolores' manner.

Felicity smiled but said nothing. She had indeed intended to hide herself away for a spell.

Cecily laughed heartily. "We already hugged a million times, Dolly. And we agreed we'd catch up in London just next week."

"A week is a dreadfully long time," said Dolly as she threw her arms around Cecily's slender neck.

It wasn't just the end of the school term. They were to become debutantes and married women, their girlhoods behind them. It was no wonder they were loath to let go.

As Usha, Gwendoline, and Jane embraced Cecily and wished her all the best, Dolores sidled up to Severin. Whispering in his ear, she tucked a folded piece of paper into the top pocket of his tuxedo jacket.

From a distance, one might have read romantic intimacy in the gestures. Close-up, however, there was no chemistry between the pair.

Severin fished the note from his pocket, his eyebrows drawing together. "Can't we stop behaving so suspiciously? We're among friends, are we not?"

"Oh." Dolores glanced at Felicity and shook her head a little. "I quite forgot. That's for Ralph. See he gets it, will you?"

Severin gave a firm nod. "He'll be pleased to receive it."

"Girls, I don't want to play the chaperone," sighed Usha, her elegant fingers teasing the petals of a corsage of silk flowers at the shoulder of her yellow satin dress, "but do you wish to see Miss Armstrong and Miss Driver dance to jazz tunes or not?"

Felicity raised her brow. Apparently, the party wasn't quite out of steam.

As Cecily and Severin finally descended the steps to their motor, the rest of the girls trotted back indoors. In passing, Gwendoline took Felicity's hand and gripped it.

"Thank you again, your ladyship," she whispered, the ice-blue of her eyes glinting in the low light. "You can't imagine what a difference you've made to me."

Felicity squeezed Gwendoline's hand. "You're very welcome, Miss Milligan." There was no other feeling like knowing one had helped.

Alone once more under the portico of Liverton's front entrance, Felicity reflected on the receding sound of the Hispano Suiza's wheels on the gravel, the distant hoot of an owl, and the faint scent of fresh grass.

It felt like an ending.

But it wasn't. Not yet.

Treading carefully in silver shoes with a Spanish heel, Felicity started down the wide stone steps. If she wished to be alone with her thoughts, she might take a walk among the neat box-hedged paths of the rose garden. It was close enough to the house to be lit by the lamps that still burned as the party continued into the night but also quiet enough for contemplation.

How might Felicity approach things in the time she had left? Was there a way to bring matters to a quiet close? It was such an intensely delicate matter. She couldn't afford to put a foot wrong.

"Cici."

Felicity stopped and turned.

Alex was under the portico, backlit by the soft light of the entrance hall. He had his hands in the pockets of his grey three-piece suit, his dark blond hair swept back, satisfaction on his face.

"Stories all filed?" asked Felicity.

She hadn't wanted to disturb Alex's reporting. Miss Armstrong and her girls desperately needed good coverage in the paper, and Alex had exercised fantastic self-restraint in holding off on reporting from the school until absolutely necessary. Now, with Miss Vincent's arrest and no other journalist on the scene, he was like a fox in a henhouse.

Nimbly, he descended the steps to join Felicity. "Just got off the line to the news desk. They're sending a motorcyclist to pick up the negatives. Should all make it into the morning edition."

"Did you not want to go into the office and put the finishing touches to your stories yourself?" asked Felicity as they descended onto the drive.

Alex gave a brief frown as they began strolling along the front of the house, feet crunching in the gravel. "I'd rather stay here. And thank you, by the way."

Felicity blinked. She'd been an obstacle to his reporting instincts over the past days. "Whatever for?"

A cool breeze deposited a lock of hair on Alex's scarred forehead. He swept it away. "For the scoop, of course. You never let me down."

Felicity let out a little laugh. "We got there in the end, I suppose."

They were almost out of the glow cast by the still-lit windows on the ground floor. Felicity came to a stop first. Alex halted in front of her, his hands still in his pockets. It was a comfortable silence.

He cast his gaze upwards. "I remember looking at the stars from the trenches. Watching my breath in the freezing air. I was stunned by the beauty of it." He looked at Felicity with an apologetic half-smile. "I realise it's odd, but there were moments like that. Among the ghastliness of it all."

The men who returned home from the war spoke so rarely about it. It was both heartbreaking and a privilege to hear about Alex's experiences.

It was also wrong to keep things from him any longer.

"Alex, I have to—"

"Cici." Briefly he touched her upper arm, his grip gentle but firm through the wool velour of her coat. "I don't want you to apologise to me. I know you think you've failed, but you haven't. You came here to listen and learn, and you've done that. You've done more than that. I mean, imagine what could have happened if you hadn't been here. Cecily might not have survived another attempt on her life."

"Alex," Felicity tried to break in. "I don't—"

"No, Cici. I won't hear it. You did as you promised and fulfilled your mission. So what if it wasn't Ogden? What happens next isn't up to us. I'll never forget the men we lost, but one can't let things fester. You saw what happened to that French teacher, so eaten up by—"

Alex stopped abruptly, his eyes wide with sudden worry.

There was a figure on the steps. They were no longer alone. Had someone been listening in?

Felicity wasn't afraid.

# Chapter Forty-Four

In a black woollen servant's dress and with her mousy brown hair swept under a white cap, the maid stood at the bottom of Liverton House's entryway steps and peered out onto the dimly lit gravel.

Upon spotting Felicity, the maid blinked nervously, the rough fabric of her skirt clutched in her fists. When she noticed Alex, who had been more in the shadows, the maid's mouth opened with surprise, and she retreated up the stone steps.

"Wait," called Felicity, crunching through the gravel towards the steps. "Miss Brown?"

The girl froze, perhaps stunned Felicity remembered her name. But Felicity had been turning the name over in her mind since she'd sneaked away from the ballroom and paid a visit to Miss Armstrong's office.

"Yes, your ladyship?"

Miss Brown was the maid who'd discovered Felicity in Mrs Ogden's room. She'd carried bags on the shopping trip to Wickleigh. She'd poured champagne at the buffet in the ballroom earlier that evening.

Felicity had overlooked her. It had been a mistake, but matters might still be put right.

Reaching the bottom of the steps, Felicity looked up at the maid. "What is it, Miss Brown?"

The maid swallowed. "I'm sorry, your ladyship." She cast a glance at Alex. "I thought you were alone. I-I'm... I'm sorry to have disturbed you." She started again towards the doors.

"It's all right," Felicity called out, but she didn't follow. She couldn't force things. "Anything you have to say to me can be said in front of Mr Cooper. I promise you, he's entirely trustworthy."

The maid halted but didn't turn around. Her shoulders were tense.

Alex caught up with Felicity. "It's all right," he said in low tones. "I'll go back inside."

The maid turned. She and Alex locked eyes.

Could she read his kindness and steadfastness in his gaze? Was it the scar on his forehead? Or had Miss Brown overheard what Alex said about his time in the trenches?

The girl swallowed, her hands still clutching at the skirt of her dress. She looked down at Felicity. Her gaze was fearful, but there was a resoluteness to her. Or perhaps a sense of desperation.

"I was there in the ballroom, when that teacher got found out for the poisoning. I saw how you treated her. You allowed her to speak, and you listened. You could have called in the police as soon as you realised what she did. They would have marched her off to gaol." Miss Brown let go of her skirt and gripped her fingers together. "But you didn't do that. You were gentle with her. You gave her a chance."

Felicity was surprised by Miss Brown's analysis. She'd imagined no one other than Miss Vincent to have been taking what she'd said to heart.

"All of us are flawed," said Felicity. "Some of us are more flawed than others."

The maid wrung her fingers tightly. Again, she glanced at Alex. He stood solemnly at Felicity's side.

"I can't carry on like this anymore. It troubles me so much I fear I'm losing my mind." The maid snatched the cap off her head. "I've done something awful. And I want to confess. I want to tell someone." Shakily, she descended the stone steps and stood before Felicity. "Will you listen to me?"

"Certainly, Miss Brown." Felicity spoke gently. "I'll listen."

Miss Brown squeezed her cap tightly in both hands. "I use the family name Brown, but my surname is actually Braun." She spelled out the name. *B-R-A-U-N.* It was the German word for brown. "I was born in England, and I've always passed as English, but my parents were both German. When the war started, my parents fled back to their country. They were dedicated to the kaiser. They took my younger sister with them, but they left me behind. Deliberately."

Felicity raised her brow. "Weren't you awfully young to have been left behind?"

"I was fourteen, your ladyship."

Alex winced. Felicity, however, was not surprised.

While the party in the ballroom was still going, and with Alex busy reporting, Felicity had crept into Miss Armstrong's office. Sneaking about was becoming a nasty habit of Felicity's, but it was simply impossible to leave the school without at least attempting to round things off properly.

During the weeks spent dedicated to her undercover mission, Felicity had asked questions. To avoid arousing suspicions regarding her true intentions, her questions couldn't be too intrusive.

For example, rather than press the servants for details about their individual backgrounds, Felicity had learned what she could from Miss Armstrong during casual conversation.

With moonlight falling on the headmistress' desk to light Felicity's review of the files kept on the school's staff, Felicity found everything Miss Armstrong had said to be utterly correct. Unwittingly, however, the headmistress hadn't shared some of the most important details.

And that was plainest to see when Felicity came across the file on Miss Adele Brown.

"Why did your parents leave you behind in England?" asked Felicity.

"They found me a position in service. At the house of a high-ranking military man. I was to spy and to share information. I had to leave messages in a—" The maid bit her lips closed, hesitant to give away information that might get others in trouble.

But it was enough. Miss Brown had made her confession, and it matched with what Felicity had seen in her records. Unlike Miss Vincent's brother, Miss Brown had been sent on from her previous employer, a lieutenant-general in the British army, with excellent references.

Alex's jaw was taut. He remained silent, his hands in his pockets.

"So you complied with your parents' wishes?" enquired Felicity.

Miss Brown nodded. She dropped her gaze to her cap, which she continued to squeeze with both hands. "I know I was young, but that doesn't excuse what I did. I realise that now, and the guilt eats at me every day."

Could someone so young be held responsible for carrying out actions they had been instructed to do by adults they trusted? Felicity had her own opinions, but it wasn't for her to decide.

"We all make mistakes," said Felicity. "It's the ability to admit to them and correct our behaviour that matters."

The maid blinked up at Felicity, then looked away. She shook her head. "I should have confessed earlier. I've been a coward."

"It's taken bravery to approach me and tell me what you've told me," said Felicity.

Miss Brown wouldn't look at her.

Felicity waited. "Where are your parents?"

"Dead, your ladyship. They did for themselves at the end of the war. They couldn't bear to see the country they loved defeated."

"And your sister?"

A hint of brightness passed across Miss Brown's features. "I write letters to her sometimes. I miss her terribly. The last time I saw her, she was twelve. She'll be a young woman by now. She tells me she has a sweetheart." A single tear ran down the girl's cheek. "I suppose I'll never see her again. Not now." She sniffed and put her wrist to her nose to stifle it, but it was no use. She started sobbing.

Felicity stepped forward and put her arms around Miss Brown

and held her as she cried, her narrow shoulders shaking in her rough woollen dress.

Alex was frozen, his dark blue eyes full of sadness and pain.

At last, it was over.

## Chapter Forty-Five

SEVERAL WEEKS LATER...

Doves as white as snowflakes fluttered against the brilliant blue sky, swooping around the tall, pointed steeple of the ancient village church. A colourful crowd of smiling people — including some of the most important names in England's aristocracy — stood on the churchyard's path, under the lychgate, and even in the grass, among the nodding daisies and the lichen-covered gravestones. Hints of delicate Parisian perfume and the freshness of midsummer greenery scented the air.

The engagement between Lady Cecily Summervale and Lord Severin Carrothers had been spoken of in the papers practically non-stop since the fateful night at Liverton House. The captivating pair might have chosen any venue in the country, but they'd chosen to get married at the little parish church halfway between the Carrothers' and Summervales' Devonian residences.

And it was chocolate-box perfect.

Felicity was happy to be attending the celebration, but her attention had again wandered to the lychgate at the churchyard's entrance, which was rather rude, seeing as Felicity was in the middle of a conversation.

She put a white-gloved hand to the brim of her picture hat, adjusting the shade to shield her eyes, and returned her attention to her conversation partner. Felicity's hat perfectly matched the robin's egg blue of her capped-sleeve silk dress.

"I was extremely sorry to read that Liverton Ladies' Academy has completely ceased to be," she said.

Miss Armstrong squinted down at Felicity from under her burgundy pillbox hat, which offered her eyes no respite from the bright sunshine.

Felicity hadn't seen Miss Armstrong for a spell. She'd read about the academy's closure in Alex's continued coverage of what had become known as the 'finishing school affair'.

"Yes. Well." The headmistress' dark hair had been vigorously trimmed to her jawline. A lace overlay on her muted-red dress did little to soften the severity of her appearance. Her tone was aloof, but a ripple of something close to satisfaction was briefly apparent in her features.

"Congratulations are in order, of course," continued Felicity. "I'm certain the Armstrong Institute will be a resounding success."

At the same time as Liverton Ladies' Academy's end had been announced, the opening of the Armstrong Institute for Feminine Achievement had been heralded.

Based at Liverton House, the new institution was still a finishing school of sorts, but its curriculum was much bolder. Students were still encouraged to debut and seek husbands, if that's what they wished, but they would enter the world with a broader skill set than dance steps, letter-writing, and household management. The school's goal was to equip its graduates to expand beyond the roles of wife and mother.

Miss Armstrong gave a firm nod. "I've got Eversley teaching medicine and first aid and Driver teaching motoring in tricky conditions and advanced riding techniques. Even Petherick's come back to teach composition." The headmistress' face darkened a little. "There shan't be any needlework classes, but a portion of the school's proceeds will be donated each year to the National Needlework Academy. We've created a scholarship to support talented embroiderers from less fortunate backgrounds. It's going to be called the Ogden Prize."

Felicity smiled sadly. "How fitting." Mrs Ogden had thankfully never known of Felicity's suspicions about her. Whatever faults the needlework teacher had, no one deserved to meet such a tragic end.

"The waiting list for the new school is already oversubscribed." Miss Armstrong couldn't suppress a brief smile. "You're not thinking of teaching again, are you, your ladyship? I'm confident there'll be aspiring journalists among the new girls."

Felicity's attention had again wandered to the lychgate. She snapped her gaze back to the headmistress.

"No." Felicity spoke firmly but smiled politely. "I appreciate the offer, Miss Armstrong, but I think not."

While there had been some aspects of teaching Felicity had enjoyed, she had her career in journalism to think about.

Since the dramatic events at Liverton, she'd covered a few village shows and the opening of a new department store in Plymouth, but Felicity hadn't yet fully returned to reporting. She used to hunger for excitement, but somehow she was thankful for a rest from it.

And there was a new project she'd been working on.

"Of course," said Miss Armstrong. "You've got your serialisation to consider."

Felicity smiled tightly. "Indeed."

A widely read lady's magazine had invited her to serialise her experiences in their publication. Not one to court the spotlight, Felicity was hesitant, but then Jasper got involved. He hammered out an agreement that was advantageous both for Felicity and for the Western Daily News, which also stood to benefit from the exposure.

Miss Armstrong quirked an eyebrow. "First time I've ever wanted to read one of those magazines."

Felicity smiled, mildly amused. "The world is changing, though, isn't it?"

"It certainly is," agreed Miss Armstrong.

Felicity had been confused about which of her experiences the magazine wished to share among the knitting patterns, advertisements for hats, and private announcements requesting companions. Surprisingly, the magazine's editor was adamant the magazine's readers wished to learn more about Felicity's adventures as an amateur sleuth.

The editor had called Felicity a 'real-life female Sherlock Holmes'.

Felicity had frowned and Jasper had twitched his moustache, both of them unimpressed by the comparison. Felicity was a keen observer, but she'd never touched a pipe or a violin. And who was her Watson?

Alex?

Having spent all her recent free time at Bradley Court writing up her experiences for the serialisation, Felicity hadn't seen her friend and colleague in what felt like an age.

Again, she craned her neck for a view of the lychgate.

"Ladies and gentlemen."

The warm, resonant voice of the vicar broke through the chatter in the churchyard. Wearing a white surplice, he stood in the arched doorway of the little granite-built church. His kindly smile wrinkled his eyes to the extent they looked almost closed. "If you would like to take your seats inside," he said, gesturing towards the doorway.

Miss Armstrong's forehead creased as she and Felicity joined the steady shuffle towards the church's entrance. "Might be rather a squeeze."

Felicity turned to look behind her. There were still people ducking under the lychgate and pouring into the tiny churchyard. Was there a chance Alex would make it, as he said he might?

Miss Armstrong had already become separated, drifting ahead into the shadows of the church's vestibule.

Felicity lurched to the side.

Someone had knocked into her rather forcefully.

## Chapter Forty-Six

"Oh, dear. Oh, goodness. I'm awfully sorry."

Jane had tripped and bumped into Felicity, sending her stumbling into the grass at the side of the churchyard's path. Butterflies fluttered up from the daisies and buttercups as Felicity regained her balance.

"Lady Jane," she said, sweeping her white-gloved hands over her pale blue dress. "What a pleasant surprise."

Despite the abrupt manner of her arrival, Felicity was genuinely pleased to see Jane. She'd been the only one to write to Felicity since the end of term — mainly with updates about visits to see her dear friend Mavis — but Felicity didn't hold that against the other girls. She'd grown quite attached to her students during her time at Liverton.

Tucking stray strands of caramel-coloured hair behind her ears, Jane looked down at her feet. Her shoes were each decorated with an enormous silk bow. Although the shade matched the floral decorations of her hat, which complimented the flowery print of her chiffon dress, the style of Jane's footwear was more reminiscent of the court of Louis XIV than of the present day.

Flexing her ankles, Jane peered down at her shoes. "Bally things. Can't quite get used to them."

"Your ladyship." Dolores and Usha arrived on the scene, both smirking, failing to fully hide their enjoyment of the mishap that had just occurred. They looked splendid, Dolores in a dark teal satin dress and Usha in peacock-green velvet.

Felicity ignored the snickering. "Miss Gastrell, Miss Ghatge. What a pleasure to see you all." She'd never imagined she would find the contents of the social columns at all interesting, but Felicity had been devouring them for updates on her former students. "How are you all?"

"Very well, thank you, your ladyship." Usha smiled brightly. "May I introduce you to Raj?"

At Usha's side was a tall, stately looking young man with a thick black moustache, sparkling brown eyes, and a mahogany complexion. His grey morning suit was exquisite, a hint of colourful paisley silk in the top pocket of his jacket.

"How do you do?" He shook Felicity's hand.

"It's an honour to meet you, your highness," said Felicity deferentially, aware thanks to the society papers that His Highness Rajeshwar Narayan was a prince and future maharaja.

"Raj has finished his studies at Oxford." Usha took her fiancé's arm, her gaze twinkling up at him. "We're going to Paris next week. We've decided it's my turn to study. I've taken a place at the Collège des Beaux-Arts. Raj and I are in no rush to marry, and I've already explained to my sponsor that I won't be taking part in the season."

Felicity lifted an eyebrow with surprise but also delight. "The Collège is lucky to have you." It was utterly fitting that a young woman with artistic talents should follow her aspirations in that arena.

The group was gently jostled as more guests made their way towards the ancient church's arched stone entrance.

Felicity cast a glance at the lychgate. Dolores was also somewhat distracted.

Jane pouted. "At this rate, it'll be just me and Mavis at Queen Charlotte's Ball."

"Isn't that actually better?" suggested Usha. "You and Mavis will be the centre of attention. You'll have yourselves fiancés in no time."

Jane looked thoughtful. "I suppose, but one must enjoy oneself. Mavis and I will be fitted for our dresses together. We'll be practising all the dances together, too."

Felicity smiled kindly. Hopefully Mavis was a little more gifted than Jane in graceful movement, otherwise there'd be quite the pile-up on the ballroom floor at Buckingham Palace.

"Will you join us for the preparations, Dolly?" asked Jane a little breathlessly.

"Are you being presented at court this year, Miss Gastrell?" asked Felicity. It was a question the society pages hadn't yet answered, and with her secret racing-driver beau, it was hard to tell what Dolores was planning.

But Dolores wasn't listening. Her gaze was on the far side of the churchyard. A small gathering of smart young men in black morning suits, buff waistcoats and slicked hair under top hats stood smoking and chatting, their nervousness and excitement evident.

"Dolly?" Usha smiled at her friend, amused. "Lady Felicity asked you a question."

Lord Severin was among the young gentlemen in morning suits, as was a slightly shorter fellow with fire-red hair and dark chestnut eyes.

Furtively, the red-haired man looked across at Dolores.

Dolores melted somewhat, her cheeks turning pink. The blush hadn't been there when she'd been handing notes to Severin. This was Dolores' man.

The vicar stepped out from a side door. He gestured for the young men to enter the church.

"Dolly?" Usha was giggling at her friend.

"Hmm? Oh. Yes." Dolores sounded briefly flustered. "Very much looking forward to the upcoming season. Of course I am." Her tone had returned to her usual ironic dryness. "Who wouldn't be?"

Felicity exchanged smiles with Usha.

Hopefully, everything would go well for Dolores and her red-haired racing driver, who clearly wasn't too disreputable, as indicated by his association with Severin. If Dolores' family came around to the idea, Felicity and the Liverton girls might all meet again at another wedding the following year.

"Where's your companion, your ladyship?" asked Dolores.

The question and tone caught Felicity off guard. It was quite clear who Dolores meant.

Felicity had been holed up at home working on the serialisation, which had been going smoothly until the edits from the ladies' magazine started coming through, which tripled the work. Alex had continued as lead reporter in the aftermath of the Liverton affair while juggling several other crime cases in the region.

He'd telephoned Felicity at Bradley Court on numerous occasions, sharing information that couldn't be published in the paper. Her heart lifted whenever she heard his voice over the line, but there'd been no time for a face-to-face meeting since the denouement at the school.

They had, however, agreed that they'd see one another at the wedding.

"Lady Felicity?"

The voice from behind saved Felicity from answering Dolores' question.

Gwendoline was resplendent in a rosebud-pink chiffon dress with a dainty V-neck and sheer sleeves. Her white-blonde hair had been swept into an elegant chignon at the back of her neck. Her lips were coloured with a dainty shade of pink that complemented her alabaster complexion. A wide-brimmed hat adorned with silk roses complemented the ensemble.

"Gwen! You made it."

Jane was the first to dash forward and embrace her friend with the other girls following soon after. Usha introduced Gwendoline to her betrothed. The pale girl beamed. She looked radiant.

"How are the preparations for Cambridge?" enquired Felicity. She'd been delighted to learn — again, from the society pages — that

Gwendoline would study English literature at the prestigious university from the autumn.

It was a fitting choice for such an intelligent, thoughtful young woman. The decision was also brave, considering the weight of the obligations Gwendoline's family had placed upon her.

"Oh, Mother and Father are simply thrilled," said Gwendoline, still smiling. "When I told them about the ratio of men to women at the institution, they realised it would likely increase my chances of marriage rather than deplete them. I didn't tell them I'll be spending more time with books than with people."

Felicity smiled. She was awfully proud of her students.

Dolores stifled a yawn with the back of her wrist. "Just the idea of a book puts me to sleep."

Jane was still eyeing her big-bowed shoes with suspicion. "Not everyone can have a fighter pilot turned racing driver for a husband."

Dolores spun towards Jane, her mouth open.

Usha and Raj smiled.

"What?" asked Jane of Dolores. "We're practically alone."

The churchyard was indeed almost empty. Felicity and the girls were among the last guests still outside in the sunshine.

"And there are no secrets between us, are there?" continued Jane. "Not anymore."

Gwendoline shook her head. "Absolutely not."

The girls had been through some exceedingly challenging times together, and their bond was all the stronger for it.

Dolores' expression lightened. She shrugged. "I suppose we better go inside. I wouldn't want any of you turning up late to my wedding."

The girls began towards the church's vestibule. With a last glance over her shoulder, and fighting a sense of dejection, Felicity followed.

Jane frowned, doubtful. "That's if you have a proper wedding that we can actually attend."

"Who says I shan't?" snapped Dolores.

Usha laughed. "Dolly, you've threatened to elope so many times I'm sure we've all lost count."

Gwendoline smiled. "Would any of you be offended if I never have a wedding?"

Dolores gave Gwendoline a light punch on the shoulder. "Don't be so hard on yourself, Gwen, old girl. You're not only beautiful, you're fiercely clever. Some young don will no doubt snap you up."

"Oh, I'm not worried about my chances," replied Gwendoline. "It's just there are so many books, and one only has so many hours in a day. I'm not sure how I could make time for a husband."

"I know exactly what you mean," said Usha. "When I have a paintbrush in my hand, I need nothing else."

Raj's thick eyebrows knitted slightly. "My darling?" He sounded only mildly affronted. "I am right here, you know."

Usha smiled sweetly. "I know, my darling."

Raj sighed.

The girls giggled, their voices and footsteps echoing as they entered the cool shade of the church's vestibule.

Felicity smiled to herself. Each girl was on her own path to happiness, all of them different. Felicity's only complaint was that she would forever be eager to peruse the society pages, wondering what her former students might do next.

"I'm right here, too."

The voice from behind echoed in the vestibule. It was a voice Felicity knew so well.

# Chapter Forty-Seven

In a dark grey morning jacket, trousers, and waistcoat paired with polished black Oxfords and a smooth grey homburg hat, Alex was perfectly attired for a village wedding.

With his broad shoulders and gleaming, dark blue eyes, he also looked incredibly dashing.

"Not too late, am I?" His chest heaved a little. He'd clearly been hurrying.

Felicity halted her advance into the church. "Never," she said, beaming. "How long has it been?"

Alex wasn't the only late-comer. Guests continued to trickle through the narrow vestibule. Felicity and Alex stepped aside, allowing them to pass.

"Too long." Alex lifted his hat and smoothed a hand over his hair. "Had to leave the motor on the edge of the village. The streets are rather full." He adjusted the brim of his homburg and watched as people proceeded past and into the church. "I thought it was going to be a quiet affair?"

"I don't know where you got that idea." Felicity peered ahead into the nave. "I doubt there are enough seats for everyone."

Alex gave a little shrug. "We can meet up after the ceremony."

Felicity frowned. She'd waited too long for this opportunity. "If you're standing, I'm standing too."

They joined the slow shuffle towards the pews.

Sunshine streamed in through colourful stained glass onto the rows of seats filled with people. Elegant hats in splendid shades nodded as the guests chatted with one another. A little pipe organ was playing a Canon in D, which echoed beautifully up into the vaulted ceiling.

The Liverton girls were already advancing along the aisle towards the pews, which were packed on both sides. Miss Armstrong was already seated towards the middle on the bride's side.

As more people crammed into the church, the space became tighter. Felicity and Alex were pressed together, their arms touching.

"Will you be writing a piece on the Armstrong Institute?" asked Alex.

Felicity cocked her head. It was an interesting suggestion. "I hadn't considered it."

"Suppose you're too busy with your serialisation. What is it they're calling it? Lady Holmes?"

"Hush," hissed Felicity, but she was smiling. She and Alex had laughed at the idea together. The comparison was overblown.

The shuffling stopped. Ushers hurried about, sourcing extra chairs.

At the front of the church, the vicar spoke calmly to the groom and his men. Severin looked a little nervous, but what young man wouldn't be on such an important day?

The organ played serenely on.

"Any news?" whispered Felicity. She couldn't leave the matter until after the ceremony, but neither could she speak about it explicitly.

Alex would know what Felicity was referring to, and it wasn't Miss Vincent. The French teacher needed little discussion, although what might happen to her was still unclear.

Now awaiting trial, it was possible Miss Vincent might receive a degree of mercy from the jury, if they were moved by her tragic circumstances and her insistence that she'd never intended to kill, only to injure. Nevertheless, an innocent woman had lost her life. The trial's outcome was eagerly awaited, and Alex would chronicle every detail.

But there was something that couldn't be mentioned in the papers. That they dared not even discuss on the telephone.

"She's still being interviewed."

The maid and confessed wartime traitor Miss Adele Brown had been taken in for questioning by British intelligence services.

Everything was veiled in secrecy, but via Jasper's connections, they'd heard that the network she'd been part of was more extensive than first imagined. While Miss Brown perhaps didn't know exactly who she'd been dealing with when passing on the information she stole, her testimony might help reveal others who were responsible for even more heinous crimes.

"She's well-looked after, though, isn't she?"

Alex nodded. "There's a facility, as I understand it. For people like her."

Felicity had faith that the British authorities would treat a woman well, even if she had a criminal past, and especially if the crimes in question had taken place when she was a child. Felicity also believed that Miss Brown's resilience and new-found bravery would carry her through whatever she faced. It was, after all, the maid's conscience that prompted her to confess.

The crowd started moving again, shuffling towards the rows of pews. Felicity and Alex were funnelled along and repositioned so that Alex was slightly behind Felicity.

"Might she stand trial?"

Alex let out a long exhale. "Hard to say. If it's done publicly, then it's no longer secret, is it? And if there are others to catch, that won't help."

The full details of Miss Brown's fate might never be known to them. Felicity had sympathy for the girl, although the consequences of her actions were more painful and real to Alex. He'd lost countless comrades and himself been wounded in the war. It was selfish of Felicity to keep pushing the topic of leniency.

"Her sister's come over from Switzerland," said Alex. "That's how they found her, you know. The letters sent back and forth between them. They were careful but not quite careful enough."

Surprised, Felicity twisted towards Alex. "Are they allowed to see one another?"

"I don't know if they've been reunited, but at least she knows she's not alone in facing whatever comes next."

Despite everything he'd been through, Alex felt sympathy for Miss Brown.

"There's at least that, indeed," agreed Felicity. It was beyond a privilege to count Alex as a friend.

The crowd lurched forward slightly.

"Sorry, old chap," said an older gentleman nearby. "Bit packed in here."

"It's all right," replied Alex.

Felicity felt a gentle hand on her back. Alex had taken the force of the shove and gently shielded her.

"Ladies, this way, please." A church usher was splitting the crowd as they reached the central aisle that ran between the pews. "Terribly sorry, but we've run out of seats for the gents. Um, this way for ladies, please?" The usher didn't quite know how to stop Felicity from streaming forward along with the gentlemen.

"I'd prefer to stand, thank you," she said quietly and politely to the usher, who looked mildly confused.

"Are you sure?" asked Alex as they moved steadily with the men to the side of the church. "These services can be a bit on the long side, can't they?"

Felicity spun towards him. "We've hardly seen each other these past weeks. I'm not letting you out of my sight."

Alex smiled. Perhaps even blushed. Was Felicity being too forward? It felt so easy to speak honestly whenever she was with him.

They found space to stand in the nave aisle. The organ continued to play.

"How does it feel to be a writer for a top-selling women's magazine?"

Felicity pulled a little face. "It's a bit like being a newspaper journalist, but with all the interesting parts removed."

"By interesting parts, do you mean the crime solving?"

Felicity frowned disapprovingly. Alex knew full well it had never been her explicit intention to involve herself in detective work.

"It's just me, my typewriter, and my memories of the things that happened," she said. "Oh, and the deadlines and the edits. There's not anyone to speak to, really. Only Lady Henrietta and Pip. Jasper's hardly ever home. I love my grandmother dearly, of course, but there are only so many disagreements at the fuchsia society one needs to hear about."

"You'll be done soon though, won't you? And you'll come back to the paper?"

An usher popped up from between the pews. "Lady Felicity. We've found you a seat."

While Felicity appreciated the efforts taken on her behalf, she didn't enjoy being singled out for a fuss.

"Thank you kindly," she smiled sweetly. "But I'm afraid I don't want to sit without my friend."

Alex smirked. Felicity supposed she had become rather bold in recent months.

The usher nodded. "That's understood. There's a seat for your, um, friend, too."

Felicity sought Alex's approval.

Still smiling, he shrugged, and they were squeezed onto the end of a hard wooden pew surprisingly close to the altar, their elbows touching.

Felicity swallowed. She didn't relish what she had to say next. "To be honest, I'm not sure when I'll be coming back."

"To the paper?" Alex's scarred forehead creased. He looked surprised, even worried.

"My grandmother has asked a favour of me." It wasn't the first time Lady Henrietta had engaged Felicity in some kind of scheme. She knew from experience there was no point fighting it.

Alex quirked an eyebrow. "Has she, indeed?"

"She won't yet tell me what, exactly. She says she doesn't want me distracted from my writing, but she's a clever old bean. She's biding her time so that when she springs the details on me, it'll be too late for me to back out."

The organ had stopped.

"That's rather a coincidence."

Felicity turned to Alex. "Why?"

The chatter in the church was dying down.

"Your brother told me I have a special reporting assignment coming up soon." Alex dropped his voice to a whisper. "Something to do with your grandmother, apparently."

Felicity huffed. Lady Henrietta hadn't meddled in rather a long while. On that basis alone, Felicity ought to have seen it coming.

"Do you have the details?" she whispered.

"As a matter of fact, I do." He spoke quietly, their heads leaning towards one another, the church now practically silent. "Your grandmother may be wily, but she doesn't have the hold on me that she does on you. I told Jasper I wouldn't agree till I knew the details."

Felicity was intrigued. "What is it then?" And a tad worried.

The organ struck up again. It was the wedding march.

Alex lifted his eyebrows and put a finger over his lips.

Whispering while the bride made her entrance was a step too far. Felicity would have to wait until after the ceremony to find out what Lady Henrietta was up to.

Everyone twisted in their seats to see Cecily approaching down the aisle on her father's arm. She looked like an angel in tiers of white lace and chiffon and a long white veil. A line of tiny cherubic bridesmaids with frilly skirts and posies of pink flowers and little page boys in miniature sailor uniforms followed her dutifully down the aisle.

Severin ceased to look nervous the moment he saw his betrothed.

As they joined hands before the vicar, they smiled lovingly at one another and looked deeply into each other's eyes.

The ceremony was moving. Felicity was glad she brought a handkerchief with her. It didn't feel long at all.

"I now pronounce you man and wife," intoned the vicar.

Alex turned suddenly to look at Felicity. For a moment, with his eyes wide and his brow raised, Alex looked happily surprised. Perhaps the happiest Felicity had ever seen him.

Then he looked down at his lap.

A wash of mild panic swept through Felicity.

Alex's hands lay at rest on his thighs. Felicity's hand was there, too. And her hand was clutching his.

Without realising it, Felicity had grabbed Alex's hand.

She met his gaze again, her own eyes widening with fear and embarrassment. Her mouth opened, about to apologise.

Then his hand squeezed hers.

Claim your free Lady Felicity Quick ebook!

Sign up for my email newsletter and you'll get **Murder at Afternoon Tea** absolutely free.

This exclusive story isn't available anywhere else.

As a newsletter subscriber, you'll also receive writing updates, special offers, and peeks behind the scenes...

Use this link to sign up and claim your copy today:
https://BookHip.com/XMGPNZC

Read the next in the series...

**Murder at a Flower Show**

A Lady Felicity Quick 1920s Cozy Mystery
Book 7

***At Bickleford's famous rose contest, Britain's loveliest blooms are on display ... and the rivalry is deadly!***

**England, 1922.** Keen to slip out of the sleuthing spotlight and refocus on her journalism career, **Lady Felicity Quick** receives a peculiar invitation. A prestigious competition between British rose growers seeks celebrity judges, and crime-solver Felicity is top of their list.

Despite a lack of interest in fame and flowers, and after a spot of meddling by her beloved grandmother, Felicity finds herself surrounded by sweet-smelling silky petals in the charming Devonshire village of Bickleford. And as romance blossoms, judging the flower show proves surprisingly enjoyable...

Until Britain's most famous rose breeder is found murdered behind the floral marquee — with Felicity's own grandma as the prime suspect! Can Felicity unearth Bickleford's secrets in time to save her grandmother? Or will our intrepid sleuth end up in her own prickly predicament?

*If you love intrepid female sleuths like Miss Marple and Kitty Worthington and the captivating 1920s whodunits of Lee Strauss and Benedict Brown, then you'll love* **Murder at a Flower Show***!*

**Murder at a Flower Show will be available soon!**

# A Note From The Author

Thank you for reading Murder at a Boarding School! I truly hope you enjoyed your time at Liverton with Felicity and Alex.

Could you spare a moment to leave a review? On Amazon, Goodreads, or wherever you prefer.

Your reviews help fellow readers discover new books. Just a few words can make a big difference.

Thank you for your support!

Gratefully,

Rosie

## The Lady Felicity Quick Mystery Series

**Murder at Afternoon Tea**

(Novella | Exclusive for Newsletter Subscribers)

**Murder on the Village Green**

(Book 1 | Available Now)

**Murder at a Country House**

(Book 2 | Available Now)

**Murder at the Tea Rooms**

(Book 3 | Available Now)

**Murder at the Ball**

(Book 4 | Available Now)

**Murder on the Coast**

(Book 5 | Available Now)

**Murder at a Boarding School**

(Book 6 | Available Now)

**Murder at a Flower Show**

(Book 7 | Coming Soon)

# About the Author

Rosie Hunt is a British author of cozy mysteries both puzzling and historical. Her books include the Lady Felicity Quick mystery series set in the green and pleasant countryside of southwest England in the 1920s.

A history addict and former journalist, Rosie grew up immersed in the worlds of Poirot and Miss Marple. This early exposure to baffling murder mysteries rather coloured her outlook on life, and it was only a matter of time before she began writing her own.

Rosie loves clotted cream, knitting, and Golden Age crime fiction, and she'll never miss an opportunity to visit a National Trust property. She lives with her husband and their four-pawed overlord on a river in Northern Europe.

**Join Rosie's mailing list:**
bookhip.com/XMGPNZC

**Follow Rosie on Facebook:**
facebook.com/RosieHuntAuthor

Printed in Great Britain
by Amazon

44764769R00172